bamboo ridge

JOURNAL OF HAWAI'I LITERATURE AND ARTS

NUMBER SEVENTY-FIVE

SPRING 1999

NEW MOON ●

ISBN 0-910043-58-2
This is issue #75 of *Bamboo Ridge, Journal of Hawai'i Literature and Arts* (ISSN 0733-0308).
Copyright © 1999 Bamboo Ridge Press
Published by Bamboo Ridge Press
Indexed in the American Humanities Index
Bamboo Ridge Press is a member of the Council of Literary Magazines and Presses (CLMP).

Front cover: "Tutuila" by Tom Okimoto. Acrylic on canvas, 9" x 12", 1995.
Back cover: "Composition" by Tom Okimoto. Acrylic on canvas, 18" x 24", 1994.
Title page: "Summer Noon" by Tom Okimoto. Acrylic on canvas, 11" x 14", 1993.
Editors: Eric Chock and Darrell H. Y. Lum
Managing editor: Joy Kobayashi-Cintrón
Book design: Susanne Yuu
Typesetting and graphics: Wayne Kawamoto
Photography: Paul Kodama

"Rockhead" copyright © 1999 by Nora Okja Keller. Reprinted by permission of Susan Bergholz Literary Services, New York. All rights reserved.
"Force Majeure" by Eileen Tabios was previously published in *Storyboard* (Guam).

Bamboo Ridge Press is a nonprofit, tax-exempt corporation formed in 1978 to foster the appreciation, understanding, and creation of literary, visual, or performing arts by, for, or about Hawaii's people. This project is supported in part by grants from the National Endowment for the Arts (NEA), the Hawai'i Community Foundation, and the State Foundation on Culture and the Arts (SFCA) celebrating over thirty years of culture and the arts in Hawai'i. The SFCA is funded by appropriations from the Hawai'i State Legislature and by grants from the NEA.

Bamboo Ridge is published twice a year. Subscriptions are $35 for 4 issues, $20 for 2 issues. Institutional rate: $25 for 2 issues. For subscription information, back issues, or a catalog please contact:

Bamboo Ridge Press
P. O. Box 61781
Honolulu, HI 96839-1781
(808) 626-1481
brinfo@bambooridge.com
www.bambooridge.com

We gratefully acknowledge the support of the following individuals and organizations for their donations during the second half of 1998:

Anonymous
Julie Chiu Au
Winifred L. Au
Fred Bail
Charlotte Boteilho
Mabel M. H. Chang
Ruth P. Dawson
Marjorie Edel
Pamela J. Fujita-Starck
Randy R. Fujiwara
Merry C. Glass
Norma W. Gorst*
Philip Kan Gotanda
Muffy Gushi
Mavis I. Hara
Violet H. Harada
Vilsoni Hereniko
Charlene Hosokawa
Lisa N. Kanemoto
Daniel T. Kawakami
Sandra Kelly-Daniel
Mary E. O. Kimura
Erin Kimura
Mildred D. Kosaki
Jane M. Kupau
Ellen Y. Lee
Marilyn B. Lee*
Pamela G. Lichty
Wing Tek Lum
Archibald MacPhail
Annette E. Masutani
June R. Matsumoto
MacNaughton & Gunn
Elizabeth McCutcheon
Grace J. Merritt

Mary M. Mitsuda
Joy M. Miyasaki*
Esther T. Mookini*
Gloria A. Moore
Mary Lombard Mulder
Audrey A. Muromoto
Amy N. Nishimura
Carrie O'Connor
Frances Oliver
Nora Y. Oshiro
Valerie Ossipoff
Alexandra Ossipoff
Joan K. Perkins
James M. Reis*
Don Rogers
Patsy Saiki
Shopping Hawaii, Inc.
Michelle M. C. Skinner
Mary A. Starck
Eileen R. Tabios
Joann M. U. Takeuchi
Talk Story, Inc.
Ian M. Tamura
Brian Taniguchi*
Bill Teter
Jean M. Toyama*
Doris T. Tsuji
Frederick B. Wichman
Elizabeth K. Wight
Irene G. Wilhelm
Kay Y. Yamada
Nancy S. Young

*indicates Special Member

CONTENTS

MARGO BERDESHEVSKY

FLYING WITH THE BAGUIO CITY ANGELS

I

What end of what world?

Manila might be one room in hell. A television special stood on its hind paws at twilight. These, the Filipino streets I'd only seen on *60 Minutes*, stagnant rivers through the spine. These, the begging babies in the traffic, the alleys of homeless, heavenless, hope turned to tin-rust and rag. Every night some eight-year-old skinny child surely sniffing glue too near our bus window to bear fearing. . . . The Victory Bus Line climbs its well-known unfenced overhang to Baguio City. Different and the same. Colder. Pines. The trees of a sky's conscience. Down there is undeletable. Satan's streets, perhaps. Here . . . a little air.

She's a born-again Filipina, looking for a home. I'm a born-again Catholic, I might say, on the road. Maybe it is the roar of the incense, the humility of the crowd, or the silence of the light, in some nearby cathedral. In fact, I like churches. All churches. My father, a Jew, politely gave up converting me once he'd passed away. Before that, it was a fight. He demanded I learn the Old Testament in exchange for my childhood ballet lessons. As soon as I could, I prayed in churches. Maybe it's a past life sort of a thing . . .

So we take a journey that might change our lives. Why not, when the world might end and we really need to be prepared, spiritually? Why not, when the world might continue forever and we might need to know a little more? It will only take a minute, in the grand scheme of things.

So, I make a Christmas bargain this year: I'll take us to the Philippines, where there are births more strange than baby Jesus going on, and faith the size of bleeding mountains. I'm speaking of us two born-agains of a different stripe: my best friend the poet-midwife, and me the poet-vagabond, using the credit card to access the money my dead dad did not tie up in perpetuity, to take us on two weeks to her mother's village. She has always wanted to go to Baguio. It's Christmas, so what is a little cash for?

I know the feeling. I had to go to see the Russian birch trees one winter, and to feel my grandmother's pale-eyed ghost kiss my head in the person of a babushka at the feet of an Orthodox icon; she then poured her holy water on my head as well. I know the feeling. The midwife wants to touch the back of her hand to the forehead of every old person in Baguio City the way her cousins do when they say goodnight to their father. We smile conspiratorially at each other's sentimentalities. What are best friends for?

Now politics has cast an ugly eye on her chosen "it takes a village" lifestyle, and sends her home to the Philippines to find her mother's street, between her not yet tattooed hands. In the market she buys a red woven *tapis* and its matching belt from a very old *Igarot*. She wants the one the woman is wearing! not the ones in the basket. She insists, demands, cajoles until there's a laughing and a play-act dancing and a little indecency as the old lady strips to her slip with her busy black tattooed fingers, to please the born-again Filipina who wants to come home. The new emigré needs cloth that smells like a grandmother, and maybe a new house, soon. She's been homing in Indonesia for these recent years, and the government there may tumble next week or next month. What is the end—of what world? How long is a minute, in the grand scheme of things?

Her hands are itching to catch another baby, to make birth gentle and world-safe in a Christmas season when *60 Minutes* has told it all or most of it, and we cannot bear to believe it. She believes in birth. My own heart is itching for Christmas, a kiss of God. We want to know more. We stretch the hour to a bubblegum membrane and hide in the pink, with terror and laughter. What else to do, three days before Christmas, a year before the millennium?

I know, go to a faith healer!

Her auntie mentions him. And I seem to have hatched the idea myself somewhere on the way across the Pacific. The Espiritus "take" on holy miracles cajoles my heart into a little more faith . . .the inner chick in me is clucking, and I wake wishing to be of great faith. I want to see the mountain. We agree to explore what is being born here, besides the obvious. The Baguio cousin drives us to a vaguely rundown hotel painted in shades of pink, and there are two unsmiling Germans in the courtyard, one with a video, one with a green baseball cap; one is a doctor, his wife is there to be healed of breast cancer. There is a chipped, once brightly painted terra cotta zoo, peopled with muddy ducks, geese, and three barking deer, all lounging on cement, over the railing below us. Soon after 9:30 in the morning, Ramon Jun Labo, the once-Mayor of Baguio, now a globally well-reputed psychic healer, now married to a pencil-eyebrowed Russian blonde named Leeza, arrives in his chauffeured black Mercedes. There are still tin shacks on the hill slopes. Still Baguio blind, crouched on near streets, and markets too dense to breathe in, too poor for tears, still people all over the world who need health and miracles. But we are in the hills and there is some sense of religion, some sense of peace and waiting in me, in the morning air. And how to be closer to Jesus than to offer our blood, to believe?

The scent of the miraculous is in our heartbeats, and roadside sunflowers so yellow they defy the ever-present dust.

The midwife-poet and I wait for Labo. "Are you ready to do this?" she whispers to me as urgently as last rites. What else to do, two days before Christmas, a year before the year 2000?

He emerges from the Mercedes in a blue silk suit tailored for a rock star perhaps. Indeed, the slicked black hair of a Presley, the round face and lips of Liberace. And the eyes of a surprised and wise child. A man of confidence. Too slick, some would say; I ignore the packaging. I am praying quietly, guided by a minute of truth that will seem to last and last.

Soon I observe his hands at work: blood spouting from beneath his gnarling fingers, from one of the now prone Germans' bellies, and the next one's left breast, more, from the leg of a man who has written ten books on the subject. Everyone may watch. I make some photographs. The light is too low.

Soon, he nods at me. "You want to come?" Soon, barefoot and humble as a maiden en route to the proverbial Minotaur, I surrender my own belly and uterus and God alone knows what else to a surge of very quiet faith. I am without question. I am certain as a simple morning. Trance, or truth, I am willingly involved, listening to the canned music, and at peace. What else to do, two days before Christmas, a year before a millennium?

"What is the problem?" he asks as I close my eyes to the red glow of the plastic Jesus which I know is real as a Sistine Chapel at this very moment. " I have an infection which returns and returns," I speak to his child-eyes, child faith. In a moment I am supine and being cleansed of all God wishes out of me, this I know, and God is watching, from not such a distance, this I know. In a long minute, a light tap on my right forearm urges me to rise to sitting and I am shown a mass of matter gross to any eye, I am glad as hell to have out of me. "What do you do with the waste?" I remember to ask him, later. Burn and bury is the reassuring reply.

"You should return one more time," he tells me matter-of-factly. "There was infection. It will all be gone then." I want it gone. I want it done. My ears focus on the tape somewhere, playing a version of Jesus music.

The midwife assures me as she helps me to dress, "That really did come out! I could see everything! And his hands were really in there! And he closed you up again without a stitch! And I know real blood when I see it, I'm a midwife!" I am wordless. A little tired. A little holy, for hours to come. I think I may have been flying with the local angels, for a long minute.

II

I palm the little coral rosary I've brought, with its skinny crucifix like a silver Giacometti in my tight right hand. I am about to enter the faith healer's salon for the second time, and I am more scared than yesterday. The midwife has whispered her doubts to me over breakfast. She doesn't like his Liberace looks. She wonders if he treats the poor for free. She hates the lace and plaster Jesuses with red lights glowing that constitute his office and his chapel. I concur. The statuary is distinctly not Italian Renaissance but Spanish influenced kitsch. Yet there's a hush in my heart that whispers, "Increase my faith, God, that's all I ask. And if it's here on this bizarre stage set, so be it. Let me be born, and born, and born."

I pause at the open entry to Ramon Jun Labo's salon and cross myself like a good Catholic child. What else can a woman dressed like all the rest in cotton panties and her black bra still on do in the circumstances? The protocol says strip to this. The holy music has started again. The Germans have already spouted their blood under his experienced fingers, and been healed, they say. The healers are donned in white coats and holy but workmanlike faces. The tape player has its own version of born-again Espiritus music and Jun Labo appears to have entered the trance I noted yesterday, his lips are moving, simultaneously praying and singing along with the music, sotto voce: a little theatre, a little inspiration. I rather like the sounds. I like Country Western when I drive my truck, too.

I lie again on his white-sheeted table surrounded by the three men in white coats, clasping my little coral beads, and close my eyes the better to feel, the better to pray, "Increase my faith, sweet Jesus, I'm a little scared this time, you know, strengthen my faith. I know that's what I'm doing here, whatever else it looks like."

The rest is silence, so Shakespeare once taught me.

I can feel the warm and liquid of what is surely my blood under his quickly moving hands. They enter, my flesh, my psychic flesh, his real hands, my real flesh, his hands . . . which seem to have more pressure, seem to be digging deeper into my unimaginable innards than yesterday.

I hear a vague click. The photographer in me is still shockingly aware. Someone is making a picture of this. I shall make my own, later, soon. I remain in prayer, still and yet I remain prone. I begin to wish that the process will be over very soon and that he will close me up very soon, but let me be healed! I believe that God has me in the right place at the right time and these are the right hands to do it, in a rundown pink hotel with its own mini zoo of maybe attending angels, in Baguio, in the Philippines, in almost 1999. . . . It's too late in my life for mistakes. What else to believe, a day before Christmas, on the road to a little more purity and the ever present millennium?

III

"O Come All Ye Faithful" still brings a choke of tears to my voice, I never know why and it always does. So I kneel and stand and sing and swallow the wafer with all the rest, forgetting what world I may or should belong to. It's Christmas morning, and my friend and I are in the cathedral where her mother was baptized. The crowded streets outside make me yearn for my hermit-life, but I am a long minute away from that; and I stand out like a marquee, blonde and hips maneuvering the masses, with a smile for babies and beggars and a sudden obsession for photographing blind people, and healers. I sing, the traditional carol stuck like a wet cracker to my throat.

IV

If once is good, and filled with unanswerables, why not observe a second, we reason? Besides, the midwife continues to make semi-ribald jokes about my experience with Labo, even as she blesses me for bringing her home. She just didn't like his outfit, or his decor, or his fee, geared, I have admitted, for the West. What about the poor, she demands. I protest, protect. For the next 36 hours, his child-face, I must call it, innocent and clean-eyed, continues to appear to my psychic inner screen, just slightly to the left. . . . It is as though to reassure me that in spite of her humored denigration, this is the self who healed me. She concurs. "He did. I know he did!" But she hates his style.

So, to another hill slope, this one with a river in the steep gorge below, and banana trees hanging onto the dirt as those who come to be healed cling to their own faith. It is a double bargain, faith plus faith, this, we know.

So to Brother William Nagog, down the steps below the police outpost. My best friend immediately likes the atmosphere better. The waiting room is jammed at 9 a.m. with all ages and variations of poor and Filipino, clutching their own wads of toilet tissue to clean up after. She whispers that she might have the courage, this time. Her lungs are scorched from the Indonesian fires, and the tensions of midwiving have accrued in her spine.

The cement-walled room huddles beneath a larger frame, for a new house which is under construction. There are open spaces where windows may eventually be. People perch in them; the space is overflowing. There is a wooden crucifix and pews where we are welcomed by shy smiles, a few giggles at our English, to sit and move forward a space at a time as each patient enters the room—over there. . . .

The small door opens and there is a beam-smiling pony-tailed man in a purple shirt and a blue work apron. His hands are at work on an old man who is still wearing the old bandaging from a hospital operation for liver cancer, which did not work. He's prone on one of the two tables. Brother William jokes. He talks. He works. He may in fact be having fun this morning. The hands are again entering flesh, there is again the undeniable crimson of splattering blood, a plastic pail of water, and two attendants who mop up. He removes a small piece of matter that looks like a clot, and flips it onto the back of his own hand, and continues to work. He moves to the second table, excises a tumor from the bulged eye of a young woman, her little son, waiting, watching, in the doorway.

"Why are you here?" he looks up amiably at us newcomers. We admit a desire to observe, I ask if it would be permissable to photograph so others might see, might understand. He looks at me directly. "God sent you today. You are very close to God. Sure," he returns to his business. Again, we are welcomed, and invited into the inner room: a small statue of Mother Mary, a donation basket, a painting of Jesus in the clouds, a clock, two tables cloaked in faint spatters of blood. A sincere and prayerful looking man dipping his hands into flesh as though it was cake batter with splashes of red. Sometimes he pauses, to concentrate, sometimes he keeps a running chatter.

Massage, the scent of coconut oil, a prevailing good humor as the good brother jokes with the children and the fearful and the elderly and the cancerous and the twist-limbed and the goitered and the belly-ached. Each receives about the same. A few receive only a touch, but no blood. Most bleed. Almost all are first rapidly cloaked with a pale not totally clean sheet which is just as quickly removed and the healer's hands set to work. He answers our questions, our looks without words. "It helps to see the appearance of what is wrong." I have a momentary thought of an imitation shroud of Turin; soon I am again fascinated and nonjudgemental of the next display of God's presence, the repeated births of faith and healing in a tiny basement room on a hillslope of Baguio.

My friend has finally screwed her courage to the sticking place and lies down to be worked upon. Surely, there are angels in the vicinity. I just don't know who is who and what is what. I make sure that my camera is workng and there is a good flash, and make the photographs to attest to the untestable. We are flying so fast, in another small room with the faithful. He pulls matter from her spine, and from her lungs and midriff. He says softly, "It was pre-cancerous." She tells me later that it feels like warm needles as his hands go "in."

"What do you do with the waste?" I remember to ask him, later. Burn, and bury, is the now familiar reply.

So, what difference?

I had heard mutterings and beliefs that there were frauds, but these were not. I have known those who follow the fads and crystals. I do not. I had heard of healers who hid tiny blades in their fingernails, but these did not. The man who had written ten books on the subject, Lecauco, bore a scar on his right shoulder from one of the "blade" frauds, yet he lay on Labo's table the day I did, to be healed by a psychic surgeon, this one. I had heard of the debunkers and the believers, and old controversies, yet I was no personal ghostbuster, and no ghost tester and haven't a science hat at this time in life. I'm an aging poetical mystic. What I came to know in its simplicity was here was a kind of collaborative trance, and a bargain in faith. What I came to know was what I and the camera I carried eyed.

One is showy and proud, sings along with a tape, has glass cases of his precious gifts, Russian eggs, Middle Eastern swords, from around the world, was videoed by *20/20*, and the tape was verified and then canceled by pressure from the AMA. This, the man of ten books and the German doctor corroborate. He speaks little, he delivers what seem like prepared and well-seasoned stories about himself, a child who didn't want to be a healer. He is neither distant nor friendly. He is experienced and busy, like many surgeons in the practical world. Yet a rarified and "safe" space surrounds the table I lay down upon. He has been doing "this" for thirty years. He seems to be in charge of a going operation. There are usually large tours of foreigners, we are told. He will leave for Mexico, then Moscow, on the 27th. We have had an opportnity to be among a very few this time. It is easy to look very closely. In adjacent cubicles there are younger assistants who would offer "psychic massage." I am less trusting of them, I demur. Despite the presentation, my body is at peace following the healing. The German doctor tells us he was cured of blindness twenty years ago, he has returned with the "incurable" ever since. The rundown hotel with its apparently useless zoo and a healer who dresses in silk suits and designer pullovers is unquestionably a place of miracles. This I know. Why? I know.

One is humble and joking, and his basement room dispenses miracles to the poor and donating, but he has also traveled, also been invited to the scrutiny of the world. He will fortune-tell for the superstitious, crack an egg into a water glass to discern the evil that may attend an illness, tease the oldest into giggles, pause, for explanations. My friend worries that he will become known and the poor will be bereft. I am content to leave the finger of fate to other hands than ours. Both serve God and the ill. Both have hands kissed by something inexplicable but known, dramatic, and holy. Labo says he was his mother's bad boy, pretended, until he was knocked over by an apparition of Jesus, and a calling. Brother William asks casually if we believe in reincarnation, then expounds that grandfather was a healer, and his great-grand-mother was a healer, and he is the both of them, now, here. A small child, he could close his friends' wounds with a touch. Being a healer is not a peaceful life, this, he warns. He has a little more youth, a little more man-of-the-people packaging. One day, massaging an old lady, his hands went "in," did what they needed to do, he pulled them out, and the wound shut. He had a calling he could not, did not want to turn back from.

The midwife-poet still likes but one of the pair. Poet-vagabond, I find I like both, Baguio beauties, angels, in a short minute in a world with distortion, and darkness that has a hole in its lung. Sometimes, I believe I can hear it breathing, rattling, nearly dying.

A speaker of many languages, I pride myself on being the lin-guist, determined to look beyond the costumes, or the languages, or even the miracles. Maybe a minute lasts forever. Maybe we can learn to fly around the birth of God, for Christmas. I do not know what cos-tumes angels certainly wear. I determine to hear the simple equation: human plus a certain longing for God and health equals a journey to strange sides of the mountains. I have climbed a few for this Christmas, near the end of another century. I've made some photographs to prove to my nervous heart or doubtful eyes that what they know, they know, for a minute. What else to do, on a voyage to the Philippines with my friend the midwife when so much must still be born, a year before our millennium, and a minute has no certain calculation, nor does the sound of near wings and wonders, in the smallest scheme of things?

NOTE:

Jun Labo was brought to Russia recently to "perform" his faith healings—as he has done numbers of times over the last several years. The Russian public is enam-ored of so-called faith healing. He was arrested, jailed in Moscow for three months, and just released. He had been suddenly accused of fraud and practicing medicine without a license, a contradiction in terms, but so it is.

—M. Berdeshevsky

REBA RUN

The stiff Tin Man paper hospital gown
     on my naked upper body.
Restless eyes saunter up to the
     spaghetti-like charts on the wall.
The heart
     that isn't Valentine shaped at all
     more like a lop-sided vacuum cleaner bag.

Routine check-up time
     five years after split sternum, artery re-routing
     bypass
Charts on the wall
     blare "patient education" warnings
CAD: Coronary artery disease
     the blood vessels to the heart are blocked, narrowing.

Arteriosclerosis
     the heart does not receive the oxygen and nutrients
     it needs.
Ischemia
     "is-KEY-me-uh"

I am confident that under the Tin Man vest
     my heart is red red
don't I feel it pulsing
     electrically wired and loaded like the VW?
Air conditioning, 6-speaker cassette stereo, dual front and side
     impact airbags,
ABS brakes
     and a bud vase
Standard.

I'm back into the spoiled world
     cruising down the H1 freeway
     Moanalua heading mauka
then I see it
The red car.
     it demanded to be seen. Ho
butting into my Beetle-friendly lane
a bashed, slinky old-model Nissan hatchback—I'd always
     hated those lizard-like things—poked itself in front
     of me.
No doubt—this car is red red.

Stopped in traffic, we're held hostage by
     the old yellow school bus lurching toward the
Bishop Museum exit
     ready to disgorge it's load of sixth-graders
     in time for a demonstration of
Polynesian celestial voyaging.

A long flailing female arm emerges from the smoke-tinted
     passenger window.
I imagine
     the jingling made by the wad of "affordable gold"
     bracelets on her arm
bracelets with Hawaiian names engraved on them
     in black Olde English lettering.
"Malia," "Pono," or maybe "Hawai'i No Ka Oi."

A head follows the arm
     with a homemade fifties hairdo, sunglasses and dangling a
     cigarette
I imagine
     the arm and the hair saying to me in pidgin:
     "Eh, try wait, ok? You gone lettus in or wha?"

I'm straining to make out the driver's silhouette
I guess right
        a frizzy double, two freeway molls
two Thelma and Louise women on the H1
        breaking up the afternoon.

Hell yes, they're welcome in my lane
        anyone with a license plate
that says "Reba"
        and a bumper sticker
"Chicks Kick Ass."

The red hatchback farts, darts, bullies
        in and out of lanes
asserting its rude energy.
I'm not their only
        freeway challenge
I'm not the only vehicle
        to be up-staged
by red red.

A feeling of sisterhood sweeps over me
        for these big roughhousing women.
Aren't we all part of the same world?
        touched by flames of daring
        marking the stations of the cross
In whatever snatches the world
        and our bodies
gift us with.

I wonder if
        some thick-necked man
with no heart for women drunk on themselves
        will someday drive them off a cliff
Like the movie Thelma and Louise.

I want to send them "patient education" warnings
        about keeping the heart oxygenated and full of
        nutrients.
I want to tell them I can smell health in
        their hatchback brag.

But just then
        they cut a swath across the freeway
        at the last minute.
A hairpin turn toward Kāne'ohe, the country.
They don't need my
        post-pulmonary check up
        advice.

Now they're gone,
swallowed by exhaust
        and Ko'olau cathedrals
throwing the unbitten coin of
        regret
back at me.

MORRIS MONIZ LIVES

I was raised up in Moroni (that's "more-own-eye," not like "macaroni"), Utah. Raised as a Saint, of course, Latter Day Saint. My father's generation hated being called Mormons; they claimed it was a derogatory type name that people in the middle of the last century called us as they were persecuting our leaders or burning down our houses and driving us further and further west, to a place nobody wanted, namely Utah. Joseph Smith himself was tarred and feathered on more than one occasion, before he was finally murdered by a lynch mob in Independence, Missouri. A true martyr. But it's okay to call us Mormons now—fewer and fewer Saints are alive that take offense at the word.

Of course, some people in my home town would say that it's not all that honest for me to even call myself a real Saint. Not that I've been excommunicated or anything, but when it came time for my missionary work I told my father I wanted to go to college directly, instead of going to Peru for two years first. He pleaded with me to change my mind, our Deacon dragged me into his office to lecture me, my mother cried for a month. That's the kind of Mormons we were. In the end I was accepted on a swimming scholarship (I forgot to mention that in high school I set state records in the backstroke and freestyle), and in the fall of 1989 I left home for good, to attend the University of Nevada-Las Vegas.

At UNLV I majored in criminal justice studies, looking to fulfill my lifelong dream of becoming a law enforcement officer. In '94 I graduated, and was immediately accepted as a recruit in the Las Vegas Police Department. After my training I was assigned to a squad car patrolling the old downtown district, the original Las Vegas. My partner was Hap Davis, also a Mormon, also from a small town in Utah.

Hap wore Ninja shades day and night, which was possible in Las Vegas, a city that spends more per capita on electric lighting than any other place in the country. Hap was an enthusiastic Saint, who carried out his mission in Papua, New Guinea (a real challenge, he liked to say), and he was always trying to get me to go with him to various LDS gatherings on the weekends. I think he sort of noticed that I wasn't really into the religion anymore, and he worried about that.

Finally I accepted an invitation to a LDS pot luck, where Hap introduced me to a woman, a friend of his wife's, who was the most beautiful woman I had ever seen up to that point in my life. Her name was Sharleen. A description of her by me is not going to come anywhere near to doing her justice, but let me at least try. She had almond-shaped green eyes, long dark hair, and brown skin that shined like satin. She told me she was of Chinese, Hawaiian, and Scottish descent. In six months we were married. Six months after that I was patrolling in a squad car in Honolulu—the direct result of Sharleen being so homesick she couldn't stand looking at the high desert anymore, and her not wanting our little girl (due in a few months) to be raised as a half-breed, when if she grew up in the Islands she'd look just like everybody else.

One of the first things I learned when I got over here is that the City and County of Honolulu includes the entire island of O'ahu, which is something like a hundred miles in circumference, and even though Sharleen and I lived in a small apartment in the city proper, I as a rookie got assigned to a cruiser way out in the country, in an area called the North Shore.

It was pretty quiet out there. Domestic calls mainly, some break-ins, some backyard marijuana eradication. My partner was a Hawaiian—Abner Poepoe—a big brown guy with perfect, square white teeth. We were patrolling Hale'iwa one weekday (actually we were stationary, watching the surfers from the beach park parking lot), when the dispatcher comes on with a bank robbery in progress. We realize it's happening just blocks away, which really excites Abner, since he knows we've got a shot at being first on the scene.

"Hey, oh boy!" he yells and guns the cruiser through the streets. Right away when we pull up to the bank we see this guy out front who must be the manager jumping up and down and pointing toward a narrow lane beside the building. As we drive past him he yells something—sounds like "muh-man, muh-man"—but neither of us is really paying attention because a second later we're out of the cruiser, standing in front of a small house at the end of the lane. Right behind the house the cane fields begin. An old man in the front yard of the house is bent over, examining something on the ground. When he straightens up he's holding a twenty-dollar bill. Abner walks up to him and plucks the bill out of his hand.

"You!" the old man protests.

"Here's another one," I shout out, moving around to the side of the house, following the trail. I find four more bills on the back lawn, and real obvious footprints leading into the newly planted cane field beyond. I take one step into the field and almost go ass-over-teakettle as my shoe disappears into the thickest, red-gum mud I've ever encountered. Abner comes up alongside me, takes in the field, the trail of money, and my shoe in a single glance. He looks at me, I look at him. He raises his eyebrows the way people over here do sometimes when they have something to say but don't want to bother with words (Sharleen does this), and then he smiles and nods when he sees that I must understand him, because I've sat down on the lawn and now I'm pulling off my shoes (no way am I destroying them, not on my salary).

"No weapon shown," he says, "but you be careful, eh? Da friggin' cane only three feet high." He scans the field with binoculars. "Da buggah mus' be crawling already."

Even with my pants rolled up as far as they'll go, the mud still reaches the cuffs, but the effect of it gooshing between my toes is really not all that unpleasant. I follow the twenties out into the cane stalks, and I've gone maybe a couple hundred feet or so when I come across a suspicious-looking mound that, upon probing, I confirm is the suspect lying face down. Immediately concerned that he might be suffocating, I roll him over. The suspect opens his eyes, smiles up at me (his teeth are dazzlingly white against the mud background). He's clutching the wad of bills to his chest with both hands—just for a second the image enters my head of a man praying.

"Howzit?" he says.

A small crowd has gathered when I get him back to the house. Abner takes one look at him and says no way are we putting that mudball in the squad car, let's hose him off first. I ask the old man if we can borrow his garden hose, but he waves me off, grabs the hose himself and begins spraying the suspect, who shows no surprise or protest and even lifts his arms for the old man to get at his pits. Everyone stands there, in anticipation, waiting for a recognizable person to appear as the mud comes off. But, although the recently acquired layer of the red stuff does disappear into a slurry around his bare feet, the jet of water has no effect on another, apparently baked-on layer underneath. I hear a guffaw from the crowd. It's the bank manager, shaking his head.

"Sucking Mud Man."

"You know this guy?" Abner asks. I realize that, although Abner is local as the day is long, both he and I are recently assigned out here, and really don't know the neighborhood yet.

One of the blond-haired surfers in the crowd begins mimicking a reggae bass line coming from a boombox speaker, working himself into a little chant.

"Mud Man, Mud Man, where you been, man?"

The surfer lays out a palm in the suspect's direction, and the suspect picks up the beat, doing a barefoot shuffle on the grass as the rest of the crowd claps in time.

"Okay, dazit," Abner says, grabbing the suspect's arm and leading him to the cruiser. By this time there are five blue-and-whites on the scene. We leave it for the other guys to do the witness interviews, and head up the hill with the suspect to the Wahiawā Station.

From the second we're all together in the cruiser and moving down the road the suspect is talking at us; there is no shutting him up. Occasionally I look back at him, through the cage, and it is definitely a weird sight, as though a clay statue could talk, a clay statue with flashing white teeth and eyes that roll around a lot and also show white, like headlights going from high to low beam. Right away he tells us his name, his real name—Morris Moniz—and his other name, we've probably heard of him, Mud Man.

"You know, you wen try foah violate my constitutional rights."

"Wat?" Abner says, not caring but bored with the drive.

"You wen try foah remove my da kine, protective shields. Widout dis," indicating the dried mud layer, "ultra-violent rays going penetrate. Bombye I get every kine cansah you can tink of."

"Oh yeah?" Abner grins, winking at me. "No worries, bruddah. Dey going put so much concrete between you an da sun, bombye you look like my partner already."

"Oh no," Moniz cries, mocking both of us, "noddat. You can do anyting to me, torture me whatevah, but no make me one haole, I stay begging you."

Abner figures that since Moniz shows no sign of settling down, he might as well bait him some more.

"Mud man, yeah? Mud is cool. But how come you wen rob a friggin' bank—da mud made you do 'em, or wat?"

"No way. Da angel Moroni wen tell me foah do dat."

I admit it, this makes me turn around in my seat.

"What on earth do *you* know about the angel Moroni?"

"Moah den I wanna know, dass wat. Why, boddah you?" He stares at me, nodding finally. "Oh, okay. You one Laddah Day dude, yeah?"

I can't help myself. "Don't blaspheme! You'll pay terribly later."

"Eh, Moroni wen tell me exactly da same ting."

We get to the station, book Moniz, lock him up, and about an hour later an F.B.I. agent shows up, it being procedure in all bank robberies. Before he interviews Moniz he takes our statements. He explains that most bank robbers are not professionals, but desperate drug addicts, which is why people like Mud Man Moniz wind up being the masterminds behind such a brilliant heist as this one, ha, ha, ha, making the agent's job a lot easier, you see, since any beat cop can usually catch them, as Poepoe and I have just proved.

Our baby arrived in March—Jessica, a tiny, perfect version of her mother, with blue eyes being my contribution. By not saying anything but the right things I managed, by June, to get reassigned to duty in the city, cruising the Kapi'olani-Ke'eaumoku district with a new partner, Samson Park, who is half Korean, half white, and looks like a movie star.

One morning we're stopped in traffic and I happen to look to my left and there is Morris Moniz, on a bicycle, waiting for the light to change. Immediately I have Samson flash the light, give two seconds on the siren, and we pull Moniz over to the sidewalk. Right away I see he recognizes me.

"Eh, Mr. Haole Mormon ossifer, how you?"

Without hesitating I spin him around and cuff him while Samson runs a computer check. But there's no warrant out, nothing. Samson is visibly upset with me, apologizing like crazy to Moniz as he uncuffs him. But Moniz is smiling, with a look that says: it's okay, just another long-suffering citizen here, minding his own business. Which is when it hits me—I can sort of *see* Moniz. Not just his eyes and teeth, but the shape of his jaw, and the hard left turn to his stubby nose. I also notice for the first time how short he is—no more than five-one or five-two.

Don't get me wrong though, Moniz is still covered, head to toe, with something (though all he's actually wearing in the way of clothing is a pair of nylon swim trunks), but the something is much darker than mud could ever be, more like coal dust—but coal dust that glistens oddly in the Honolulu noontime sun and clings to him like semi-gloss latex paint. Like semi-gloss that hasn't quite set up yet.

"Eh, no touch me!" Moniz yells, slapping away Samson's hand. Samson recoils, utterly surprising himself, unaware that he was even reaching for Moniz, that he too is curious as to the composition of the covering. He gives Moniz an innocent, questioning look; Samson seems to be about ten years old at this moment. Moniz clearly likes this. He ignores Samson while directing his explanation at me. Unfortunately he starts at the beginning.

When he got up before the judge on the bank robbery charge he took the stand in his own defense. He explained about the angel Moroni, at which point the judge says wait one minute, did you say Moroni? and Moniz says yes, and Moroni told me exactly what to do, and, since it was an angel doing the talking, I did what I was told, and your honor knows the rest. The judge does kind of a strange thing and asks Moniz, how many times did the angel Moroni speak to you, and Moniz says just once. Just once? the judge says, looking at him hard. Well, actually three times, Moniz says. Which was it, the judge says, getting plenty excited now, three or once? Three times, Moniz says, but all in one night. Then, Moniz tells me, the judge just sits and stares at him, and you could hear a pin drop in the courtroom. And, although I'm standing in the hot sun in the middle of a busy sidewalk talking with a madman it's just the same for me—my mouth is hanging open and the world has stopped and all there is is Moniz, who for once has ceased talking.

"You, you read that," I finally say to Moniz. "You read that in The Book."

Samson Park has long since lost interest and is over at the cruiser, checking out his hair in the side view mirror.

"Dass exactly wat da judge wen say."

"And?"

"An' wat? I cannot read shet. Not da newspapah, even. Everyting, da words, foah me, da kine, upside-down backward mix up already."

"You're dyslexic."

"Watevah."

"Someone told you the story then."

"Watevah you say."

The judge, who Moniz claims was sort of shaky by this time, remanded him to the state mental hospital at Kāne'ohe (apparently Moniz had already spent time there). After five months he was released to a half-way house in Makiki, in the middle of the city, which is where he is now. The state even bought him a bicycle, this bicycle, which although actually a girl's bike he likes a lot, especially the wire basket between the handle bars, which he uses to hold the aluminum cans he collects from trash bins along Waikīkī Beach, cans he crushes with his bare feet to reduce their bulk. The tourists sometimes stop to watch him do this. Some even throw coins at him after he's done.

Yes, Moniz is a full-fledged townie now, forced by the terms of his parole to remain in the city and actively seek employment. No regrets over this, the authorities do what they have to do, as always, but the lack of mud on the streets of Honolulu makes things difficult at first. He could remain indoors, of course, but this would kill him faster than any rays you could mention, he being a nature boy at heart; and besides, jobs don't come to those who just sit at home, so some new protection had to be devised.

Eventually he finds a friendly gas station owner who supplies him with waste oil—mostly ninety-weight gear oil from manual transmissions—which he applies to his exposed body parts (and, unavoidably, his swim trunks) by filling up a plastic bucket and dumping it over his head. This works. He can feel the rays bouncing off him and back into space where they belong, but now his body is so slippery that his feet slide off the pedals of his bike every time he tries mounting it, and he can't open doors on the first try or even eat a hamburger at McDonald's without the burger slipping out of his hands and falling to the ground where he is forced to get down on his hands and knees and eat it like a dog. So what he does is he goes down to Ala Moana Beach Park to the circular concrete pits where the picnickers dump the ashes from their hibachi fires and he takes the charcoal ash and lightly dusts himself from head to foot. Instantly he re-connects with the planet, gets some friction back in his life so to speak, and, although he has to carry a small pouch filled with the ash and periodically re-dust himself, he is happy with the new approach, no additional problems to report. He even likes the new look, even briefly considers changing his name from

Mud Man to, well, something else. But no need, no need. Petroleum being, after all, just a deeper down kind of mud, mud from the center of the earth, and charcoal dust being burnt wood, trees being the source of wood, and trees growing, that's right, out of the mud, makes him still Mud Man. And now he really has to take off, since unlike cops he has no union, no breaks, no pension, no health plan. Aloha!

I wasn't really worth much as a law enforcement officer for the rest of that day. Even Samson Park noticed that I was out of it, and Samson never notices anything. When I got home I ate dinner without knowing what I was eating or what Sharleen was talking about. After dinner, instead of watching TV and cuddling with baby Jessica I went into the bedroom and pulled out Sharleen's copy of *The Book of Mormon* from the nightstand drawer. I already knew the part I was looking for—every Saint knows it. It's right at the beginning, where Joseph Smith is explaining about the origin of the Book, how the Angel Moroni appeared before him in the night with directions on how to find the golden plates, upon which the Word was inscribed. The particular paragraph I wanted was this one, where, talking about Moroni, the Prophet Smith writes: "After this third visit he again ascended into heaven as before, and I was left to ponder on the strangeness of what I had just experienced. . . ." Three visitations. In one night. By the same angel. This is what made the judge (who, as I suspected, turned out to be a Saint also) do a double-take, and also stopped me in my tracks when Moniz told me about it. Of course it's right there in black and white for all the world to read—millions have and accept it as the truth. But I believed Moniz when he said he couldn't read. Which brings me to another strange thing, probably as strange in its own way as an angel appearing to an unlettered farm boy in the 1820s. Sitting there on our bed, reading the Prophet's words, I suddenly realized (scaring myself quite a bit) that I believed everything Moniz had told me. Absolutely everything. I cannot, of course, defend this belief. It's like the feeling I used to get from going to church—filled to the brim, with no space left for rational doubt. Which scared me even more, when I thought about the source of my newly found faith: that is, one Morris Moniz, felon.

It's a week or so later and Samson Park and I are cruising down Pensacola Street, heading into the setting sun, when we get a call on a robbery in progress at Ala Moana Shopping Center. A jewelry store has just been hit, the suspect fleeing on foot, headed makai (toward the sea). I tell Samson to floor it, and in two minutes we're at the beach park, where three or four cruisers and a couple of Cushmans are already on the scene, and a sergeant directs us to search on foot the area around the duck pond. The sun has dipped below the horizon by now; mothers and fathers are gathering up their blankets and hibachis and kids and heading for home. We question several people, but nobody's seen anything unusual. Fifteen minutes later we're standing next to the pond, Samson smoking a cigar (I've told him not to, it sets a bad example), when a little kid comes up and tugs on my pant leg.

"Eh, da straw wen move!"

We look where the kid is pointing. In the fading light it's hard to see, but out there in the pond, sticking straight up out of the duck-excrement-colored water a plastic drinking straw is, yes, the kid is right, moving along, leaving a telltale wake, like a miniature periscope. Several other officers have joined us by now. There is an awkward moment, while everyone looks at everyone else, mentally ordering rank and seniority. Then Samson Park swears, yanks off his shoes, rolls up his pants, and, after a brief struggle, drags Morris Moniz to shore.

At just this moment a mobile TV news truck pulls up to the near-by curb and shines a blinding floodlight on the whole scene. With his hands already cuffed behind his back Moniz grins through the layers of gear oil and duck scum, winks, and speaking directly into the camera, says, "Howzit?"

The next part I have to tell concerns the strangest period I've experienced in my life (up to now). True, I may have had some secret doubts about certain things before this, things I didn't tell Sharleen or anyone else about. Sharleen is a very devout person (maybe I forgot to stress that), and I guess I wasn't ready to go into my problems with her concerning my loss of faith in the Church that both of us grew up in. I mean, my doubts in that area came along before we met, but after I let so much time go by it became impossible to talk about it without it seeming like she was somehow involved, somehow to blame. I know her, and that's just how she is.

So, I continued to go through the motions, attend services, etc. But somewhere deep inside I had that same gnawing doubt. I kept thinking about the early Saints, about the purity of their exodus across the continent in the 1850s. It took a real community to do that, every-one watching out for everyone else, sharing burdens, arriving in the

Great Salt Lake Basin with little more than the clothes on their backs, but elated, home at last in the Promised Land. This was how I had wanted to feel, how I did feel when I was young. Connected to something that stood apart from everything else, from the world as we know it. My personal sanctuary of pure goodness.

So maybe I already had some kind of secret life going on, and Moniz was just like the next level, I really don't know, not yet anyway. I just knew that he was important, even though I couldn't say why exactly. Anyway, what happened was, after Moniz was arraigned and indicted on the jewelry store job (we found a diamond ring in his swimsuit pocket and recovered two Rolexes from the pond) I went out and secretly hired him a very expensive, very well-known trial lawyer, who agreed to tell the press and anyone else who asked that he was taking the case pro bono, because he felt that all too often rich people were able to buy justice in this country and every once in a while he needed to defend someone like Morris Moniz, just so he (the lawyer) could sleep at night (while billing me weekly). Meanwhile Sharleen had started working nights for an accounting firm downtown, in order for us to build up a nest egg and qualify for a loan on our dream house.

And it gets worse. I decided to take sick leave in order to attend Moniz's trial, which was getting plenty of publicity because of the prominence of the lawyer, the comedy of the arrest (witnessed on TV by everyone in the state), and the nature of his defense. No way could I show up in court as myself; the TV cameras were there every day, not to mention that quite a few people in the criminal justice system knew me, at least by sight. So, I shopped around as discreetly as I could in second-hand stores and turned myself into a middle-aged hunchbacked Caucasian woman with thick glasses and a trench coat, sort of a composite of the regular crowd I saw all the time in the District Court gallery when I had to appear there as a police officer. I threw in the hunchback (foam rubber attached with masking tape) because I figured no one questions cripples, and I was right—people gave me one glance and then looked quickly the other way, leaving me to watch the proceedings, secure in my disguise.

Moniz was led in by a guard. He wore a threadbare grey suit a couple of sizes too big and a grin so wide it seemed to extend several inches on either side of his face. What my (Moniz's) lawyer did was to concentrate, right from the beginning, on the voice, the Angel Moroni's voice speaking to Moniz, directing him to rob the jewelry store because the jewelry store represented Mammon, and Mammon must fall before the Kingdom of Heaven can be restored. The lawyer called three different psychiatrists who all testified that they had examined Moniz and found that he really did hear a voice. And, Moniz being a devout Mormon (I almost choked on my chewing gum), and therefore believing fervently in Moroni—an angel who had also spoken to Joseph Smith over one hundred and seventy years ago about the lost tribes of Israel and where to find the golden tablets which told of their wanderings in the New World—Moniz had little choice but to believe and obey. And remember, you doubters out there, that Joseph Smith had also not been believed initially, but nevertheless had gone on to found a very successful, very popular religion with millions of converts worldwide and enough cash to start up businesses like Safeway Stores and elect influential and respected leaders like Orin Hatch to the U.S. Senate. If so many millions of people could believe and invest in Joseph Smith's vision (based on a conversation with a certain angel), then who are we to say that Mr. Moniz, a man of faith, shouldn't believe and follow the orders of the very same celestial being? Weren't we, in essence, trying the wrong entity here? Wasn't Mr. Moniz merely a misguided victim, a victim of frivolous commandments, issued on a whim, by an irresponsible (from a secular, legal standpoint anyway) deity? Think about where we'd all be now if Moses had had the bad luck to have been singled out by Moroni, instead of Yahweh.

Wait one minute here your honor, the prosecutor jumped in. The angel Moroni never told Joseph Smith to rob a jewelry store, never ordered him to commit a felony in the name of the Lord.

Oh no? the defense countered, what about polygamy?

Your honor, the angel Moroni never ordered Joseph Smith to take multiple wives. This is ridiculous.

Oh really? What about society's response to Smith's other alleged "crimes?" Smith and his brother Hyrum, shot dead by an angry mob, while the law sat on its hands. Is that what the prosecution has in mind for Mr. Moniz—a lynching? Martyrdom?

At this point the judge told both the attorneys to sit down and shut up, and called a recess for lunch.

After lunch the defense presented closing arguments, our lawyer approaching the bench with both hands out, palms up. Your honor, we've presented expert testimony indicating that Mr. Moniz heard a voice that directed him to commit a felonious act. Let's put the religious argument aside for now, since I think we've established that no one can say for certain that the voice was or was not the angel Moroni. What we *can* say about Mr. Moniz is that he possesses a psyche fed by a potent combination of religious fervor and a belief that rays, generated by a distant star, will cause him deadly harm if he does not cover himself with mud or a mud-like substance before venturing outdoors. Add this all together, your honor, and I think you'll agree that Mr. Moniz is in no way an appropriate candidate for traditional incarceration, and instead should be remanded to the Hawai'i State Hospital for further observation and treatment.

Fast forward six months. We had just marked Jessica's first birthday, which over here in the Islands is a very important event, celebrated by Sharleen and her family with a party called a luau, attended by over two hundred people, including several of my co-workers and their families. For the first time since I'd moved to Hawai'i I felt like I might actually belong here, like my wife and I had created something in Jessica which could be a kind of bridge—one that I could walk across to acceptance.

I hadn't thought too much about Moniz since his trial, hadn't once visited him in the mental hospital. It was as though helping him had been something I had to get out of my system, but then was too confused about (or ashamed of) to pursue. I even started to feel a little more positive about the Church. Maybe, I thought, if enough time went by, I could regain what I'd lost and be a normal member of the faith again. Anyway, I was working on it.

Then one evening I got off an early shift and was just walking in my front door as the evening news was beginning on TV. Sharleen was in the kitchen fixing a quick dinner for us before she went off to work. I was unbuttoning my shirt and sort of absently watching out of the corner of my eye when the lead story—about a robbery at the Kapi'olani branch of First Hawaiian Bank—came on. I immediately gave it all of my attention because up until a month earlier that area had been my beat (I had just been rotated to Kalihi), and as the usual grainy black and white surveillance video of the crime came on the screen my gut tightened into a ball of concrete and my head felt disconnected from the rest of my body, my eyes still functioning however, watching as the video froze and focused on Morris Moniz, wearing a big floppy hat and sunglasses, at the teller's window, scooping bills into a grocery bag. I blinked in disbelief. Now the picture was gone, replaced by the newscaster, who was flashing one of those fake grins they sometimes put on when the story they're reporting has some cute angle they want you to laugh along with. The suspect, described by witnesses as a local male approximately five feet tall, his face and body covered with what appeared to be military type camouflage make-up, was seen pedalling away at high speed on a bicycle—that's right, a bicycle—heading in the direction of Waikīkī. Police are asking anyone with information. . . .

Sharleen found me there several minutes later, my fingers still on the same button of my shirt, eyes glued to the TV but not seeing anything. She had been calling my name from the kitchen, and had actually become a little frightened after I didn't reply. To tell the truth, that's how I felt too—frightened. I was scared of myself, of the feeling I had at that moment. Because I realized that there was no way I was going to call the office and I.D. Moniz. And, knowing that, I also understood that I was no longer a full-fledged member of the Honolulu Police Department, that I was a traitor to the oath I took, the oath I traded for a badge. All this rushed up at me at once and I fell to my knees, in front of the TV and Sharleen, and cried like a baby.

The next two weeks were the worst of my life (so far), as the man the newspapers called *The Bicycle Thief* went on a crime spree the likes of which the city had never seen, hitting five banks in eight days. After the second heist the Department identified him as Moniz. (He'd gone missing from the mental hospital two weeks earlier, and his old bicycle was reported stolen from a resident of the halfway house soon after that; and besides, how many five-foot tall males covered with gear oil and charcoal dust could there possibly be in a city the size of Honolulu?)

The entire force was in an uproar by the time he hit the fifth bank. The newspapers and the TV stations were having a field day, and HPD was catching all the flack. The victimized banks were all in the Kapi'olani area, Moniz was making no effort to vary his m.o., he'd been seen making his getaways each time and pursued by everyone from security guards to patrolmen to common citizens, but they all reported the same thing: one minute he was there, pedalling his ridiculous three-speed bike down the street and the next minute he turned a corner or slipped behind a bus and was gone.

The Chief formed a special task force—because I had been in on two previous arrests of Moniz I was picked as a team member. We set up a command post in the basement of the main station on Beretania Street, and opened up a bank of phones we manned twenty-four hours a day to take care of the reports that were pouring in of Moniz sightings. He was seen pretty much all over; we sent officers to every part of the island to check out every single report. Nothing. When he robbed bank number six the Chief himself came down to the basement and yelled at us for half an hour straight.

The next day we got our first real break. A beat patrolman downtown had been questioning a street person about something else and the guy, hoping to avoid being dragged in for whatever misdemeanor they had him on, mentioned that he knew the girlfriend of the "Portagee midget" we were looking for in the bank robberies. He didn't give an exact address, but he had a name—Dolores Bright—and the detectives on the task force were able to trace her to a public housing project in Kalihi. I found myself practically begging the SWAT team guys and the two FBI agents assigned to the case to be allowed to tag along when they busted down this Dolores's door, and for some reason they said okay.

We sneak into the housing project in four unmarked cars—it's two a.m. and quiet. Although Moniz has never been seen with a weapon, the SWAT team is of course armed to the teeth (though under strict orders not to use deadly force if at all possible, since Moniz has become kind of a comic character by now with the public and the Chief is concerned not to appear to be overreacting).

The SWAT team deploys itself, front and rear, around a two-story complex at the end of a short cul-de-sac. As one of the F.B.I. agents and I watch from a car, several team members silently climb the concrete stairs single file and bunch around one of the apartment doors. The two biggest officers swing the iron battering ram once against the flimsy door and then all hell breaks loose, the SWAT team shouting and piling into the too-small space, residents pouring out from every door on the lane, dogs barking, kids crying, the whole scene suddenly lit from above by the powerful search light of a police helicopter, which has been hovering out of earshot behind a nearby ridge and is now drowning out all other sounds with the scream of its turbine.

It's several minutes before the SWAT team begins emerging, one by one, from the apartment, and by now there are more than a hundred residents gathered, not to mention two TV news trucks. One of the officers has a woman in tow—this must be Dolores Bright—but there's no sign of the man everyone is craning their necks to see. The helicopter, I notice, has moved to an area just behind the projects, and several of the officers are running in that direction. The other F.B.I. agent opens the driver's side door and slides behind the wheel, telling us that they are pursuing a suspect into the thick brush of the ridge. We've got him now, the agent says, might as well go back downtown for the interrogation. As we speed out of the projects the last person we steer past is one of the TV reporters, microphone held dejectedly at his side while he yells into a cell phone: "Not yet, not yet!"

Sometime after dawn of that same morning I got the story of what happened from a SWAT team guy who was one of the first through Dolores Bright's door. This guy is big, Chinese I think, with huge shoulders and hardly any neck, but a sweet high voice almost like a girl's. When they push into the tiny apartment the first thing they hear is a woman's scream from behind the bedroom door, so they break in there, just in time to see the dark shape of a man jump up off of Dolores Bright and dive headfirst out the second-story window, right into the arms of the officers waiting below. The Chinese guy sticks his head out the window to watch what he figures will be a quick and successful finish to the raid, but instead he compares it to the greased pig event at a county fair, six big men taking turns trying to tackle a very small, dark, four-limbed critter that rolls and twists and squirms and finally breaks free and starts running faster than he's ever seen anything run, toward the next building, where several residents are already coming out of their apartments, which makes firing on the suspect impossible.

Around nine in the morning of the same day the captain heading our task force called a meeting to announce that, after an exhaustive search of the hills behind the projects, involving fifty officers, several dogs, and both of the department's helicopters, Moniz had eluded capture once again. We're sure it was Moniz, he explained, because Dolores Bright gave him up (after not being able to satisfactorily explain why the entire front of her body was smeared with gear oil and charcoal dust). Where do we go from here, the captain asked. We redouble our efforts, track down every lead, stay up for a week straight if we have to, until we get our man. Because worse than the ridicule in the press, worse than the cheap-shot comments of politicians or the sneers of the public, is the idea of the bad guys out there, the slime balls, laughing at this Department, disrespecting every single one of us who wears a badge. It's time we took back this city and let everybody know who's in charge. Let's get to it.

The last time I saw Morris Moniz was two nights later. I had stepped out for a bite to eat around eight o'clock, and was on my way back down the stairs to the station basement when I almost ran into the captain, rushing to his car. Moniz had been positively identified, on his bicycle, pedalling over the Ala Wai bridge, heading into Waikīkī. The two patrolmen who had spotted him had followed in their cruiser, but then lost sight of him as he entered the congested area around Fort DeRussy. I asked the captain if I could ride with him, and he said let's go.

We drove down into Waikīkī, listening to the calls coming over the radio every few seconds, various units checking in, already an incredible amount of people involved, from the Cushman drivers to the bicycle squad guys to officers who had left their cruisers double-parked and were out working the sidewalks and probing the bushes. Everywhere we looked there was a policeman looking back at us, giving the captain the thumbs up or a shrug and a nod. And then we heard it—a positive sighting, man fitting the description surprised by a security guard in one of the big hotels on the beachfront attempting to break into the penthouse suite, the guard giving chase but losing the suspect somewhere between the eleventh and twelfth floors, the guard almost sure it was our man since he was naked and very slippery. The guard also reported the suspect had a knife.

We're in the alley behind the hotel in what seems like thirty seconds. Several three-wheelers and a single cruiser are pulled up in a rough circle around an open service door. The captain and I run inside, charging down a long, low-ceilinged hallway, through a couple of doors, bursting suddenly into the main lobby of the hotel, where a manager-type in an aloha shirt stops us.

"No, no, officers, please! The service elevator, please—our guests."

"Fuck that," the captain yells, surprising me and the manager equally (I'd never heard him swear), "where the fuck is everybody?"

"I think they're on ten," the manager squeaks.

"Let's go!"

We ride up in the main elevator with three terribly sunburned Japanese tourists; when the door opens on the tenth floor there's no one in sight. We run down the hallway, push open the door to the stairwell and here the captain grabs my shirt sleeve to hold me up.

"Shhh. Listen."

Above us, maybe two floors up, we hear the unmistakable scuffing of cop shoes on cement accompanied by heavy breathing and then a single "Shit!" The captain nods at me and we run up the stairs to the twelfth floor—just as we enter the hallway we see a police pant leg go around a corner. The captain yells, the patrolman comes back, and we follow him to where five or six officers are clustered around room number 1212. The first thing I notice about these guys is how young they all are. I figure they must mostly belong to the Cushmans—that's typical duty for rookies. The second thing is the smell of fear coming off them like a chemical cloud. The third thing, which makes the fear rub off on me, is that they all have their weapons out of their holsters.

"He's here," one of the rookies tells the captain.

"We got him—da buggah keep coming back to dis floor," another one says dreamily. "We saw him go in—he nevah come out."

"Did you check it out," I ask, "is there a guest in there with him?"

Nobody answers. They're too pumped up to care. I see that the captain is caught up in it too, more a part of the group now than leading it.

"Captain, this may not be Moniz. The security guard saw a knife. That's not Moniz's m.o."

"Hey, this shithead don't know an m.o. from asshole," the captain spits.

One of the rookies laughs at this, and as I quickly turn to look at him I find myself staring into the grinning face of the devil. The devil has the mannerisms of a killer punk, high on crystal methamphetamine—he throws his head back, and winks at me, waving his nine-millimeter automatic.

"Time to get it on," the devil says to me. "Where's your piece?"

"Right here," I answer, and I'm part of a chorus, the rookies and the captain all leveling their guns, all eyes now travelling past the evil one to focus on the hotel room door. To my horror I see that the door knob is turning. As if on cue, three of the rookies forming the front line go down on their knees, guns extended, and as the door opens to reveal Moniz I feel my own finger pull gently on the trigger and then my mind goes to jello in the roar of firing and the choking smell of gunpowder and the drowned-out screams of my fellow officers. For a second or two I see nothing in front of me—it's as if the bullets have passed through thin air, through a ghost—but then Moniz is there, standing in the doorway. He is looking down, confused, at the volcanoes of blood that have suddenly erupted all over his chest and abdomen. He lifts his head to gaze upward at the ceiling, then turns his attention to us. As his glazed-over eyes scan the group of officers he nods slowly, as though committing their faces to memory, then stops when he gets to me, breaking into a slow smile.

"Eh," he says, as though from a great distance, "how you?" He pitches forward and lands with a sickening thump onto the floral print carpet of the hallway.

In the first few weeks following the shooting, the department received quite a bit of criticism over the fact that Moniz was unarmed (the key to a bicycle lock was found in his closed fist, although we never located the bike). But the critics were fewer in number and less vocal than back when Moniz was loose and on his spree. There was an internal investigation—a rubber stamp kind of thing, designed to quiet the bleeding-heart types and the advocates for the poor who were making all the noise about police brutality.

As for myself, I tried as hard as I could to forget what happened that night at the hotel, to forget Moniz—in particular to forget the look he gave me as he was dying. I started paying more attention to Sharleen and Jessica, and tried to become a fully engaged Saint again, attending every function and even exploring ways that I might still be able to fulfill my mission, even this late in life.

Professionally, I got a new partner (Samson Park having left for Seoul to pursue an acting career)—Buddy Ching, a chubby, cheerful guy who introduced me to the intricacies of local food. We were rotated to the Kapiʻolani-Keʻeaumoku district, my original town beat, and things pretty much went back to normal.

One morning about ten we're cruising Kapiʻolani Boulevard. I'm driving, Buddy Ching slurping over a bowl of saimin, when I see this familiar figure riding a bike on the sidewalk. I hit the brakes so hard that some of the noodles Ching is eating fly out of the bowl and stick to the inside of the windshield, Ching turning and yelling, what, did we hit something, what?!, but by now I've stopped the cruiser, blocking one lane of traffic, and I'm out of the car and now I've got my hand on the sticky shoulder of the dark-skinned bicyclist, who looks up at me with the gap-tooth grin of a stranger, a grin that shines like a bea-con through some unknown substance smeared all over his face and body and pokey hair. He keeps on smiling and nodding in an odd, knowing sort of way. Neither of us says a word.

Finally I take my hand away and walk back to the cruiser, where Buddy Ching is retrieving noodles from the back seat. I slide in behind the wheel, but make no move to go, although traffic has piled up behind us and the drivers who can are going around, giving us every kind of dirty look. Which I'm aware of, but somehow not really, myself having left the area (travelling to a place I've never been before).

I crane my neck out of the cruiser window and peer straight up into the bright blue sky, past the clouds, past our atmosphere into deep space, where, even as we speak, certain rays are racing toward us, up to no good, no good at all.

JACINTA GALEA'I

BOOT CAMP FOR SAMOAN GIRLS

Don't hang your hair; put it up or braid it; don't be late for choir practice; don't wear shorts to the faifeau's house; put a lavalava over it; don't pluck your eyebrows; don't wear football jerseys to school; when you sleep over Lei's house, don't wear her clothes; wear your own clothes; pick up the trash every day after school; don't forget to pick up all the cigarette butts and bottle caps; everything that's not a rock is garbage, so pick it up; dry your hair before you put it up; shower before evening prayer; wake up early on Sundays and fofola the mats for to'ona'i; wear your school uniform; it looks better; faifeau's daughters don't go to parties; do your homework; get a sponge and wipe the table; sweep the crumbs onto your palm not the floor; rinse the sponge again and wipe the table again; get on your hands and knees and wipe the toilet clean; it won't hurt you; feed the dogs and cats; bathe the dogs and hang their towels in the sun; open up a can of mackerel, mix it with rice, and feed the dogs; hang up your play clothes so you can wear them again tomorrow; you don't need to have your ears pierced; don't read in the dark; don't hang around the older girls; don't talk in church; wear a mu'umu'u or a puletasi, not a lavalava, to to'ona'i; don't wear tight dresses; when you use the jam, don't get it all over the jar; wipe the ketchup bottle; it's dirty; wash the cat's eyes and inside her ears; pray before you go to bed; read your Bible every day; don't go bus riding; good girls don't go bus riding; don't wear shorts in Kanana Fou; wear a lavalava over your shorts; say "tulou" when you walk in front of people; don't throw the fan; bring it to me; say "Manuia lava, Faafetai" when people ask, "How are you?"; speak with a "T" not a "K"; take the old ladies home, they don't have rides; serve the faifeau's drink on a saucer; serve the toeaina's food on a tray; run to the store and buy some fruit cocktail for the old ladies' drinks; go help Sala sweep the church; she's sweeping it by herself; don't eat nor drink while you're walking in public; fold your legs and pull your dress over your knees; don't wipe the table with the kitchen towel; you'll get it dirty; use the sponge instead; save all the rags; you can use them to wash the cars and windows; this is how you hold a broom so the bristles won't bend to one side; this is how you store a broom so the bristles won't break; hold the salu like this when you sweep; don't go in the sun; you'll get sick; don't turn the burner up so high; you'll burn the bottom of the pot; wipe the stove clean; keep your room clean; you're not a boy; Saturdays are for chores, not football games; oil the pan well and cover it with flour so the cake won't stick; cut the chicken leg in half so it will cook faster; don't go out at night; you're a girl; tell your friends not to call; the telephone is for adults and emergencies only; this is the church's telephone; don't buy those magazines; you'll just end up wanting everything in them; don't watch soap operas; they're for adults; put your dishes in the sink after you eat; don't bring your friends inside the house; play under the mango tree; drink out of the plastic cups; save the glasses for guests; don't put your feet on the couch; if you don't know how to sit on the couch, then sit on the mat; do your feaus before you turn the TV on; share your candy with the kids; when you fold the blankets, make sure all the corners are the same; scrub your body with the pulu when you shower; place the soap on the shelf so it doesn't melt; don't poke holes in the butter; put the scissors back where you got them from; no TV on school nights; don't eat your mangoes with soy sauce or salt; go help your cousins with the dishes; when people bring food over, wash their dishes and return them immediately; don't wait till the next day; don't eat the head of the fish; that's for your father; don't eat the fish at all; you might choke on a bone; don't feed the fish to the cats or dogs; they may choke on the bones; see if the dogs have clean water; smile; don't be fa'asau; don't talk about other girls; if you find quarters or anything else around the house, ask if it belongs to somebody; if you don't have money, then don't go into the stores; don't talk back to your parents; read the Ten Commandments; don't think about boys; be a good daughter; I'm a good mother; Am I not?

NORMA W. GORST

ROWAN

This young deer with his eyes
equal to the eyes of homeless children
looking out at us
& knowing the forest . . .

from "Young Deer"
Hilda Morley

The discarded apples shriveled, went brown and wrinkled like weathered cheeks. This time of year Sam tossed the apples into the grove of Scotch pine beyond the vegetable garden. When blue shadows lengthened under the trees, deer came to feast, wraithlike, their nervous white tails the only clue to their coming.

Evenings, Sam and Stella sat on the back porch, which was hidden by morning glory vines, and waited for a glimpse of Rowan.

"Sam," Stella whispered. "Is he there? Has he come back?" She pressed close to him as he peered through the vines into the garden gloom.

"Can't tell. Have to wait 'til the moon comes up." Sam shifted so Stella could see through the place he had cleared in the vines, then brought out his pipe. "It'll be up in an hour. Full, too." He fumbled at his shirt pocket for tobacco and matches.

The air lay still about them, winey with the scent of apples from Stella's kitchen where she'd canned sauce and apple butter all day.

"So many apples this year." Stella sighed. "Reminds me of the year Robbie was born. I used to lay him in a drawer of the kitchen bureau, so's I could watch him while I canned." She rubbed a leathery hand across her face, then pulled a strand of white hair back toward the bun at her neck. "He'd be twenty-five now. He'd be in his prime."

"Huh, probably woulda left home by now." Sam pulled at his pipe. "Left us so we'd be no better off than we are. Two old people on a bit of land in the north woods. Well, I never asked for more."

"Oh no, Sam. Robbie would've stayed to help us. I know he would, we would've raised him to it, raised him right."

"Can't know what they'll do when they're growed, Stell."

Blue smoke spiraled above their heads as Sam puffed matter-of-factly. Stella seemed to ignore his remark. The garden was still dark, although the sky was beginning to brighten as the moon rose. Down by the pond, a whippoorwill's monotonous skirl began.

"I knew," Stella persisted. "Even though he died when he was only twelve, I knew what he was. D'ya remember how he never complained, even when he was sick? He didn't want to worry us. I respected that."

"You believe what you want to believe," Sam grunted, shifting his bulky frame on the hard bench. "You always have and you always will. I tell you, young people these days don't want to be saddled with their parents' lives. I didn't. I wanted my own life, I made my own life, and would of wanted Robbie to do the same if he'd lived."

"But what if he'd wanted to stay? Would you have thrown him out?"

"By God, woman, you can worry a man to death. Leave off."

Stella drove him wild sometimes, never leaving things rest, always searching for ways to "put things right." When Robbie was diagnosed with leukemia, she'd told Sam she was sure they could beat the odds. That's what she'd said. She'd said, "Why would God go and give Robbie to us so late in life only to take him from us so soon?"

Now Stella shivered and said, "I'm sorry, Sam." She clutched her elbows with her hands.

"You still thinking about Robbie? It don't do no good. It don't change anything." If I could blame someone or something, this pain might ease off, he thought. As it is I never did believe in your God. There's no rhyme or reason to anything that happens in the world.

He touched Stella's hand. "We did all we could, Stella. I just wish we coulda seen how he turned out. Maybe you're right. He loved working on the trees with me. I still remember the day I taught him how to prune and gave him some pines to care for."

To celebrate Robbie's seventh birthday, Sam had taken him to the grove beyond the garden.

"Robbie," Sam said, his hands on the boy's shoulders. "These trees are as old as you. It's time to prune 'em so's they'll grow thicker.

Most people like Christmas trees that're bushy, well shaped. If we prune just right, they'll sell a lot better when they're big enough."

Robbie looked up at his father. "Can I do it? Pruning?"

"That's why I brought you here. I'm gonna show you how." Sam indicated four trees set slightly apart from the rest. "I'm going to let you care for these four trees, and when you're about twelve you can sell 'em yourself."

Robbie reached out to touch one of the new shoots at the end of a branch. A brighter green than the rest of the branch, its tip showed pale yellow where the next new shoot would form.

"It's so soft, Dad. I thought it would be prickly. It looks prickly, with all those needles."

"That's 'cause it's young. Those new shoots are the ones we'll trim off so next year two will grow instead of one. Here's what you have to do."

From the porch, Sam could see the four pines silhouetted against the night sky. Must be twenty-five feet tall, he mused. Won't never cut 'em now.

Stella put her hand on Sam's arm. "I see them. The deer have come. Maybe Rowan's there."

The moon had risen over a corner of the barn. Pale and round, its silver lit the garden. Dry cornstalks stood attached to deep shadows, and in the pine grove white tails flickered.

"He won't come," Sam said in a low voice. "He's too wild now. He lets his does come and he's probably not far off, but he won't let hisself be seen no more."

Stella jerked her head back. "Sam Strickland, sometimes I can't figure what keeps you going. Don't you have faith in anything?"

Sam grunted. How can she go on believing after what happened to Robbie, he thought. Darndest thing I ever saw, the way she saved that fawn after I found it near its run-over dam. But she couldn't fight leukemia and she can't change a deer's nature, no matter if she did raise it.

He'd carried the poor thing into the house, had made it comfortable in a box by the kitchen stove. "I'll take it to the Wildlife people in a bit," he'd said.

Stella had looked at the frail, red-brown, spotted bundle of bones, and her eyes went all soft. He could tell she was set on something.

"Sam, there's a purpose to this. We have to keep him. He was sent to us and we have to do what we can for him, not pass him along to someone else. He was meant to come to us."

"For God's sake, Stella. It's a wild thing. You can't go messing with nature. Even if you did raise it, it'd never be fit to live in the wild again." He lifted the box. "It would be too trusting of people, its worst enemies."

"Sam, you put that box right down." She knelt to stroke the narrow head with its huge, frightened eyes. "I know I can do it. And when it comes to his living in the wild again, we'll just have to see. Anyway, the Wildlife people wouldn't have the time I can give to him. He'd die in a few days."

Sam remembered how he'd stumped out of the kitchen. He'd denied all responsibility for the fawn. He'd grumbled about the crazy woman he'd married. But he had to admit she'd gone and done it, crazy or not. Even so, he dreaded the day Rowan—named for Stella's favorite tree, the mountain ash—would up and go for good.

Sam dug at the bowl of his pipe. "Well, I'm sorry. I still say he won't come now. Sorry I ever let you get attached. Probably got a rack two feet across by this time. Be lucky if he stays outen the way of the hunters this year."

Stella pressed her fingers to her mouth. "I don't know, Sam. Maybe I should've let you take him to the Wildlife people after all." She paused, then her eyes widened, "No, no. It would've been wrong. Now at least he has a chance. And he's breeding!" Stella paused. She hugged her arms to her chest.

"Robbie missed so much," Stella continued, then burst out, "Why wasn't I allowed to say goodbye to him, Sam? Why wasn't I there when Robbie left us?" Stella couldn't forget that. How she'd fallen asleep for a bit, in the chair by his bed, holding his hand. How it slipped out of hers as she slept. "D'ya think Robbie thought I had left him? Oh, I couldn't bear it if he thought that! I couldn't bear it!"

"Stella, Stella, ease off. You'll make yourself sick." Sam took her hand in his, trying to think of what words to say. "It's no use, Stell. It was a long time ago." What could he say to ease her pain, when his own still gnawed at his heart like grubs in a dead tree? He pressed her hand.

To divert her, he said, "I can't believe Rowan was so tiny once. Last time I seen him he musta been four-and-a-half feet at the shoulder." He tried to make his voice steady in the dark. "I knowed it was him from the nick in his right ear where he got caught in the wire fence. Remember when he followed you to the neighbors and got set on by sheep dogs? You had to lead him home and tie him to the clothes pole."

Stella brushed a hand across her eyes before answering. "What I remember most is when he came back after being gone a week. Oh, you'd warned me, but it was hard."

The whippoorwill, closer now, began its churning cry again.

Sam glanced at Stella to see if she had got over her bad spot. "Now that he's growed, we'll see him less and less."

"I think he's out there, Sam. Look, over by Robbie's trees. D'ya see that darker shape? The moonlight on his antlers." Stella stood up slowly so as not to startle the deer. "I'm going out to him, Sam. I want to touch him again, see if he's all right."

"Stella, no! You'll scare him off for good. This way, at least we get to see him once in a while." But Stella was already off the porch. He watched as she waded through the cornstalks, moving slowly in the direction of the four Scotch pines. They stood pale bluish-green in the moonlight, dense shadows clustered on the ground underneath. Then he saw it—a dark shape next to the pines. A large shape, tall.

He saw Stella, white as the moonlight, glide toward it. Some does moved off, staying within sight of the four pines. She raised her hand, holding it out, the fingers upturned as if giving or taking something from the night. The whippoorwill's call died. In the silence, Sam heard the murmur of her voice.

Rowan stood his ground, motionless. Stella inched forward, her hand almost to his neck. When his head jerked up, tense, quivering, Stella stopped. Then, very slowly, she lowered her arm until both hands hung at her sides.

Sam stared, pipe halfway to his mouth. He let out a slow breath as he watched the old woman and the stag face each other in the chill, wine-scented night. Finally, the tall, dark form faded into the trees and Stella turned toward the house, alone.

ERMILE HARGROVE and KENT SAKODA

THE HEGEMONY OF ENGLISH

or

Hau kam yu wen kawl wat ai spik ingglish
wen yu no no waz

This paper was presented at the Society of Pidgin and
Creole Linguistics meeting in conjunction with the
Linguistic Society of America Winter 1999 meeting in Los
Angeles.

The creole which has developed in Hawai'i has had a rough history and has at this time come to be known as Hawai'i Creole English
(HCE).

Before we proceed any further, definitions are necessary for
clarity. A **pidgin** language is nobody's native language and comes
about when people who speak different languages try to talk together
(how does this differ from foreigner talk?). It initially is makeshift and
very abrupt and abbreviated (pre-pidgin). Through frequent use, it
becomes more regularized and gradually can become a second
language (e.g., Nigerian Pidgin, cf. Siegel).

A **creole** has its origins in a pidgin but is somebody's native
language. It arises when the children of pidgin speakers acquire the
pidgin as one of their first languages.

A Very Brief History

Hawai'i's pidgin and creole development(s) came about through
a series of contacts with outsiders. The first European contact was
made in 1778, during an exploration of the Pacific. Soon after that initial contact, Hawai'i became a regular stopping place for whalers and
traders. Three kinds of pidgins—Pidgin Hawaiian, Chinese Pidgin
English and other seafarers' foreigner-talk such as Pacific Pidgin—
were part of the mix of languages available among speakers in Hawai'i
from the late 1700s to the early 1800s.

The early part of the nineteenth century was a turning point for the Kingdom of Hawai'i and probably the development of Hawai'i's pidgin(s) and creole. There was more and more contact with the outside world. The monarchy had begun to be influenced by external factors. And commerce was increasing. If the population had remained native and foreign, HCE might not have had such a complicated history. Traders probably used some kind of trader-talk with the natives. With more frequent visits, this trader-talk probably regularized into some kind of early pidgin (e.g., Pidgin Hawaiian). However, the language of commerce was (and still is) English and some form of English had to be used. So some kind of English-influenced pidgin (e.g., Pidgin English) probably arose as a later development.

In 1820, the American missionaries arrived. Hawai'i at that time was still a Kingdom. Politically, the American missionaries were ambitious. Twenty years after their arrival, they were fully involved in the Hawaiian government. By 1887, the Kingdom of Hawai'i was forced to accept a constitution and by 1893 the Queen was overthrown and taken prisoner. The monarchy was replaced with a provisional government and Hawai'i became known as the Republic of Hawai'i. In 1898, Hawai'i was annexed to the United States of America and became a territory.

Literacy and Schooling

The early literacy training missionaries did was using a Hawaiian orthography they had created in translating the Bible into the Hawaiian language. This literacy training was aimed at teaching adults and through the interest of the monarchy gained wide acceptance. As the interest of adults waned, children were targeted for literacy training. At the same time, a number of schools began to spring up—the "common" school for the general population of natives and the "select" school for the chiefly class of children. Children in the "common" school were taught using the Hawaiian orthography. Children in the "select" school were taught English.

> In 1840, the hundred or so American *haoles* (originally the Hawaiian word for "stranger" or "newcomer"), who were seeking changes in government and protection of their property rights in Hawai'i, proclaimed a constitution

authorizing an elective House of Representatives (Dodds and Sikkema, 1994:16).

Having a constitutional body allowed them to create "The General School Laws of 1840" and establish a public school system. This was not the first educational system in Hawai'i but the first school system, mandated by western law. "Education was said to be compulsory up to the age of fourteen" (Dodds and Sikkema, 1994:21). This required children to be sent to school.

Rev. Richard Armstrong, the third educational leader (Minister of Public Instruction, 1847–1860), stated as one of his aims the need for Hawaiians to learn English. "English instruction, he said, would enable the Hawaiians to enter commercial and industrial work and 'earn more money'" (Dodds and Sikkema, 1994:23). By his suggestion, laws were enacted which introduced English as the medium of instruction. Although it is not clear whether these laws covered both the "common" schools and the "select" schools, it is quite clear that "by 1855, public education in Hawaii was well organized and systematized . . ." (Wist, 1940:11). By 1870, "American textbooks replaced earlier materials written in the Hawaiian language" (Dodds and Sikkema, 1994:28) and public education in Hawai'i took on the characteristics of American public education.

The first signs of the racial nature of hegemony occurred in 1899. A paper written by Henry S. Townsend, inspector general of the schools, entitled "The Educational Problems in Hawaii" clearly states this attitude. "Townsend pointed out that 'Asians were not expected to, nor were they welcome to, assimilate with the Caucasians; the Hawaiians, now considered passive, were classified with the Asians by the Americans who were the aggressive group'. . . . The problem, as Townsend saw it, was adjusting these elements to one another in a common civilization" (Dodds and Sikkema, 1994:39).

> To teach all our people the English language, and thus make Anglo-Saxons of them, would indeed, be a very simple solution to our race problem. . . . But the educated Irishman of today is more Irish in everything else than in language. He may not be able to speak the Keltic, but he thinks, feels and acts as an Irishman. . . . The despotisms of Europe reason but superficially when they attempt to crush the Polish spirit by crushing the Polish speech. Although

English education for Hawaii . . . is an absolute necessity, it offers but a small part of the solution of our problem. Polynesians and Asiatics cannot be made to think and feel as Anglo-Saxons by the simple process of teaching them the English language.

So by the end of the nineteenth century, the force of proselytizing had diminished but attitudes were firmly in place that Hawai'i's non-Anglo-Saxon people would not change even though they were taught the English language.

The BOE, in 1880, felt the need to defend its decision to continue to establish English day-schools—the Board of Education does not admit that in the establishing of English schools [we] aim at the suppression of the Hawaiian language. Walter M. Gibson, president of the BOE, drew the issue sharply, noting that the learning capability of students was judged by their ability to speak and communicate in standard Anglo-Saxon English.

Demographics

If the population had remained native and foreign, HCE might not have developed. Hawaiian more likely than not would have been replaced by English. However, the land attracted plantation developers and agricultural industrialists. Sugarcane was introduced to Hawai'i in 1825 and with it came the importation of foreign labor to keep up with the production. The Chinese were the first to arrive (around 1835). The first sugar plantations began in 1835 but by 1875, with the Reciprocity Treaty (allowing Hawai'i, which was then still the Kingdom of Hawai'i, to export sugar to the United States duty free), sugar dominated the market. With the rise in productivity more workers were needed so along with the importation of Chinese laborers, Portuguese were imported (1872) and other Europeans, mainly Norwegians and Germans. Following the Chinese Exclusion Act of 1882, Japanese labor began to be imported (1884). This was followed by Puerto Ricans (1900), and Koreans and Filipinos (1910). (For reference, see Siegel, 1998b.)

By 1884, the demographics of Hawai'i were at a turning point. The number of Hawaiians and part-Hawaiians was just a little more than half (55%) of the total population of 80,578. By 1896, there was a significant difference in the demographics (36% Hawaiian and part-Hawaiian, 22% Japanese, 20% Chinese, and 14% Portuguese). Interestingly, by 1896, of the non-Hawaiian, non-white population, 20% were locally-born. Many of these locally-born children presumably went to school. (See "The General School Laws of 1840.") (For reference, see Siegel, 1998b.)

Languages of Hawai'i

By the end of the nineteenth century, plantations were in their heyday. Sugarcane was the main export crop and pineapple was being established as another cash crop. The need for labor was extensive. Plantations were set up similar to the plantations of the South with workers being provided living quarters on the plantation proper. The plantation "camps" as they were called were generally ethnically divided. With the increase in population, small businesses cropped up as well.

The native population still spoke some Hawaiian, although that was diminishing with the decline in population. Pidgin Hawaiian could still be heard. A few varieties of Chinese (e.g., Hakka and Cantonese) and some Chinese Pidgin English could be heard. There were speakers of several dialects of Japanese. Portuguese was still being spoken by some, as well as German and Norwegian by other Europeans. English was heard. And a pidgin was in its adolescence with a few creole speakers beginning to emerge (mostly in mixed language families and in families who had immigrated in the mid- to late-1800s).

Out of this seeming cacophony of languages and the hegemony of English, HCE emerged, first as a pre-pidgin, then as a pidgin which became a second language, and finally nativized as a creole. Its lexifier might have begun as Hawaiian but was probably replaced by English as the lexifier. In spite of the fact that American and British populations were only about 6.5% of the total population, English was, after all, the language of power—of commerce and of government. School also played a major role in the dominance of the English language.

It is this preponderant influence of English which is being addressed in this paper and which we claim is the cause of the confusion which exists today for native speakers of English. We will use three separate but overlapping perspectives to view this issue. The first is awareness (partial understanding of language), the second is prescriptivism (appropriate use of language), and the third is voice (imbalance of power). Throughout this discussion, however, you will notice a single motif of how hegemony shapes perception.

The twentieth century has seen Hawai'i Creole English challenged over and over again. It has been blamed for children's low verbal test scores. It has been used to deny employment (e.g., weatherman positions that went to court). It is a bone of contention that flares up every now and then in the daily newspapers (e.g., letters to the editor). In 1987, the Board of Education tried to ban the use of "Pidgin" in the public schools but public outcry and convincing testimony from some of the people from the academic community dissuaded the Board from following through on a policy to ban the use of "Pidgin." However, the Board did reiterate the policy that English is the language of instruction.

Awareness and Partial Understanding of Language

A dialect has been defined as a subset of a language. That is, it is a variety of a language. The variation might be in pronunciation, grammar, or vocabulary or a combination or it might be in the discourse but the assumption is that dialects of a language are mutually intelligible. It is understandable that the Hawai'i creole (Hawai'i Creole English) might be mistaken for a dialect of English since it uses English as its lexifier. However, many lexical items probably were relexified (substituting new vocabulary for old) from Hawaiian or Pidgin Hawaiian but not reconstructed (changing from one syntactic structure to another). If this is the case, and because of its history, there are system differences that exist between HCE and English. (The word is still out on whether HCE developed from a substrata or from some universal.)

Ignoring the language children came to school with, the goal was to teach the children in English. However, since educators had little understanding of the language the children came to school with and thinking that they were dealing with English, educators were inclined to relexify the children's language, since it contained English lexical items and could be partially understood by some of the teachers. (Of course, many of the teachers were native-born and trained in Hawai'i.) This practice ignores the grammatical differences which exist between HCE and English. It continues to confound language development in

Hawai'i. After one hundred and fifty years of relexification, it is hard to determine what is and what is not the creole. Some have labeled this phenomenon the post-creole continuum and continue to relexify the creole toward the target—English.

This practice (of relexifying the creole to English) is disappointing for two reasons. The first reason is that we have missed an opportunity to study a new language in natural development and instead have the potential to study a language death. The second reason is that we have failed to understand the uniqueness of the situation. What we are left with is a language which has been so altered that we are now asking, "If it sounds like 'Pidgin' is it 'Pidgin'?" (Even though in writing it looks like English, "she is feeding the horse," using Odo orthography you see the difference, "shi iz fiding da haws.") and "If it looks like English (in writing) is it English"? ("He had similar experiences that his friends had.")

Yet, it is a unique language, emerging out of a need for a group of people who have come together for a variety of reasons to form a union with the host culture, Hawaiian, yet maintaining a separate "local" language, not Hawaiian, while at the same time acknowledging the prestige of English. It is this accommodation which is reflected in the language (HCE) and in the culture ("the aloha spirit") which gives it a unique world view. It is also the inclusivity which makes HCE a linguistic enigma, as it tries to reconcile with the hegemony of English.

Attitude and Remediation

Day (nd) describes HCE as "a nonprestigious form of communication, usually associated with members of cultural groups of middle to low socioeconomic status. . . ." This is the general attitude of most people in Hawai'i, whether they are HCE speakers or not. This attitude has been fostered by the constant use of remediation of children's language in school. For example, it was noticed that children in the early 1980s did not have a plural form ending (not needed in HCE), so they were taught to add the plural form to their noun endings when plurals were needed. So rather than saying, "*Get tu dag ova dea*," the child learns to say, "*Get tu* dogs *ova dea*." *Dag* has been changed to dogs. And through generalization, one can find the following example: "And den two feets together and den one feet" (Rynkofs, 1993:143), feets analogous to dogs.

There were other instances of remediation when relexification was not involved but instead the addition of grammatical constructs. For example, it was noticed that the verb "be" is not present in HCE. So it was taught as an addition. Instead of saying, "*Shi fiding da haws,*" the child would be taught to say, "*Shi* is *fiding da haws.*" What you end up with when constructs are added are utterances such as this:

> "—he doesn't sti' yet come his school, yeah." (Day, 1974, L42-1-184/7)
> (—*hi* doesn't *stiyet kam* his *skul, yae?*)

Day glossed the utterance as: "He doesn't continue to go to school" and notes that the "*[d]oesn't* is not usually regarded as HCE in nature" but does not acknowledge the use of "his." (Another gloss for the utterance might be: He doesn't come to school anymore.)

A lot of research was done to remediate HCE to include English constructs such as the past tense marker, the "be" form fronting present progressives, the contracted form of negatives and other negative forms, yes-no question formation, passives, indefinite articles, indirect question formation, and pronominalization. It is uncertain what relexification and insertion of English grammatical structures does to a "minimal distance" language other than English but strange constructions are found in HCE. The following are some of the strange findings.

1. English past tense marker inserted into HCE sentence.
   e.g., *Ma sista haed tichd mi tu swim.* ("My sister had teached me to swim.")
2. English negative forms. HCE has different negative forms.
   e.g., *Ke not laik go bich.* ("Kay not like go beach.")
3. English passives. HCE has a different passive construction.
   e.g., *Jawn wen get bit ap* by the waves. ("John wen get beat up by the waves.")
4. English indefinite articles replacing HCE *wan* (changes the meaning).
   e.g., *Shi tol mi shi laik ple so ai wen get a bawl.* ("She told me she like play so I wen get a ball.")

Most of the remediation has been superficial and fragmented. In addition, the nuances of HCE are ignored and the effectiveness of HCE usage is diminished so that sentences such as, *"Ai laik chrai fo raid yo baik,"* gets translated as "I want to ride your bike" and loses the politeness and perhaps elegance of the statement such that it might be perceived as, "It would give me great pleasure if you would allow me to ride your bicycle."

Appropriateness and Prescriptive Language Use

Such applications of relexification and remediation to HCE have their roots in such prescriptive concepts as "correctness." In more explicit form, prescriptivism would often manifest itself in strong attitudinal commentary such as calling the creole "bad English" or "bastardized English" or its speakers as being "lazy" or "unable to learn." In a more implicit milder form, one often reads in the editorial pages of the local newspaper about the detrimental effects of "Pidgin." For example, a businessman, Nelson Nekomoto, is quoted as saying:

> Young children in school should never be taught pidgin. It becomes a handicap throughout their working career. Growing up in an environment where pidgin is a daily routine is like being sentenced to a life of poverty. They are doomed to struggle. (*The Honolulu Advertiser*, 1995:B-1)

But perhaps the most prevalent, mildest, and yet most insidious practice is to juxtapose and contrast HCE with "proper" English, totally unaware of its prescriptive nature and its consequence. In this scenario, the dominance of English commonly meant "at the expense of the elimination of the creole."

Attitudes—Historical Perspective

Although the number of Caucasians gradually grew at the turn of the nineteenth century, their influence was felt in every aspect of Hawai'i's society. The use of English for commerce and government and the use of English as the medium of instruction in schools (by the early part of the twentieth century practically every child went to school), demonstrate clear evidences of the hegemony of English.

In 1924, the Department of Public Instruction established the first "English standard" schools in Hawai'i. In 1927, the Territorial Legislature passed a law to provide for these schools (Act 103 of 1927 for

English standard schools). Children were admitted if they were able to pass the entrance examination which was an oral examination.

> There can be no question but that English standard schools and sections are regarded by some persons as a means of maintaining social and economic stratification and discrimination. Ability to speak good English has become associated with status, at least to the extent that use of "pidgin" sets one off as not "belonging" to the middle class group. This standard for gauging one's social position is utilized not alone by haoles, but by other racial groups, as well.

This system was eliminated by law in 1949 (Act 227) and phased out completely by 1961. But the attitude persists.

Gradually, there has been a change in attitude, probably brought about by the effects of the Hawai'i Board of Education's series of hearings in the late summer of 1987, in an attempt to mandate that standard English be the mode of oral communication for students and staff in Hawai'i's public schools.

> Never before in Hawai'i's history had such a diversity of voices been raised, in a formal institutional setting, in defense of Hawai'i Creole English. Taken aback by this extraordinary display of feeling against the policy, the board eventually adopted a much weaker version which simply 'encouraged' the modeling of SE [standard English] by teachers and staff members in the Department of Education. (Sato, 1993:133)

What came about after the hearings and the plethora of editorials, articles, interviews, and debates over the media was a qualified respect for HCE—a legitimization of sorts in the eyes of the community; the result being a foregrounding of both HCE and the use of the term "Hawai'i Creole English" to represent what was now a legitimate object, subject to rational discussion.

In a recent interview with a local journalist, a well-known Hawai'i author talked about how she was put down by teachers and some students for speaking "Pidgin." The journalist provides evidence of how this attitude of "there's something wrong with the way you talk" is perpetuated when she wrote, ". . . after she'd learned proper [the emphasis mine] English, she made a decision to write in pidgin."

Did the author have to learn English before she wrote in "Pidgin"? Perhaps . . . just as it is beneficial to learn a foreign language to better understand your own language. But the use of the term "proper" signifies that there is something improper about HCE.

The Hawai'i author goes on to say:

> "I don't think my teachers meant to be mean," she says now. "They just didn't want us to use pidgin. They told us we wouldn't get a good job. They suggested that if you can't speak properly you can't think. You get the message that your family is wrong, if they speak pidgin. So you grow up not knowing why you feel bad about yourself, why you feel inferior.
>
> "Even if they say pidgin is fine for some occasions, you get a picture of standard English on the right and pidgin on the left, or English on top and pidgin down there." (Kathy Titchen interview with Lois-Ann Yamanaka[1], MidWeek, June 3, 1998)

Hence, in many writings today, both academic and popular, HCE is compared and contrasted to "standard English." This perception of a subordinate relationship together with the long held view of the decreolization of HCE set the scenario for this "variety" or non-dominant dialect to be incorporated into the dominant "standard" English. The intent to use "standard" English may have been a technical decision, that is, to distinguish it from other varieties of English. However, local HCE speakers' exposure to English has predominantly been the so-called "standard" variety. This, together

---

[1]   As an aside: Lois-Ann Yamanaka's writing has faced a lot of criticism. The following paragraph from an article by Scott Whitney, Honolulu, December 1998, explains the circumstances.

. . . the American Association for Asian American Studies took back its 1998 fiction award nomination for Blu's Hanging, saying that it stereotyped Filipinos. This was the third time the association awarded, then dis-awarded one of Yamanaka's books. This public feuding turned peevish and unveiled some of Hawaii's dirty family linen: like the tensions between local ethnic groups—who have learned to share a public pidgin culture and a public Standard English DOE/Media environment, but who still mock and distrust each other in private. The irony was that the opposition to Yamanaka was headed by Japanese-American academics, who for years have been criticized for dominating the Pacific Islander and Filipino members of their scholarly associations.

with the popularization of the name "Hawai'i Creole English" which suggests a creolized English (as opposed to Hawai'i English Creole—an anglicized creole) strongly implicates that when juxtaposed, a subordinate relationship exists. A Honolulu writer and curriculum researcher, Edith K. Kleinjans, in response to the controversy of HCE in the classroom says on the editorial page of the *The Honolulu Advertiser:*

> All this does not mean that a school should insist that its student use the more public, formal variety of English all the time. But it is the kind of English that kids are sent to school to learn—the kind they are less likely to pick up outside of school. . . . It is arrogant to believe that "dialect speakers" need only understand standard English, while "leaders must know how to speak and write it well." (*The Honolulu Advertiser,* 1995:B-1)

In the same series of articles, Millicent Y.H. Kim, who was then the chairperson of the State Foundation on Culture and the Arts, shares a different point of view. What she has to say is akin to the next scenario and quite conveniently sets up the following set of discussions:

> Do I think pidgin should be used in schools if it helps students and teachers to communicate? YES! As long as it is presented in the context of TWO languages of equal status, one being preferred for classroom use but not to the preclusion of any other means of communication that will further the basic goal of learning. (*The Honolulu Advertiser,* 1995:B-1)

The following discussion is within the context in which HCE is in a coordinate relationship with English. In other words, it is its own language. Unfortunately, due to the hegemony of English, a lack of equal status between these two languages can only mean a scenario in which the non-dominant language is relatively marginalized. Marginalization occurs when people hold the commonplace view that HCE and English differ in being appropriate for different purposes and different situations. It is this concept of "appropriateness" which is a form of prescriptivism; a newer, more subtle form. Norman Fairclough (1992) very convincingly deals with this concept of "appropriateness" in language and critiques theories of sociolinguistic variation that center around it. Although the community under scrutiny is Britain, and the concept of "appropriateness" is institutionalized, the arguments put forth by Fairclough are quite applicable to the sociolinguistic situation in Hawai'i. He argues that models of language variations based upon "appropriateness"

> derive from a confusion between sociolinguistic realities and political aspirations. In no actual speech community do all members always behave in accordance with a shared sense of which language varieties are appropriate for which contexts and purposes. Yet such a perfectly ordered world is set up as an ideal by those who wish to impose their own social order upon society in the realm of language . . . appropriateness is an "ideological" category, which is linked to particular partisan positions within a politics of language— within a struggle between social groups in a speech community for control of (or "hegemony" over) its sociolinguistic order. (Fairclough, 1992:33–34)

Even in well-intentioned situations in which the assimilationist ideology is rejected in favor of a pluralist position as a way of legitimizing the educational experience of language minority groups, there are problems. In aiming to extend the range of children's language experiences and to enable them to do more with their language, the teaching of English is viewed as additive rather than remedial. The goal is to add English to their repertoire not to replace their language and/or dialect and to do so in a way which respects the children's language experience. But Fairclough (1992) asks if it is possible to add without replacing. Is it possible to teach children English which is more prestigious and powerful than their own HCE without any detriment to the latter? A possible solution (at least on the surface) is an orderly division of labor between English and the creole and any other language or variety. The different languages are appropriate for different contexts and purposes and have the legitimacy of being appropriate for some contexts and purposes. The problem is when the appropriate contexts and purposes for the languages other than English are listed. For example, M. Wrenn, a fourth-grade teacher in Kalihi [a district of Honolulu] voiced her opinion in a local newspaper:

> Don't criticize me as being ignorant or having a lack of understanding for the "beauty" of pidgin. Yet, pidgin has a right to exist—at home, on the playground, in original

> pieces of literature where pidgin is the chosen style of writ-
> ing, and in Frank DeLima's [a local comedian] show, but not
> in my classroom on a daily basis. (*The Honolulu Advertiser,*
> 1995:B-3)

For non-dominant languages, the list generally includes those contexts in the domain of the private and the quaint and excludes those that are public, formal, and socially prestigious. The message is clear to HCE-speaking children. Their language may be "appropriate" but it is also marginal and even irrelevant. The concept of "appropriateness" at its introduction into sociolinguistic studies as explained by Hymes (1972) is part of the domain of language attitudes. It is a kind of judg-ment that is made by speakers of a speech community about language use. It is about what is judged to be appropriate by speakers and not about what is or should be appropriate in a speech community. This is not to say that HCE speakers should not be aware of or scrutinize poli-cies and attitudes about sociolinguistic practices. In fact, judgments based on appropriateness should be assessed and evaluated in terms of their social genesis and functions, speakers' own sociolinguistic experiences, and the possibility, risk, and cost of denying dominant judgments (Fairclough, 1992:54). HCE speakers should have a clear picture of dominant judgments of when English is appropriate and how widely such judgments are shared and followed in practice. They should develop their ability to be able to use HCE (or any other lan-guage/dialect) for the prestigious purposes and contexts where English is said to be appropriate. They should not be condemned to disadvantage and marginalization—the final choice should be theirs to make. Lisa-Anne Lung, a Wai'anae High School [rural school on O'ahu] teacher, puts it quite succinctly:

> I don't agree with "authority" dictating what will or will not
> be spoken in school. I believe that as long as true learning
> takes place, no matter through what vehicle, that the stu-
> dent has gained through the experience. (*The Honolulu
> Advertiser,* 1995:B-1)

It is this history of prescriptivism—of "correctness," of "subordi-nation," of "appropriateness," underpinned by the hegemony of English that has shaped (or misshapen) the sociolinguistic experiences of speakers of Hawai'i Creole English.

Literacy

One reason for the persistence of prescriptivism is the insistence on literacy. Suzanne Romaine claims that without a writing system, "HCE is represented as if it were a deviant or non-standard variety of English. In other words, HCE is forced to be a literary *dialect* rather than a literary *language*" (Romaine, 1994:527). If the previous discussion is relevant, then, even if "Pidgin" had a writing system of its own (and it does have an orthography called "Odo"), it would not be legitimized in spite of an understanding of the nature of language and literacy if a prescriptive attitude endured.

What Rynkofs found in studying the second-grade children of one class of a rural school was that although they spoke in HCE, they wrote in SE. "Even those students who spoke extensive HCE with Ellen [the teacher] in the classroom still wrote primarily in standard English" (Rynkofs, 1993:63). Elsewhere Rynkofs states:

> Furthermore, Ellen never told her students that she expected them to write in standard English so the codeshifting between the oral language of Hawaii Creole English and the more formal written language of standard English was primarily done by the children themselves. The students developed this expectation for written language in SE by hearing stories read aloud to them, reading stories themselves, encountering varieties of print in SE and watching teachers demonstrate writing, among others. (Rynkofs, 1993:164)

Menacker states that the SE acquisition environments "tend to be typified by a great deal of exposure to the standard variety through mass-media and teacher models, but relatively little interaction with peer speakers of the variety. Overt correction and recasting are also likely to be present in these environments" (Menacker, 1998:5). Menacker also states that:

> The acquisition of formal written English as an additional register is an integral part of schooling in English speaking countries and in countries where English is the language of schooling. . . . It [is] often characterized in terms of language socialization and initiation into a discourse community. Like the "language awareness" approaches to standard lan-

guage acquisition by speakers of nonstandard languages (cf. Siegel, 1997), instruction in the register of formal written English often involves drawing learners attention to differences, large amounts of exposure to the target variety and recasting or correction of learners approximations of the variety. (Menacker, 1998:3–4)

Although it seems possible to acquire two or more varieties, as is demonstrated in the Rynkofs study, it would seem that the closeness or minimal language distance between the two varieties might lead to subtle linguistic differences and interpretation and translation differences which could lead to confusion and academic underachievement.

Voice (or Imbalance of Power)

If it is true that speakers of any language can hold conversations on any number of topics, then it should be true that there is no language hierarchy. However, when it comes to literacy this is not a proposition that many hold true. In spite of the fact that linguistically there is no basis for a hierarchy, academics and laypeople alike lay claim to certain languages as holding more power than others. Romaine (1994:545) claims that "HCE has yet to be seen as a language fully appropriate for certain literary genres like the novel; even within drama, we have seen how the authorial voice writes stage directions in Standard English." Would Yamanaka's *Blu's Hanging* be considered an HCE novel?

On the one hand, there is the literary strength of "Pidgin" stories. On the other hand, there is the underlying schizophrenic attitude that English hegemony has created. There are those of us who want to hear the "Pidgin" stories in spite of their raw tellings. At the same time, there are those of us who want to not be reminded that "Pidgin" refers to the "nonprestigious form of communication, usually associated with members of cultural groups of middle to low socioeconomic status . . ." (Day, nd).

As we give voice to our local characters through literary works, issues of attitude come to surface. Some of the criticism can be heard in an article by Candace Fujikane (1997:55) as she criticizes a local writers' publisher for not publishing more works by Filipinos and Hawaiians.

> In his account of the history of Bamboo Ridge Press, "The
> Neocolonialization of Bamboo Ridge: Repositioning
> Bamboo Ridge and Local Literature in the 1990s," Chock
> makes several highly problematic arguments about con-
> temporary Hawaiian literature, but ends the essay with an
> important self-critical point: "It is the job of editors to select
> what they see fit; we want to be open to diversity, but we'd
> like to publish only the best of that diversity. We also want
> to be open to suggestions. Perhaps we need your essays to
> educate us on our aesthetics, because, ultimately, the aes-
> thetics of the editors define a magazine." (Chock, 1996:25)

Is Fujikane suggesting that she has not heard voices she can identify with even in local publishers' works? Elsewhere, Fujikane (1997:57)
writes:

> We can think about the ways that the term "local" emerged
> in order to account for peoples in Hawaiʻi who are not
> "Native," and that its roots lie in a recognition of that cru-
> cial distinction between immigrant and indigenous groups.
> We can ask the question, how can non-Hawaiians claim a
> local identity and a commitment to the peoples of this place
> without supporting indigenous struggles in Hawaiʻi?

Fujikane suggests that attention should be given in support of the
indigenous efforts. But does the "Pidgin" speaker identify with the
indigenous group or with a group termed "local" which Fujikane herself claims "emerged in order to account for peoples in Hawaiʻi who
are not 'Native'"? Fujikane does not define who she is generationally
but does define herself as "local Japanese." The use of this phrase "local
Japanese" distinguishes her from Japanese nationals who come to
Hawaiʻi primarily as tourists and ethnically are different. (It also distinguishes her from mainland Japanese Americans.) But it also
includes her in the "local" category, specifically to the Japanese group.
She states:

> our teachers tried to instill within us a pride in the fact that
> we were all Americans and could claim and celebrate as our
> own the American revolution for freedom from British
> tyranny. Yet this land upon which we based our identities as
> "Americans" was inscribed with Hawaiian heiau [defined
> by Fujikane as pre-Christian place of worship] and burial

sites, as well as with the Hawaiian stories generated by these and other sacred sites. . . . (Fujikane, 1997:42)

Fujikane's words remind us of another kind of hegemony—a non-indigenous view—and she defines herself not as U.S. American but places her personhood within the context of the claim for Hawaiian sovereignty. In trying to shift the balance of power, we are faced with the dilemma of using the voice of the powerful or using other voices not usually heard who speak out for a cause.

Tamura (1996), in her article entitled, "Power, Status, and Hawai'i Creole English: an Example of Linguistic Intolerance in American History," asked several questions:

> What has been the role of speech in determining who has gained privileges and preferred positions? What have been the various perspectives on Hawai'i Creole English held by people in different positions of power at different times in the past? What roles have race and class played in the development of Hawai'i Creole English and the debate over its use? (Tamura, 1996:431–432)

These are interesting questions and some of the answers have already been alluded to previously in briefly describing the "English standard" schools, in citing the example of the weatherman's case, in citing some of the struggles with literacy and prescriptivism.

Tamura further states that "linguistic intolerance has been one way in which dominant groups have maintained their power and status."

> despite considerable advances in the field of sociolinguistics and pidgin and creole studies, middle- and upper-class Americans have continued to use their dialect of English as a gatekeeper to positions of authority and privilege, illustrating the primacy of power and status in the politics of language. (Tamura, 1996:432)

This attitude is much more pervasive than the gatekeeping that Tamura posits on the middle- and upper-classes. It is an attitude that many HCE speakers share and can still be captured in a quote in Tamura's article:

> If we speak good English, our friends usually say, "Oh you're trying to be hybolic (i.e., to act high and mighty), yeah!" . . . Consequently, those who moved to Standard English often experienced "cultural anomie."(Tamura, 1996:440)

Although it would seem that bilingualism should have been possible, schools in their attempts to teach English built potholes in people's language knowledge base. Tamura points out:

> educators in Hawai'i were ignorant of linguistic differences between Standard English and nonstandard English varieties, and did not know how to teach Standard English to nonstandard English speakers. (Tamura, 1996:437–438)

It is probably more serious a case than ignorance. It is a case of not having a voice to talk about the differences between HCE and English. Again taking from Tamura (1996:452):

> Ten of the thirteen elected schoolboard members were born and raised in the islands [at the time of the article]. Ironically, most agreed with their mainland-born colleagues that Hawai'i Creole English was inferior, even if they themselves grew up speaking that language. In believing that Hawai'i Creole English was substandard, these board members were in effect rejecting a part of their past. This was an instance of Antonio Gramsci's concept of cultural hegemony, in which minorities willingly accept the norms of the culturally dominant and become, as David Carson states, "accomplices in their own domination."

In order to end this kind of "cultural hegemony," we have chosen to point out the English hegemony which persists. It is not the monolithic nature of English to which we object, but the desire of certain speakers of English to assume that a creole which has an English lexifier is English. The label, Hawai'i Creole English, although given as a linguistic identification for place, type, and lexifier, continues to perpetuate the notion that the creole is English. This, of course, stems from its linguistic folk history and from calling it "pidgin English" or "broken English" but there is no reason to continue to perpetuate this myth. It does students a great disservice to continue to remediate the creole with English constructs and to not help them give voice to their stories in their language. We can call the creole which has its genesis in Hawai'i, the Hawai'i English Creole.

Educators' Responsibilities

Siegel (1998) quotes Coelho (1988:146) as stating:

> The teachers' task is to become more knowledgeable about the language background of their students, to understand the important link between language and identity, and find ways to assist students to become aware of language differences without loss of self-esteem.

That is just one aspect of the educator's responsibility. Teachers must become aware of their own language(s) and their own language backgrounds. Using the Rynkofs study again, we have a quote from the teacher, Ellen.

> I know I use it [HCE] but seeing it written there surprised me. It's funny to see it written down. It's not the real heavy pidgin [HCE], a here and there kind of thing. I know I do it and maybe that's why I'm hesitant to speak to other people too. I don't do it to patronize the kids. I'm trying to be natural with them and get them to give, too, and it comes out [Interview 3/16/92]. (Rynkofs, 1998:88)

This paragraph is particularly insightful because it provides the full range of attitudes which underlie this paper. Here is a litany:

> ". . . seeing it written there surprised me"—Although the teacher knew she slipped in a few HCE comments now and then, she probably didn't realize how often she did.

> ". . . funny to see it written down"—The teacher was not accustomed to seeing HCE written. HCE does not have a history of literacy.

> ". . . not the real heavy pidgin"—The teacher is aware that there are degrees of pidgin-ness and, if our assertions are correct, of relexification and remediation.

> "I know I do it and maybe that's why I'm hesitant to speak to other people too"—The teacher knows she is an HCE speaker. She also has accepted the stereotype that HCE is a less acceptable form of communication.

"I don't do it to patronize the kids"—Although accepting the stereotype, she does not want the children to feel the stigma she feels, so in using some HCE she feels she can affirm their use of HCE.

It is this dilemma HCE speakers, particularly educators, feel that needs to be addressed in further studies about English hegemony. Grace (nd:223) wrote:

> I should not end this discussion without calling attention to the special status that the monoculture has among us—the very strong culturocentrism that surrounds and supports it, and the high positive value which it, _itself_, places on culturocentrism—i.e., culturocentrism which invidiously views all other cultures from the perspective of the monoculture.
>
> The assumptions of the monoculture are represented as nothing less than the truth—reality itself, and it encourages no tolerance of vernacular cultures, except as adding nonessential touches of grace to the lifestyles of its (the monoculture's) adherents. . . .
>
> This culturocentrism itself encourages the support which linguistics is giving the promotion of the monoculture. It encourages it most directly in that many people may take it quite for granted that if the monoculture expands its domain, that is a good thing, and that if linguistics abets this expansion, that is all to linguistics's credit.

Further on, Grace (nd:224) states:

> we tend to project our own characteristics onto others. That is, except where we have been provided with clear evidence to the contrary, we automatically attribute these same characteristics to any other people and any other culture. Second, where it is clear in a particular case that the characteristics of some other group do _in fact_ differ from ours, we then automatically assume theirs to be unnatural—unjustified (unless they offer convincing proof to the contrary) departures from normality.
>
> Thus we are led to pay particular attention to monoculture standard languages and monoculture linguistic skills and to accept them as the measure of normalcy. Once we have done that, it becomes dangerous to suggest of any other people that they do not have the same skills, because

that is tantamount to suggesting that they are less than normal.

It is only if we admit that there is much that is cultural artifact in monoculture standard languages and much cultural conditioning in the linguistic competence of properly enculturated members of monoculture societies that we can admit other languages and their speakers to their legitimate role in defining the nature of language.

Bibliography

Day, Richard R. (nd) "Can Standard English Be Taught? Or What Does It Mean to Know Standard English?" Manuscript, Kamehameha Schools Bishop Estate.

Dodds, Cecil K. and Mildred Sikkema (1994) *Challenging the Status Quo. Public Education in Hawaii 1840–1980*, Hawaii Education Association.

Fairclough, Norman (1992) "The Appropriacy of 'Appropriateness'" in N. Fairclough (ed.) *Critical Language Awareness*, NY: Longman Publishing.

Fujikane, Candace (1997) "Reimagining Development and the Local in Lois-Ann Yamanaka's *Saturday Night at the Pahala Theatre*," *Women in Hawai'i, Sites, Identities, and Voices, A Special Issue of Social Processes in Hawai'i*, pp 42–61, Department of Sociology, University of Hawai'i.

Grace, George (nd) *Culture in Language and Linguistics: Linguistics's Role in Monoculture Imperialism*, Manuscript, University of Hawai'i.

Hymes, Dell (1972) "On Communicative Competence" in J. Pride & J. Holmes (eds.) *Sociolinguistics*, NY:Penguin Books.

Kleinjans, Edith (1995) "Standard English Critical in Education," *The Honolulu Advertiser*, 29 January, B-1 & B-3.

Menacker, Terri (1998) "Second Language Acquisition for Languages with Minimal Distance," unpublished paper.

Romaine, Suzanne (1994) "Hawai'i Creole English as a Literary Language," *Language in Society*, v. 23, 527–554.

Rynkofs, J. Timothy (1993) *Culturally Responsive Talk Between a Second-Grade Teacher and Hawaiian Children During Writing Workshop*, U.M.I. Dissertation Services.

Sato, Charlene (1993) "Language Change in a Creole Continuum: Decreolization?" in K. Hyltenstam & A. Viberg (eds.) *Progression & Regression in Language*, Cambridge: Cambridge University Press.

Siegel, Jeff (1998a) "Applied Creolistics in the 21st Century," paper presented at the Symposium: Pidgin and Creole Linguistics in the 21st Century, SPCL Conference, New York, January.

Siegel, Jeff (1998b) "Substrate Reinforcement and the Development of Hawai'i Creole English." paper presented at the Symposium on Language Contact and Change—ALI '98, 1–35.

Tamura, Eileen H. (1996) "Power, Status, and Hawai'i Creole English: An Example of Linguistic Intolerance in American History," *Pacific Historical Review*, v. 65, no. 3, 431–454.

Whitney, Scott (1998) "Naming All the Beasts: Lois-Ann Talks Back," *Honolulu*, vol. 33, no. 6, 56–61.

FOURTEEN

I wore high-top sneakers and ripped jeans.
I walked the halls of high school with cigarettes in my back pocket,
my hair long and blonde with natural waves.
The boys in the courtyard who smoked with me
offered thin joints if I'd make out with them behind the stairwell,
but I didn't do boys.
Dawn met me each morning before homeroom,
she'd smile and ask if we were watching a movie later.
I'd say: Yeah, a horror movie, come over at eight.
After school, I'd sit in the back of the bus with Jesse.
Wanna go to the park tonight, I got some sweet hash,
his voice yellow, like his eyes, his face scarred from picking his acne.
I'd take my breasts and squeeze them together.
Why? So you can touch these, I'd ask, and seize his neck.

At home I'd make pizza bagels and figure out science,
then I'd flip my hair upside down and back again to heavy metal,
until the doorbell rang and I looked out the window
to see Dawn holding a bottle of Mountain Dew.
We'd go in the den and sit on the couch,
she'd cross her legs and I'd spread mine,
her shirt cropping up to reveal her bellybutton.
I'd press play with a bowl of popcorn on my lap,
our fingers touching around each kernel,
then moving away to our mouths.
I'd watch her lick the salt off her lips with her tongue
as someone painted murals in my stomach,
and I grabbed her hand as a girl screamed—
our bodies the weight of flowers curling into each other.

AN EXTENSION OF

My mother said that men
are an extension of their size—
that everything's a pissing contest.
When I'm in the men's room,
there's no challenge—I go to a stall.
If a man holds himself out, I look through
a small opening to see how he does it—
his palm engaged, and fingers curled
like a defunct spider. I've watched a man
investigate like this, careful as an ant
who uses its antennae to taste.
He looks over with the agility of a soldier,
then retreats, his neck snapping back to center.
It's his nature to wonder—a need to understand
this organ, that makes it dangerous.

LIVE AS A BOY

I watched the boys run through sprinklers,
their bare chests and small nipples moist.
I lived as a boy:

I had my first crush on Nancy, and told my friend
to tell his friend to tell Nancy that I liked her.
I reached the top of the rope in gym class,
and didn't have to walk the balance beam
or change with the girls in the locker room.
Nobody called me "tomato tits" at recess,
and I swung from the monkey bars—
my body right, my timing perfect
to win chicken fights with other boys.
I went swimming in shorts,
and didn't have to worry about pads or tampons.
My shoulders grew wide, and I got taller
as girls sat on the bleachers
talking about me and my friends,
and how cute we looked playing soccer in the mud.
I picked my date up and met her parents and
put my arm around her during the movie.
We kissed in my car and she moved my hand away.

I watched the boys run through sprinklers,
their laughter stainless—
free as water, and just as clear.

JEFFREY HIGA

CHRISTMAS STORIES

My father spoke of the Hakoloa Sugar Plantation like he spoke of death, something immutable that taunted him at every risky venture, greeted him at the end of every failure, and loomed like a buzzard over him, waiting for him to stumble so that it could pick his bones. Having grown up in the Japanese section of the plantation camps, I was used to this kind of traditional morbidity but my father's fatalism was different. He embellished his specters, animating them and seizing my imagination so securely that I continue to dream of death not as a rattling skeleton, but as a hidden cane worker, sweating flesh and dirt, his square hammertoed feet leaving bloody tracks on the porches and floors of my nightmares. We thought of the plantation as part of our family, a wicked stepfather, perhaps, someplace we could always go back to but without our self-respect. So, in January of 1923, when we left the plantation for the third time, we had no way of knowing for sure that it would be for good.

My parents moved into the Pālama area of Oʻahu, an area filled with Filipino and Japanese plantation expatriates, people like ourselves who possessed the immigrant's vision, like a blindered horse, of only looking forward. My father used to say that he didn't have time to look where we were, only where we were going. It would be many years before I realized that was because where we came from was too deeply inscribed upon his memory. But for me, away from the plantation, a whole world had opened up. Luxuries that I had only heard about and never believed, such as children's shoes, suddenly entered my life and all things seemed possible.

As his own boss, my father worked harder than ever, keeping the hours of his cane working days, sunrise till sunset, six days a week. He worked as what we called a "yardboy"—cut the grass, trimmed the hedges, tended the flowers. They're called gardeners now, but yardboy is what the haoles called it and to call it anything else would have been useless. He prided himself on being quiet and efficient, keeping immaculate flower beds and rarely chatting with the other domestic staff. I imagine the wealthy families in Mānoa that he worked for thought well of him, "a credit to his race," passing his name along to their friends, speaking of his reliability and industry. What they never discovered were his little acts of defiance: our eggplant vines growing amidst their hibiscus groves, the rose gardens he would let die and blame on the insects and later replace with tropical plants, the ponds he created upon request never warning them about the mosquito breeding.

As the oldest son, I helped him in November and December, so that he could charge a little bit more and try to pay off all our debts before the new year. I helped him for years, happily abandoning my schooling during those two months, eager in the promise of more "firsts"—our first radio, first icebox, first automobile, first house— which was the way we really measured our lives. My father's plans, however, were different, as he secretly squirreled away most of the money in the bank, waiting for that day when he could purchase us an entirely new life overnight, that first foothold in the American Dream.

So that December of '23, we were working the grounds of the VanHarding estate in upper Mānoa. It was the biggest place he worked for and he usually spent his Saturdays there, preparing the grounds for some kind of gala event: the welcoming of a new industrial pioneer to the islands or the hosting of a private charity. I liked working with him on Saturdays; it meant missing Japanese school, but mostly I enjoyed the bus ride from the fevered alleyways of our dusty community up into the cooler reaches of the Ko'olau Mountains and into the shaded valleys of oak and banyan trees. Once there, I was never very much help, just followed him around with the rake or rubbish bag, picked up fallen palm fronds, or watered the hibiscus. But I liked to go with him because sometimes I got near enough to the VanHarding house to catch a glimpse of the inside.

My mother used to call it the *Ichiban* white house, because although the other haole families had white houses, the VanHarding house was the biggest, the whitest, and the cleanest. My father, how-ever, had another name for it, the *obake* house—ghost house. "Too white," he would say. "No more anybody there during the day. Just like one ghost house." Shaking his head he would go on, "Why anybody want a white house in the first place? So unnatural, like that. And hard for take care, every time chip and gotta repaint." He would conclude by spreading his arms and saying, "More better have one house like this. If little bit chip, little bit dirty, no matter. Brown paint anyway." Every time he said that I would look at our house and think how poor it looked next to the VanHarding's, like newsprint next to linen, and I would hunger even more for what I thought cleanliness and whiteness could buy: prosperity and satisfaction.

That Saturday, as my father piled bananas on top of me while I made a basket with my shirt, I planned my approach to the white house. I would have to run and stay out of sight until the last minute, because if I walked or crossed the open lawn too early, Otsu-san the maid would see me coming and meet me outside the kitchen door. But if I ran and knocked on the door, sometimes Mrs. VanHarding would answer and let me into the kitchen. This time I got lucky.

"Oh, it's the yardboy's son," Mrs. VanHarding said as she held the door open. "Come in."

"Okay," I said. My father would have wanted me to say "thank you" but at that age, I was only polite to people who scared me, like my father and his friends. It never occurred to me to be scared of Mrs. VanHarding. She was one of those haole ladies with a big bust, but the dresses she wore made her look soft, like an overstuffed futon pinched too tightly in the middle. Her dresses were fringed in layers of white lace, more lace, I imagined, than in all the dry goods shops on King Street. And she was always powdered and perfumed, even for just staying at home. As she took the bunches from me, I stood close to her and inhaled and was instantly reminded of the plumeria tree in our yard, wet with dew and still riffling in the morning breeze. It was an intoxicating but soothing fragrance, and once I was there, I didn't want to be anywhere else.

After she finished unloading me, she pulled two bananas from the bunch and offered one to me. "Banana?"

"Okay," I said and then remembered, "Thank you."

We both ate standing up. It was part of the ritual. When she was done, she stepped back and looked at me. "Good?" she asked, "The bananas, I mean?"

I shrugged. Big bananas were okay eating, but they couldn't compare to the sweeter and smaller apple bananas that I stole from our Filipino neighbors. "Anything else?" I asked. My father instructed me that anytime Mrs. VanHarding told me to do something, I was to ask if there was anything more I could do.

"How is your mother?"

I then gave her the answer my mother told me to say whenever the haole ladies asked about her, "My mother is good and thanks you for your generosity to our family."

Mrs. VanHarding smiled at me and looked like she wanted to say something else. In all previous encounters, nothing ever came out. Usually, a minute of silence would pass where she looked around the kitchen nervously, and I would inch closer to smell her better. "Well, goodbye," she would say and I would say bye, and walk out the door. The ritual complete.

This day, however, in the middle of my sniffing, she said, "Stand up straight."

"Hahh?"

"Stand up straight," she said, as she walked around me and looked. The smell of lavender had completely surrounded me. "You are eight?"

"Ten," I corrected, which I was, although I felt like I was lying. "Ten, missus."

"Yes, of course." She stood in front of me again, nodding her head. Her lips were a thin line as she looked me over, top to bottom. "Of course." She looked over her shoulder into the heart of the house, and then turned back to me. "Do not move. I will be right back." And she left the kitchen.

I didn't know what to do. My instincts told me to leave because good surprises rarely came from my father's employers. Extra hours, pay reductions, reprimands, and odious tasks were the kind of surprises I was used to. But I also knew that if I disobeyed Mrs. VanHarding and my father found out, I would be lucky to live the night. Even if I did manage to survive, I could foresee a long week of lectures on responsibility and the precariousness of our financial situation, punctuated by additional emphatic physical reminders. It seemed I had but one choice, so in the few minutes she was gone, I tried not to move. Soon I saw her coming towards me, but I still did not move until she handed me a brown paper bundle wrapped in string.

"Here," she said, "I think these will fit you."

The bundle was soft and I turned it over, but I couldn't see what was in it. I looked up at her and wanted to say something, but I didn't know the proper thing to say. No haole lady had ever given a gift to me before. I could only think of what my mother would have said. "Thank you for your generosity to our family."

"I have a son that is your age," she said. "He outgrew these a few years ago, and they were just taking up space in his wardrobe, so I thought. . . ." she paused and looked around the kitchen and then at me again. "Well, your mother might have to alter them a bit."

"Thank you," I said and bowed like my father did when he got paid. "Thank you for your generosity to our family."

"Don't get them dirty when you get outside."

I nodded, bowed again, and ran out the kitchen door, across the lawn, and into the banana grove. "Look," I said to my father as I held up the bundle. "Look at what she gave me!"

"Who?" he asked.

"The haole lady," I said, "Mrs. VanHarding. She said she also had a son who was ten and that he didn't need these anymore because they too small for him now and. . . ."

"Gimme that!" he said as he dropped his sickle to the ground and threw off his gloves. He wiped his hands on his shirt and snatched the bundle from my arms. "Why you accept this? We taught you better than that!"

"But . . . but she said she didn't need these. And I thanked her for it. I did. I said, 'Thank you for. . . .'"

"No." He shook his head. "No charity. We no can accept this."

"But how do you know?" I knew my father would give the bundle back without even opening it. "She said they were too small for him. She said they were just sitting around. They're probably only *boro-boros* anyway. . . ."

My father turned to me with a glare that stilled the rest of my thoughts. "Don't say stupid things, Ma-chan. Put away all our stuff. I going take this back." He turned around and walked towards the house.

I didn't try to stop him. I picked up the sickle and gloves. I knew there was no sense even hoping that he would change his mind. He couldn't accept the gift for some Japanese reason, and I knew from past experience that it was useless to try and convince my father out of his Japanese reasons. I just had to accept them.

Even now, I don't know if he could have explained his "Japanese reasons" to me anyway. In times of uncertainty, these traditions, rooted in his custom and history, were the springs he touched upon to propel all of us into our new future. It was a way I could never fully embrace and I would have to create a new way, balancing the forces of my past with those of my future.

After I finished putting the sickle, gloves, and ladder in the shed behind the white house, I started toward the kitchen door, knowing that my father would wait there, hat in hand, for Mrs. VanHarding to pay him. When I got to the door, my father was still trying to give the bundle back to Mrs. VanHarding, who was shaking her head furiously.

"No," she said. "Please take it. These are just old clothes. I must insist you take it."

"No. Too generous. We no deserve such kindness."

"No. This is not a gift. Christopher has outgrown these clothes."

"Then please take the cost out from here," Dad held out the week-ly salary Mrs. VanHarding had just given him. "To pay."

"No!" A horrified Mrs. VanHarding looked at me for help. I shrugged. She couldn't win. "Please take them," she repeated.

"No charity," he said. "Not right."

"Yes," she said. "It is right." She took the bundle from my father and thrust it at me. "Anyway, I was giving them to your son. Doesn't he want them?" She turned to look at me. "Don't you want them?"

I couldn't believe that she was trying to get around my father. I knew if she had not been a woman and also haole, that he would have been very insulted and have left. Instead, he turned toward me and I could see the violence brewing in his eyes: I better not even raise my arms to accept the bundle—or else. But the look on Mrs. VanHarding's face was equally clear: She was not used to being disobeyed, and I was to take the bundle from her. It was up to me to do the right thing, and for the second time that day, I did not move.

"It would make my son very happy," she said to my father, "if your son would accept this gift from Christopher."

I almost laughed then, thinking, that's not going to work. You have to think of something better than that. But when I turned to look at my father, he had turned away from Mrs. VanHarding and was look-ing at the ground. He seemed suddenly bashful, something I had rarely seen, and after looking at his shoes for a few seconds, he lifted his head and asked, "How your son? Good, yes?"

She nodded her head but said, "No." And then added quietly, "The doctors say this might be his last Christmas."

My father looked back down at his shoes and then turned to look at me. "My son," he said as he nodded at me, "honored by gift from your son."

I stepped forward and then the bundle was in my arms.

The following Sunday and the entire rest of the week was frantic as my parents argued about what I should give Christopher. In the bundle was a white shirt and a pair of white shorts. Both of them were too big for me, and my mother refused to alter them because she said the material was too expensive and too nice to cut up. Instead, we draped the clothes over a chair set up in the living room, and all our neighbors came over to see and feel the silk shirt and linen shorts from Christopher VanHarding.

We knew that we could not afford to buy him anything that would be as fine as the clothes he had given me. We also knew that we could not make him the kind of food he was used to. So it was decided that I would give Christopher the koa carving that one of my father's friends had carved for me when I was born. The carving was of a carp twisting and fighting against the current, its tail flexed as it thrust its body out of the turbulence, determination and power barely restrained under its scales. It was a carving that had always frightened me as a child; its ferocity was more demon than fish. But my father thought it was an appropriate gift for a sick boy like Christopher.

The next Saturday on the bus, I asked my father why he had never mentioned that the VanHardings had a son my age. He said that he had seen Christopher only once, when Mrs. VanHarding had my father wash the windows. Christopher was lying in bed in a bedroom that faced the back lawn. He said he could see that Christopher was very sick but figured that the VanHardings could afford expensive haole doctors to take care of him.

"So is that why you decided to accept the gift? Because Christopher is sick and might not get well?"

"Yes," he said. "When number one son dying, it is a very sad time. Doesn't matter if they Japanese or not. Everyone sad."

I nodded my head and we remained silent the rest of the way to Mānoa.

My father waited until the afternoon before he sent me to the white house with the gift. The carving was heavy in my arms and was wrapped in the same brown paper and string that Mrs. VanHarding had given us. As I made my way across the back lawn to the kitchen door, I looked into the windows but did not see Christopher in any of the rooms. Mrs. VanHarding answered my knock and led me into the kitchen.

"How are you, Mrs. VanHarding," I said from the carefully prepared script that my parents had devised.

"Fine, Masa."

"My parents thank you for the beautiful clothes you have given us." I offered the present to her, "And hope your son will accept this meager gift in return."

"Oh." Mrs. VanHarding looked over her shoulder and then back at me. "You did not have to do that."

"It is nothing so fine as the gift he has given me," I said. Then in proper Japanese fashion, "This gift is worthless and of poor quality." I bowed and held out the present in front of me. "Please accept this token of our gratitude."

According to the script, Mrs. VanHarding was supposed to take the gift, after which I would take a step back, bow again, and then leave. But as I waited, bowed over, she didn't take the gift. I was worried that maybe she wouldn't accept this token of our gratitude because of what I said about it being worthless. These proper Japanese things are always getting me in trouble, I thought.

"Masa?"

I raised my head without straightening up. "You don't want this? It's actually very nice. My mother made me say that part about it being worthless. It's not really. . . ."

"This present is for Christopher?"

I nodded.

"Then maybe you should give it to him yourself."

I didn't know what to say. Meeting Christopher was not in the script. I was curious about seeing him, maybe through a window, but I wasn't sure I wanted to meet him. I wouldn't know what to say to a sick, rich, haole boy. I straightened up and tried to think of a tactful response, when Mrs. VanHarding said, "It would make him happy to meet you."

I knew then I had no choice, and said what my father would have wanted me to say, "You honor me."

Mrs. VanHarding motioned for me to follow, and for the first time, I walked out of the kitchen and into the VanHarding world. Even now, it is still hard to describe what I saw there. I can't really describe each room through which we passed. I remember thinking that it took a long time to cross the rooms, and there was something new to look at with every step. At the time, I had never seen so much material used to cover a window, with the excess allowed to spill out onto the walls. I had never seen a wooden floor shine. I had never seen chairs where cloth covered the entire thing, not just the seat. I had never seen doors made of glass. I had never seen plates and bowls and cups and pitchers that reflected like mirrors. I had never seen walls made of books. I had never seen an overhead light made up of diamonds, too numerous to count. But all of that did not prepare me for a sight I had never even seen in my dreams.

"There's a tree in your house," I said to Mrs. VanHarding but she had already moved to the other side of the room. It must be a mistake, I thought. Why would someone grow a tree in their house?

"Christopher, you have a visitor," she said to someone lying on the couch.

I knew that I was supposed to follow Mrs. VanHarding to the other side of the room and give Christopher his present. But I did not want to stop looking at the tree. It was, of course, a pine tree, but at that time all I knew was that it was a tree shaped like a green mountain, pointy on top and broader on the way down. I was going to touch it and make sure it was real, but I knew my father would not like me touching anything that belonged to the VanHardings.

"Masa," she said, "Masa, we are over here."

I carried the present to where Mrs. VanHarding was calling me, but kept my eyes on the tree.

"Christopher," she said as I got closer. "This is Masa. The yardboy's son. He is ten, also."

I turned my eyes away from the tree to the boy on the couch. I was surprised to see that Christopher, propped up by pillows, was not the tall, fat boy I had envisioned. Judging by the clothes he had given me, I had expected to see someone who was much taller and much heavier than I was. A boy version of Mrs. VanHarding. Instead, Christopher's skin looked like it didn't quite fit, like he had shriveled inside from staying too long in the ocean. Against his white clothes, his skin took on an ashy hue, like a shirt that had been worn and washed too often.

Even his hair looked weary of fighting the advancing white which had taken over his blond roots. When he looked at me, I felt I was looking into the worn-down eyes of an old plantation worker. Eyes that saw everything but kept it on the horizon.

"Hello, Masa."

"Hi . . ." I didn't know what to say next. I was trying to remember the beginning of the script so I could restart, but the tree and then Christopher made me forget. ". . . Christopher."

"Only my parents call me Christopher." He smiled at his mother. "Everyone else calls me Chris."

"Yes . . . Chris," I said and then frantically tried to think of something to say. I watched Mrs. VanHarding squeeze Christopher's hand, and walk past the tree, out of the room. "The tree," I said to myself, then I noticed Christopher looking at me. "You have one in your house . . . Chris."

"Yes, do you like our Christmas tree?"

"Oh yeah, Christmas." I had heard of Christmas. My parents had used the word once or twice, and one of my friends had said something about Christmas, something he had learned in school, but I always missed school during the last few months of the year. "A Christmas tree."

"This is the biggest tree we've had yet. How big is your Christmas tree?"

Our Christmas tree? I wondered if I should tell him the truth. "Not as big as this one."

"Yes, yes, but how big is it, anyway?"

I was about to reach up with my hands and say, about this big, when I realized I was still carrying the gift and had no way to gesture. "We don't have one."

"Your family doesn't have a Christmas tree?"

"No."

"Why not? What do you do for Christmas? How can you have Christmas without a Christmas tree?" Christopher pushed himself a little higher up on the pillows.

Although I didn't know what he was asking, I didn't like the way he was asking it, so I shoved the package at him and said, "Here, here's your gift." I knew it wasn't the proper thing to say, but I didn't care. It was my father's fault for getting me into this in the first place. Why did we always have to give something back? "Here, take it."

"Is this a Christmas present?"

Christmas present? What do I answer? Yes? No? Which answer did he want to hear? I chose, "Yes."

"Well, you have to put it under the tree, then." Christopher frowned at me. "Didn't you know that?"

"Yeah," I said and put the gift next to several other boxes that were beneath the tree. It didn't make sense to me, but if he wanted me to put it under the tree. . . .

"Don't you know anything about Christmas?" he asked.

I wanted to say yes because it sounded like I should know, but saying yes got me in trouble last time. "No."

Christopher continued frowning while I stood next to the tree. The tree had a pleasant scent, and it reminded me of my sister, Naomi, and the powder we put on her newborn skin.

"You don't know about Santa Claus or Bethlehem?" he asked. I wasn't sure if he was asking me or himself. "Don't you get presents either?"

"Well," I said as I considered his question. "I usually get presents on New Year's Day." Christopher swung his legs off the couch and sat up. "And then there's Boy's Day."

"But that's not like Christmas," he said.

"No." I thought about the tree behind me. "I guess not."

We then looked at each other. I could imagine my father kneeling among the orchids, wiping his brow, and wondering what was taking me so long. I was thinking I should probably leave now that my mission had been accomplished, and was just about to make that suggestion when Christopher said, "Come here. Sit down."

"Why?" I asked, even though my father had scolded me many times for asking "why" so much. No good ask too many questions, he would say.

"Because I'm going to tell you about Christmas." Christopher smiled at me. "I'm going to tell you a Christmas story."

I still don't know why Christopher decided to do what he did. I don't think he was trying to convert me to Christianity, because he barely mentioned the baby Jesus and Bethlehem. Or if he did, I didn't remember that part as much as the story about decorating trees and the flying animals and the fat haole man with the white beard and how he came through a hole in the ceiling instead of the door and gave you presents, everything you wanted if you were good and had listened to your parents that year. As Christopher told the story and I followed his voice and hands, I forgot that he was sick, that he was haole, and felt as if I were with any of my Pālama friends just talking story. When he finished, he closed his eyes and leaned his head against the back of the couch. Suddenly, neither of us had anything to say as he breathed heavily and slowly as if asleep. We sat in silence until Mrs. VanHarding appeared in the doorway a few seconds later.

"Masa," she said. I stood up from the couch. "Your father is waiting for you outside."

I nodded at Mrs. VanHarding and turned to say something to Christopher. He had opened his eyes and was smiling weakly at me.

"I was just telling Masa a Christmas story," Christopher said to his mother as he slid his legs back on the couch. "But we ran out of time before he could tell me a story."

"Well, perhaps next week Masa can tell you a story." She turned to me, "You are coming back next week?"

"Yes," I answered although she didn't really seem to be asking me. "To tell Christopher a story."

"Good," she said and then to Christopher, "I will be right back with your medicine after I show Masa out."

Christopher nodded. "See you next Saturday, Masa."

"Yes, next Saturday." I nodded. "Chris."

My father did not say a word to me at the VanHarding's kitchen door or during the entire bus ride home. Even through dinner, he did not once look at me. So later that night after my mother had cleared the dinner dishes, I was relieved when my father finally said, "Why you cause trouble for the VanHardings?"

"I didn't. Mrs. VanHarding told me to give the gift to Christopher. She said that he wanted to meet me, so . . ."

"You see inside the house?" my mother asked.

"Yes," I said and proceeded to tell them all I could remember. My father did not say anything as I described the things I had seen, but my mother kept interrupting me for more details. What color were the walls, the rugs, the furniture? How big were the rooms, bigger than this house? Was Mrs. Van Harding wearing lots of gold and diamonds? When I got to the part about the tree, my father snorted.

"No make sense, I tell you," he said. "These haoles. Make me cut down live tree and put tree in house. After new year come, make me take tree out of house. Throw tree away."

I knew I had to wait until he was finished. But he didn't say anything else, so I continued. Then, in the middle of my description of Santa and the presents, my father blurted, "And how you throw tree away? Cannot. Got to burn." He lifted his empty teacup. My mother reached over with the teapot and refilled his cup. "Wasting tree, I tell you," he said.

"Go on, Ma-chan," said my mother, and so I did, ending with the part where Christopher had finished his story and Mrs. VanHarding was back in the room.

"Mrs. VanHarding," I took a deep breath, "wants me to come back next Saturday."

"Hahh?" Like most Japanese fathers, my father didn't like surprises from his children. "What you mean?"

"It's for Christopher. Mrs. VanHarding wants me to help Christopher."

"Help? Help with what?"

"She wants me to help him . . ." For the first time in my life, I lied to my father, ". . . learn Japanese."

My father started to stand up, "No *shibai*, you!"

"I'm not lying," I lied. "She wants him to learn Japanese."

"Why? Why he like learn Japanese?" He was standing now, looming over me.

"I don't know," I said, scared that this was starting to get away from me like an unraveling ball of yarn rolling downhill. "You told me never to ask why, especially to haoles."

"Don't say dumb things!" He raised his arm. My mother started tugging on his shirt but he ignored her. "Haoles no like learn Japanese, they like everyone learn English!"

"Let him go, let him go," my mother pleaded. "Maybe she pay extra for teaching."

I nodded at him, knowing that if I opened my mouth again, that hand would come down. He glared at me and I lowered my gaze to my feet. Neither of us spoke and I didn't raise my head until he exhaled loudly and said, "No embarrass us."

I nodded again and started to leave the room. I was almost out when I heard him say, "And no get me fired."

I didn't want to tell my father the truth because I didn't want him and my mother to tell me what story to tell Christopher. I knew they would pick a story about one of Japan's glorious samurais who did this or that brave deed and then died violently. Or some story about a child who did not listen to his parents and was tricked by demons and was now enduring eternal punishment. I wanted to tell Christopher a story like the one he told me: a story where animals had magical powers, and good things happened to children, and at the end of the story everyone was happy.

However, I did not know a story like that. All the stories I had learned from my parents or their friends were not happy enough, and Christopher probably knew all the stories I had learned in school. Every day until Saturday, while working with my father at one of the estates or afterward at home, I tried to make up a story. But every story turned out to be a thinly disguised version of the Christmas story, except with a fat Japanese man or flying mongooses. Saturday afternoon found me at the VanHarding's kitchen door, with no story to tell.

"Hello, Masa." Mrs. VanHarding opened the door. "Christopher has been waiting for you."

"Is he too tired to see me?" It was my last hope. "I don't have to see him today. Maybe next week?"

"Nonsense," she said. "Come, he's waiting for you in the sitting room." She turned and motioned for me to follow.

I slid my feet after her, barely looking at the things around me. This time, the VanHarding house did not seem so wonderful, just confusing and forbidding. I suddenly understood what my father meant by the *obake* house.

When we entered the sitting room, Christopher was on the couch near the Christmas tree. The tree had been decorated with ribbons of red and green, paper cutouts, white candles, garlands of silver, and glass balls that reflected the sunlight. The festivity of the tree only made me feel more empty-handed, like the hollowness I felt when I won a game by cheating. The carving I had given Christopher stood unwrapped on a table. Mrs. VanHarding whispered to Christopher, turned to smile at me, and left the room.

Christopher pointed to the end of the couch. "Hello Masa. Come sit here."

"Hello, Chris." I was hoping that he forgot I was supposed to tell him a story.

"So, what story are you going to tell me?"

I tried a change of topic. "Your tree looks very nice. Very Christmas."

"My father helped me decorate it," he said. "I did the bottom and he did the top."

Having exhausted all my knowledge on that topic, I switched to another. "Did you like the gift we gave you?"

"Yes, my mother was just telling me that I should remember to thank you for it." We both turned to look at the carving. "So thank you for this very nice . . . fish."

Both of us started laughing, but stopped almost immediately when Christopher started to cough. He coughed for a long time, and I waited until he was breathing normally.

"That's why we gave you this fish," I said as I stood up and took the carving off the table. "So you would get better." I handed the carving to Christopher. "It's a carp which is good luck for boys."

"Good luck for boys?"

"See this," I pointed to the base of the carving. "This is the water, the current." I pointed to the flank of the fish. "See this? The carp is bursting out of the water. It is a strong fish and can fight off the rough water."

I put Christopher's hand along the carved side of the fish. "Can you feel it? It is alive, full of power." He caressed the carving. "The carp is not afraid and does not give up."

And then it came to me. The story I needed to tell.

I drew up my legs onto the couch. "Once there was an old couple who lived in the countryside of Japan. Everything was good, and they lived simple and peaceful lives, farming rice year after year. But there was one thing that was missing. One thing that they really wanted but never had. Something that would make their lives much happier." Out the window, over Christopher's shoulder, I could see my father pruning the hedges. I watched him move from one bush to the next, each swing of the sickle fluid and assured, a movement he practiced hundreds of times a week. Then somewhere in a dim portion far back in my ten-year-old mind, I thought that if I were lucky, I would be able to move like he did in the world: deliberate and without shame.

"What!" Christopher shook my arm. "What was it?"

"A boy," I said. "They wanted a son." I told him the story of Momotaro, the boy born from a peach found by the old couple. I told Christopher of how Momotaro grew and brought much happiness to the couple, their lives made brighter by his presence. How Momotaro excelled in school and at games. How he was an expert wrestler and a good swordsman. "Then," I said, "when he was still a young boy, Momotaro decided to kill the demons stealing from his village." I told Christopher of Momotaro's journey and of the talking animals he befriended: the dog who could bite through anything, the monkey who was slier and trickier than any man, the bird who could see further and fly faster than any other animal. I explained how Momotaro was not afraid and sailed to the island where the demons lived and killed them all with the help of his animal friends. How Momotaro returned to the village and gave back everything the demons had stolen. And how, now that the demons were dead, the entire village celebrated but none more than Momotaro's parents who were just happy that their son was home with them.

When I had finally finished, Christopher looked up the from the carving he was still holding. "That was a good story."

I nodded, "When you get better, maybe we can play Momotaro sometime." I saw my father brush off his clothes, and walk across the lawn toward the house. "Like I do with my friends at home."

"That would be fun," he said. "As long as I get to be Momotaro."

"All right, it's more fun being the monkey anyway." And as soon as I'd said that, Mrs. VanHarding appeared in the doorway.

The next Saturday was the first week of the new year and I returned to Japanese school. I wish I could say that despite our differences, Christopher and I had become steady friends but in reality I never went back to the VanHarding estate and I never spoke with Christopher again. I didn't forget him, my days just became too busy. Regular school during the week, Japanese school afterward and on Saturdays, adventures with my Pālama friends on Sunday—it seemed I always had something else to do, something too important to postpone. Then one Saturday halfway into the new year, I came home from Japanese school and found my father already back from work.

"Didn't you go to work, today?"

"Yes, but I had to come back."

"Why?" I asked but I already knew.

"VanHarding boy die two days ago." He shook his head. "Very sad. Funeral today, so no work."

Suddenly, I wanted to tell my father what had really happened between me and Christopher and of the story I told. But as the impulse to confess welled up in me, I knew that I wouldn't be able to tell him. I thought of the promise I had made Christopher and then abandoned. And as that wave of guilt sucked me out into an ocean of remorse, I turned away from my father, confused.

My father and I never talked about the VanHardings again; I suppose he felt there was no need. I did not understand what it meant that Christopher had died and my father could not afford the luxury of dwelling further upon it.

In a few years, my father saved enough money to open up his own restaurant in Pālama, The Palama Inn. He gave his old clients to a friend of his, a recent immigrant to the islands. One day this man told my father that the VanHardings had decided to move back to the mainland. Massachusetts, the man said.

Now years later, after an old man's lifetime of knowing people and then letting them slip out of my life for no reason other than my own laziness, Christopher's is the friendship I think about the most. I wonder if I might have become a different person, if I had gotten to know Christopher better. So in my regret, I do the only thing I am able to. Every year, with my children and now with my grandchildren, I tell them the Christmas story. I tell them also of the boy, Momotaro, and his fearlessness while facing his enemy. And then, when they are ready, I show them the white shirt and shorts and tell them this story.

MURIEL M. AH SING HUGHES

HAWAIIANS EAT ROCKS

Hawaiians eat rocks
The universe-encompassing crunch that
     isolates all other sensations
Taste the bitter salt of a'a, the honeyed strips of pāhoehoe
Eyes sniff the velvet lava fields baking in the sun,
     fragrance of salty tears and sun-bleached bones.

Hawaiians eat rocks
The fish-eyed coral reefs echo death throes
     screams of poisoned polyps
Sands swish as tourists fan their fins chasing convict fish
The lei seller, the busboy, the surfer feast on
     green paper palu that tourists toss.

Hawaiians eat rocks
Cold hollow tile universes devour life's energy and
     multiply more of their own kind
Cases of Lysol keep the deviant away and sanitized
Keep our young people at home, build a bigger, newer, more secure
     prison in Hawai'i.

Hawaiians eat rocks
Money for the people squandered by trustees who
     do battle like a'ama crabs in a bucket
Keiki learn their culture from books and Kepanī teachers
Poor fools wait patiently for liberation they think is
     sovereignty.

LAURA IWASAKI

MY SUMMER ON AN ISLAND OF GHOSTS

My grandfather left Hiroshima Province for Hawai'i in 1905. As soon as he arrived, he sent a letter to an uncle who was living in Kohala, but after receiving no response, he quickly struck out on his own, encouraged by the ardent warmth of the tropical air on his skin, the flagrant boiling of color, and most of all, impelled by the powerful confidence of his own youth, which exerted an influence as strong as any tide. He was sixteen years old.

I heard this story some time after he died, at age ninety-six, one of the last Issei left in the state. A few years earlier, at a ceremony honoring his longevity, he'd been photographed with the governor, I was told. I never saw the picture, but I've imagined how he looked in it—a fragile man reduced to basic elements by a lifetime of island weather: toughened skin stretched across bird bones, two agate eyes blinking in the sun.

From his obituary, I learned he spent three years on a sugar plantation until recurrent bouts of fever forced him to leave. He went to Hilo then, where he bounced from job to job—first a hotel dishwasher, then a sewing machine salesman—before finding steady work in an ice cream parlor. Unfortunately, the owner ran off without warning after four years, along with three months of my grandfather's back pay.

At that point, he began setting type for a Japanese newspaper. I guess he stumbled into it, the same way I did. I grew up in California, half an ocean away from him, so I can't say for sure if his hands held the blueprint for mine—small, but quick and strong, equally suited to manipulating little blocks of lead or summoning letters from a computer keyboard. I felt strange reading about that, as if the old man and I belonged together in spite of ourselves. Since neither one of us had wanted to claim the other while he'd still been alive.

"If you do come to Hawai'i, I don't want your children associating with the rest of my grandchildren," he wrote to my father, who was testing the waters for a family visit in 1968. "They might contaminate their cousins," he added, by way of explanation.

Of course we *were* exposed to a greater variety of germs on the mainland, but I didn't believe for a moment that he was referring to any physical disease. I waited for clarification from my father, sitting across from me at the dinner table with the letter in his hand, until his downcast silence convinced me that he wasn't about to reveal anything more. So I sneaked a glance at my sister Joyce, who bit her lip and raised a penciled eyebrow at me. She knew exactly what he meant. In fact, although we quickly chose to drop our eyes and change the subject, we all knew what he meant.

The California-to-Hawai'i grapevine began with a benign purpose in mind—to hold broken families together across miles of ocean. But in our case, the results were more efficient than kind, for we had a distressing list of woes to transmit—from six months in a residential drug-treatment facility to a particularly unwise first love affair on my part. My grandfather was as good at that kind of social arithmetic as anyone, and the way he figured it, so many minus signs added up to only one thing: we were fatally infected with iniquity. He hadn't willed a life out of black rock and his own youth by being sentimental; he'd done it by making the necessary hard choices. He still knew how to make them. This time, to cut his losses and focus his affections where they wouldn't go to waste, on our sound and more available cousins.

I didn't give a thought to how my father must have felt, and personally, I was too young to experience anything more complicated than scorn, quick and pure as a lightning flash. I was eighteen and filled with a potent self-assurance of my own. I waved my hands at him, that old man sitting on a tiny piece of rock in the middle of a big ocean, at all of them, from my impeccable grandmother to my disapproving aunts and uncles and their precious, pristine children. Already estranged by distance and ancient frictions, it was easy to . . . well, not exactly make them disappear, but just *diminish* them a little. In an instant, I obliterated all depth and detail, leaving nothing but blank outlines colored in with Hilo rain.

"You don't mean anything to me, *ojii-chan*," I mouthed back at him, mocking the rarely used childhood term by flinging it sarcastically into his stranger's face. For me, his life as a ghost had begun long ago. I was just making it official.

But there were consequences I hadn't considered.

I never guessed that a family of ghosts would give birth to a phantom child and woman. Restless and without a home, uncertain whose songs and stories circle in her veins, she will be hungriest for those she denies most strenuously, a lonely ghost, the worst kind to be.

Years later, along with a pair of ancient suitcases and too many lumpy cardboard boxes, I arrive in Hawai'i with my children. I say our trip is a special kind of extended vacation, but the girls are less tourist than hostage, on loan from the land of the living, a place I've come to fear and despise.

Long past the simple certainties of youth, I'm now as close to dissolution as all the other ghosts who wander into and out of my life. I watch their hollow hands pass through me, listen while they chatter pointlessly in obscure languages I no longer have the heart to understand. Day after day, I play at feeling kinship in their touch, then dream of biting off their heads and gulping down their blood like water. Yet even in dreams, their feeble substance fails to satisfy me. I've made them what they are, just as I've made myself. Outside, the fading shell of our programmed physical responses; on the inside, nothing. It's like air swallowing air.

Worn and adrift, I reach for the same piece of volcanic rock my grandfather first set foot on nearly ninety years ago. Is it instinct? I wonder. Yet when I ask myself what I've come looking for, I know only this much: that if I'm not taken in by spirits—acknowledged, embraced, reclaimed—then after so many uneasy years, I just want to find a place to rest my troubled head.

The road down to Laupāhoehoe is paved, but narrow and curved. If you meet a car traveling uphill in the opposite direction, both drivers must make allowances. Black cliffs sprouting thick rain forest unfold into the distance like the crinkled edge of a fan, trimmed with more black rock and the blue ocean.

In 1946, the same tidal wave that demolished downtown Hilo gobbled up the children who had arrived early for school and were killing time on the field behind the seawall at Laupāhoehoe. I approach a memorial plaque listing the names and ages of those who died. Reading the raised inscription line by line, I am struck by how easily the gods of earth and water can reach out and twist their fingers through the painstaking warp and weft of our lives, leaving a tangled ruin behind. Here, a mother and her infant. There, several children bearing the same last name, the oldest on the verge of graduation.

Meanwhile, my two daughters have scampered down to the water's edge. They don't know yet how much there is to fear in the world. Anyone can see it's not a friendly beach. The ocean is too unruly, too gaudily blue, as if it doesn't really know how to behave. Still, they stand tilting seaward, gazing provocatively out at the waves, which break short in a thwarted writhing of foam against the tumbled rocks. Shivering, I call them back, but the wind snatches the words from my mouth.

My grandfather's boat docked at Laupāhoehoe after stopping first in Honolulu, late in 1905.

A few weeks after my arrival, my body sloughs off its sense of snow and forest, skyscrapers and concrete, like a moth shedding its chrysalis. On slow, hot days, watching dry-tongued geckos stalking flies on the kitchen windowsill, my skin makes overheated promises I'm desperate to believe: *This is where you come from, this is your home.*

At my father's favorite restaurant in Honalo, the owner, a woman in her eighties, stops at our table to reminisce.

She recalls my father as a young man of thirty, when he spent several nights on this side of the island to codirect public speaking classes for a well-known self-help institute. After each session, my father, his teaching partner, and most of the participants gathered at her restaurant for dinner followed by a long evening of beer and storytelling.

The two faces—one plump and fair, framed by ripples of gray hair, and the other baked brown and close to the bone—smile serenely, cheered by the shared memories.

"Ah, those were the days," my father says at last, while the rest of us nod amiably in agreement.

"I remember your grandfather, too," the old woman adds unexpectedly, turning her bright eyes on me, "coming over from Hilo to stock up all the stores."

"That's right," my father confirms. "Every couple of months, he had to make the rounds."

I gaze with fresh appreciation at this unknown woman who apparently knew my grandfather better than I did. Far from being the disembodied phantom he'd been in my life, he'd no doubt eaten and drunk in hers, maybe even laughed, all things no ghost ever does. While I morosely and inexplicably visualize my grandfatherless years as a line of empty telephone booths standing side by side, she continues to study me.

"You know," she says at last, "you are all over your grandfather."

My grandmother was a great beauty, the old people say. Still, she has no claim on my imagination, so I'm pleased to be told that I resemble my grandfather.

In my only clear memory of my grandmother, I run into her at dawn in a hallway of her house in Hilo. She looks spooky to my four-year-old eyes, materializing out of the shadows, her face covered with a mucous substance that glistens like one large snail track in the silvery light. ("Some kind of beauty lotion," my mother theorized later.) She is wearing a dark kimono and white *tabi*, and her tiny feet whisper rhythmically across the bare floor.

"Ah," she exclaims in a musical voice when she sees me.

I shrink back against the wall, staring up at her with the kind of dismally bone-deep gaucherie my grandmother automatically disdains, even in someone so young. Yet her smile never wavers, the same petal-lipped, beatific smile she wears all day. With faultless poise, she dips her head and glides past me into the murk of the dim hallway.

That's all.

As for my grandfather, I have no specific memories of him from that time. Most likely, he was out fishing.

My father tells this story about my grandfather.

Early one morning, he is fishing for *ulua* out near Kalapana, the old black sand beach. To reach their favorite spot on the coast, he and a friend crawl across what seems like miles of black rock, picking their way in the half-light over boulders, fissures, and the scored swirls of old lava flow. As they settle down with their lines in the water, my grandfather feels compelled to look over his shoulder. He sees two women, dressed all in white, moving across the lava field as swiftly and smoothly as if they are strolling on pavement. *These are not ordinary people,* he tells himself and, seized by a penetrating chill, quickly turns away. He opens his mouth to speak, then decides against it because he doesn't want to frighten his friend. When he glances back, the women are gone.

"Did that really happen?" ask my daughters, their eyes wide.

"Oh yes," my father assures them. "My father told me. And he never lied."

In an old family album, my mother finds two small photographs I haven't seen before—snapshots of my grandparents, taken separately, standing on the porch of their house in Hilo in 1940.

My grandmother has parted her lips, exposing slightly crooked teeth for the camera. She looks relaxed and assured, with her soft, fine-textured cheeks, rounded nose, and pale, plump hands resting comfortably at her sides. Black hair curves up and away from her face in two smooth wings. Her kimono is patterned with thin vertical stripes, the glossy kind that runs through stick candy, and is cut horizontally at the waist by a wide, floral obi. On the back of the picture, she has written in Japanese, which my mother translates:

"'This person is smiling.' I wonder what she's so happy about?"

In the second photo, my grandfather stands in the same corner of the porch, wearing a dark suit and a light-colored shirt buttoned up to the collar. His hands, too, are at his sides; the thin fingers curl in toward the palms, almost, but not quite, clenched. His hair is cut short enough to show scalp above the ears and stands up stiff and straight on top. He is not smiling; in fact, a small wrinkle is beginning to form between his eyebrows. In the narrow face, its long lines punctuated by angled cheekbones, a sharp nose, and the steady chin of a man who always tells the truth, I see my own reflection. I understand now why I couldn't come up with a single "pretty" feminine expression that seemed to fit my teenaged face no matter how hard I tried, practicing one look after another in front of the bathroom mirror. There's simply no place for it there.

I turn the picture over.

"'This person is a difficult parent,'" my mother reads aloud. "Well, I wonder what she meant by that?"

My sister Joyce, who moved from California to Hawai'i with my parents, was the only grandchild from our family to attend the old man's funeral.

"How did you feel?" I ask her curiously.

She shrugs, drags deeply on her cigarette, then blows the smoke into the whirling blades of a fan, which is thoughtfully pointed out an open window.

"I wasn't sad or anything," she replies candidly, without a trace of false apology. "I was just sorry we didn't get the chance to know him."

And in the end, that's all there is. I wonder, suddenly, what else I thought I'd find here.

The dead make no original moves, after all. They are bound to a set number of stories, which we recite for them over and over again. Old men and women, forever the color of Hilo rain, this is as close as I'll ever get to you: mute photographs, anecdotal scripture. Regardless of what I want, you can offer nothing more. My skin, drunk on sun and sweat, was either delirious or lying. This may be where I come from, but it will never be my home. All at once, I can't think of one good reason to stay.

By summer's end, hurricane season scents the wind; I linger on, listless and undecided. I seem to have lost my taste for momentum after beaching myself here, on this island of ghosts.

It is my daughters who finally remind me. They alone refuse to be less than real. They fill my empty hands with their small, warm grasp and tug instinctively in the only direction they know. *Hold on,* they whisper, *keep moving. Together we will make the place where we belong.*

So I leave my spirits with their burning mountains. Disguised as clouds, they shrivel to a white wrinkle on the sea.

Now everywhere I look, it is blue. And between blue air and blue water, there will always be the persistent hands of children.

DARLENE M. JAVAR

THIS TOILET OUT OF ORDER

So you wanted to end
it all, take your shit, your
pain, your life and flush
them down the toilet
knowing the plumbing
was fucked
and the back wash was thick
with yesterday's crap.
You took the pills
with water from your kitchen
and attempted to unclog the drain.
Hah!
The pipe was
too small
and your shit
didn't go down.
I stood at the side of your gurney
after your stomach was pumped.
You reached in your pocket for
letters in envelopes, envelopes in
Ziploc sandwich bags
to me and your children.
How could you imagine
I could replace
you,
that you may
leave us here
without you?
How dare you presume
I'd be your plumber
and wipe the muck
spilt over?

Your glazed eyes were sad.
Your spirit was broken.
I'm glad the charcoal
was disgusting,
made you vomit
in the bed pan.
I'm glad
I still have
your ass
to wipe.

DARLENE M. JAVAR

KNOCK FOUR TIMES IF THE PHONE RINGS ONCE

Kiss
your third knuckle;
knock on wood
four times;
kiss your knuckle again
if the phone rings once
then stops
to prevent the caller
from redialing.
His name is Diablo.

On a late night errand
at the supermarket,
as you walk past the telephone booth,
the phone rings
once
then stops.
You know it's for you.
You kiss
your knuckles,
suddenly stop—
asphalt, concrete, glass
surround you.
Your eyes wildly search
for a wooden wall,
a wooden plank,
or any splinter of wood.
The phone rings again,
stops.
Diablo is returning his call.

You run
into the store frantic,
knuckles still at your lips,
teeth biting down in agitation
as you are oblivious to the blood
trickling down your wrist.
The aisles are filled
with color and cans,
plastic bags and
words you can't recognize,
yet the price tags lurch out at you
like a boxer's right jab,
again and again,
$1.64, 49¢, $4.25, 4@$1.00.
Cutting boards, hangers,
wooden spoons, toothpicks,
you know they are there
in the store
somewhere.
You can still hear the phone ring
once.

ROCKHEAD

My baby's head is so round—round as a rare and perfect piece of obsidian found on Waimānalo Beach, polished instead of flattened or fractured, by the force of water.

I love her round-headed perfection, my daughter's head shape so like mine, and my mother's when she was a child.

While I was growing up, my mother would study her daughters for signs of herself, then make pronouncements binding us to her and to our fates. To oldest sister, she would say: Our hair is like seaweed, so black and slick it can never hold a comb; Watch that you don't fly away. To second sister, she'd say: You've got my dimples; Life has to pinch your cheeks hard to make you happy.

My mother would tell third sister to hold out her hands, fingers pressed tightly together. See, she would sigh, see how the light shines through the cracks? Like me, you'll have trouble holding onto what you most want.

When she would look at me as if she was seeing both me and a memory, I knew what would come out of her mouth: Rockhead. Just like me, she'd say, shaking her head. You'll have a hard life, always banging against the current. Worse than a boy, more stubborn than a stone.

But she would say these things with pride so I would know that she loved me.

And everytime she called me Rockhead, I'd ask her, "why? how come? how do you know? what does it mean?" pestering her for a story, hoping to learn more about my mother and, in turn, about the secrets of myself.

At night, when my mother unwound her hair, combing through the heavy silk with her fingers, I'd press against her, close as she would let me, and wait. If I was lucky, she would notice me. Baby Girl, she might say, pick out my white hairs. Or Youngest Daughter, massage my temples.

I'd sit cross-legged on the floor and wait for my mother to lie down and slip her head into my lap. I'd stroke her forehead, the sides of her face, the top of her head where the spirit escapes at night. When she'd begin to tell her story, I'd part her hair into sections, using my nails to find and pluck the white strands. As she talked, I'd stick the oily roots onto a sheet of one of the underground papers, either the *Korean Independence* or the *Student Revolutionary*, that found its way into our village outside of Pusan. And after the story, after my mother fell asleep, I'd crumple the paper into a ball and burn it in the flues that warmed the underbelly of our home. As I drifted off to sleep, breathing in the scent of hair and smoke, I'd imagine that words wrapped in my mother's hair drifted into our dreams and spiraled up to heaven.

I am still trying to find order in the stories my mother doled out in bits and pieces, in the hopes that in doing so I can find significance and sanity in my own life. And so that I can warn my daughter, and protect her. Because what I remember most strongly from my mother's storytelling is not something that she told me, but something that I felt: her head was no longer round.

My mother was told that the most famous fortuneteller in Seoul, paid to read her head at birth, said that she was the most round-headed baby she had ever seen. In a round-headed family that valued head shape along with money and auspicious birth charts, this was the highest praise.

The fortuneteller predicted that because of her roundness, because of the class she was born into, and because of the sign she was born under, my mother would be very spoiled and very happy. Everything would roll her way.

This was true for perhaps the first seven years of her life.

My favorite fairy tales when I was growing up were my mother's own baby-time stories. When we played make-pretend, my sisters and I pretended to be our mother, whose early days were filled with parties in Seoul and candy and fancy Western dresses. I pictured most of the things she told us about by finding something in my own life to compare it to and thinking, same thing only one thousand times better. When she told us about a doll from France with blue eyes painted in a porcelain face, I took my own pine and rag doll, put a cup over her head and imagined a toy a thousand times better.

The one thing my mother talked about that neither my sisters nor I could imagine or comprehend was ice cream. We just had no reference for it in our own lives, and when we'd push our mother for a definition, her descriptions left us even more dubious and mystified.

It's like sucking on an ice cold, perfectly ripe peach, my mother once tried to explain.

Then why not just eat a peach, we asked.

Because it's not the same, my mother said. That's just what it feels like in your mouth. It feels like a ripe peach and like the snow, and like how a cloud full of rain must feel if you could bite into it.

I remember biting into my own honey and nut candy that my mother made for us during the harvest and watching her talk. She would shut her eyes, but I could still see them move back and forth, back and forth under their lids. She seemed very magical, like a princess from heaven, when she talked about ice cream.

When I married my GI and came to Hawai'i, I was surprised to see how common and how cheap ice cream was. Once I found out what it was, I bought a carton of each flavor I could find—cherry vanilla, strawberry, banana, pistachio, Neapolitan, chocolate chip, macadamia nut. We'd have ice cream every night after dinner. At first my husband encouraged me, glad that I was becoming American. But then he found out that I was also eating ice cream for lunch and for breakfast. And that I cried after eating a bowl of a particularly good flavor because it reminded me that when my mother was a round-headed child princess, she took a bite out of heaven.

After he found out these things, my husband put me on a diet.

I try to maintain my baby's round head. I make sure her hats and headbands aren't too tight. When I shampoo her hair, I am careful that I don't use too much pressure and leave unintentional dents. I make sure she sleeps on her stomach so her skull won't flatten out in the back, and I maintain a constant vigilance, checking on her throughout the night so that I can catch her when she flips over. This is hard work, and I do it in secret because I do not want to hear my husband talk about god and genetics. I know better, because of my mother, than to think that head shape is fixed for life.

In the years before her head changed, my mother's father was a middle school official. He was the one who gave my mother her doll from France, fancy dresses, a taste for ice cream. He was also the one who taught her her lessons, drilling her in math and history. Because of him, my mother wanted to be the best girl student in the primary school.

"I studied, studied, studied," my mother would say, "so I could be the best. But everytime we took the tests, I always placed second. Number one was always my best friend, who I hated at that time of year.

"Every year," she said, "I wished to be number one. One year, though, I figured out that my wishing it wasn't enough to make it happen, because my best friend was also wishing to be number one. Her wish was blocking my wish. So that year, when it came time to write our wishes on the paper we would burn and send to heaven, I told my best friend she should wish to be the prettiest girl, since she was already the smartest. When she said okay and I saw her write this down, I snuck away and wrote on my own paper, I wish to be number one in the school."

My mother would always become sad at this point in the story, and when my sisters and I asked if she got her wish, she'd always say, "yes, and I'm sorry."

The year my mother's wish came true was the year Japan invaded Korea. The year her father and his colleagues were taken away. The year that her best friend had to drop out of school because her family could not afford to pay the education fee demanded by the New Japanese Provisional Government.

My mother had to learn a new alphabet, and new words for everyday things. She had to learn to answer to a new name, to think of herself and her world in a new way. To hide her secret self.

These are the things my mother taught me, and these are the things that have enabled me to survive in this new country. Because of my mother's early lessons, I can eat crackseed without making a face or spitting. I can look up at the shopboy at Woolworth's who says

"Watcha like, lady?" and hide my fear. And I can smile when everyone talks too fast with words that make no sense, when all I really want to do is scream and scream and never stop.

This is the way my mother also survived, but she paid a price. I think this, the way my mother hid herself, the way her lived life deviated from the person she was born to be, is what changed the shape of her head.

In Korea, the elders warned those of us haunting the American PX for work or handouts about mixing our blood with the foreigners. Though nothing specific was said, my girlfriends and I imagined that big-nose, blue-and-blind-eyed monsters would sprout from our wombs if we mated with the Americans. Still, that did not stop us from going where the money and food was. I know I was willing to risk anything because I was hungry, even marrying a foreigner and leaving my home country.

When I became pregnant, I could not help worrying about what my baby would look like, wondering if she would be a monster or a human. Korean or Other. Me or not me. Even walking the streets of Honolulu, seeing for my own eyes the normal-looking "chop suey" children, I could not stifle the voices of the village elders whispering, "monsters, monsters."

Now, as I look at my daughter, I do not know how I could have doubted her perfection. Her hair is reddish brown, not black. Her eyes, though brown, are cut differently than mine. But her head is round.

I cup her tiny head in my palms and whisper, "I am so proud of you. You are a rockhead like your mother and your mother's mother. Only a thousand times better."

WHITE KITE FLYING

I. Red Shoes

I lost my red shoes.
Left them on the running board
of Dad's truck and he drove off
because I wanted to run barefooted
on the cinder road up Pele Lane
to chase Roy Asato
who looked up my dress.
Could beat him up
for doing that.
Catch him by the neck
on the fly.

II. White Kite

In the open field
on the Kino'ole side
of the Macaroni Factory,
I go, fly kites
with the neighborhood boys.
Days before, I had slit
Dad's old bamboo fishing pole
and made a crossed brace.
Bowed the frame with grocery twine.
I then covered the kite with white
Christmas tissue found
in a KTA Dry Goods box.
From an old pink mu'u mu'u
I stripped material
and tied bows for the kite's tail,

a trailer for weight and high balance.
Made it long. To it, hidden, I tied an old fishing
blade to cut loose the boys' kites.
"C'mon, we go," they called.
Mine flew the highest—soared—
the string snapping in the force
of wind, only to disappear
into the clouds like a faint day moon.

III. Green Fish

Easy to catch with throw net, the school
of green fish under Coconut Island bridge.
But try catching them with a pole
one by one. Need patience
to put the California shrimp bait
on the small hook and watch the fish suck it
in the mouth. You have to know
when to jerk the line to hook
the lips pressed out like a kiss.
There's a picture of me,
a line of mamo on a cord,
the boys in the background.
Some envious, their faces.

FROM A TO ZITS

"Asayama, sit up front."
I always first or second row.
"When I call you, say your name out loud.
Enunciate."

Boy girl, boy girl. Dale Aoki always
in front of me, unless a new girl with A-name
comes to class, but no chance for that.
No new families come Hilo. Most
moving out—go Honolulu. Los Angeles.
Annette Abe, she in A class.
Never going come ours.

"Catch the ball good, eh?
Donno how for play Dodge Ball o wat?
Girls useless. No choose her for play our team."
Dale Aoki chases me away. Yanks my pigtails
down. "You going broke my neck," I wail.

"Dumb ass. Who tol' you for cut yo' haya yourself.
Look yo bangs." My father dragged
me to the barber to straighten them out as best could.
But I look like one samurai,
hair pokey, head like one bird nest. Tawashi.
I don't want to go school.

Echoes through the house, sad way she cries.
"This how I going die, too," she says of her father
who's dying of cancer.
"You craaazy," scoffs my father.
I run to the church to burn senkō.
Years later, my mother dies
of the same cancer.

Falsies made of Kleenex tissues. False eyelashes,
mascara, lipstick to look like Japanese Marilyn Monroe
but too shame to show nothing kind cleavage except
Marge Mukai who had bumboolas. Guys
follow her so she bend over, maybe they can "spaaak,"
get lucky, catch a glimpse. Cheap thrills.

Good. Be good. "No be one easy fish."
But you want to be popular. You want to have a boyfriend—
he take you prom, maybe one football game
at Ho'olulu Park.
You want to be seen. Adored.

High heels. Almost broke my ankles.
Fall down like big Waimea eucalyptus tree—
trapped between the branches of girlhood.
How to grow up?

I. I want. Why can't I? All the other girls can.
They can go out. You don't want me to have fun.
Can't do this. Can't do that. This house is a prison.

J starts your name. Name so fancy.
How did your eighth-grade-only educated mother find it?
What did the name, in giving it,
hold for her daughter? Juliet.
Did my mother love in saying it?
My father couldn't even pronounce it.
It got caught in his throat like a fish bone.
For him, it was easier to use my Japanese name.
Written in katakana, not kanji, it meant nothing.
It was ordinary, for someone ordinary.
The ordinary letters made it easier for poor imaginings.
No inscription, no mark of Chinese-complicated characters.
I learned this, later, secretly,
that were my name in kanji
it would have meant the "heart of rice."
If only my name were written in kanji.
Imagine, having a name so beautiful, to soar, to grow into.

Kiss. And it was all over school.
The boy talked and soon others like "chance."
I had heard about girls who had done more.
Girls gossiped. Boys bragged. Everyone, dangerous.

Love. What does it mean? Myrtle and Kevin
are two hearts in a slam book and yearbook,
arrow running through. But no one comes.
Your parents withdraw to work, sister has a steady.
You wish someone would even look at you.
The boy you like is already taken.

M R S degree. That's all the girls talked about.
If you weren't married by when you were out of college,
you were out of luck. Old maid—
the croney-looking woman
on the face of the cards we played in school.
We don't want to be like that.

Norman. Chinese. "No good go out with Chinese,"
says my father. "Go out with nice Japanese."
You want to be a good girl.
You want to please your father.
But good Japanese boys hard to find. They spoiled,
wear ducktails, kabe-silk shirts,
satin jackets, stick black combs in back pockets.
They fool around street-racing cars,
want to make out in the backseat.
He puts your hands on his dick.

'Ōpū. Big 'ōpū.
"Edith, what's her name, you know which one,
pregnant tenth-grade year.
No be like her.
Big shame, for the family."

Papaya. Same thing as big ʻōpū.
"No be like her, you hea? Give you one whack.
The kid, some big, already. The motha and baby—
why, just like brotha-sista."

Question so big, seventh-grade year.
Where do babies come from?
"You dumb or what," says my neighbor.
She explains. I'm shocked!
"I neva know," I confess.
Can't get it out of my mind.

Rape happened to lot of girls my school.
Make yourself not yourself.
Hide behind your sweater.
Don't let the guys with *rep* date you.
You never know when it can happen.
Lock yourself up. It's dangerous out there.

Silence is golden, but my eyes still see.
My Chinese boyfriend cheats on me.
Maybe I'll marry one Japanese after all.

Toot toot, Tootsie, good-bye.
My mother stuck this nickname on me.
"Mama, stop calling me that," I plead.
"Shame, you know,"
but you don't know why.

Understanding—a perpetual lack thereof.
Growing up, so hard to understand how to be.
No one explains. *Can* explain.
The Japanese are an inscrutable people.

Violent to you, but you marry him, anyway,
this Japanese boy.
He is violent when you want to sing a song
or write a poem or grow a tree. He smashes
your typewriter and burns all of your pictures
of twenty years as if you never existed.
Be a good girl. Be a good mother.
Be a good wife—fish, battered, ole lady, no name face.

What happened?! First you are one, next 43, then . . . .
Children die and parents, too.

X is the head, the target, the gun put to it
for the releasing.

Yosh is your father's name. His nickname "Asa,"
spelled Biblically. Now there is no confusion:
girl, woman; father, husband.

I had many zits on my face growing up,
the scars still on my face.
When I wash my face in the morning,
the zit-scar shadows remind me of all our faces intertwined,
the scars, the pits of patience,
of forgiving,
of letting go.

THE ABCS OF IN SICKNESS OR IN HEALTH

Arrival
        One week after my mother's death,
the cleaning woman jumps out from my mother's room.
"She's sitting on the chair," she says
of my mother. "She's smiling, so I guess it's okay."
The cleaning woman goes back into the room
with her broom and dust cloth.

Bedpan
        I put it under my father's heavy 'ōkole.
He says "too cold." He complains
he's backed up like the old cesspool,
snakes of intestines having recoiled in the cold.
It's the first time I see his penis.
It's purple—like nasubi.

Circulation
        So poor. He's diabetic
and always cold. My mother calls him samugari,
wearing his cold. As if he can help it.
No wonder his dick's purple,
his lips blue, fingers cyanotic.
I Can't Get No Satisfaction plays in the background.

Do not resuscitate
        DNR. Tattoo these letters on his
forehead or on his chest. Make sure, so there's
no mistaking—there'll be no reviving.

Enjoy
        Enjoy your food. Live to eat. Not eat to live.
My mother feeds my father his death:
Spam, New Zealand Corned Beef, Vienna Sausages.

Finesse
        None in our house. Father
shovels food into his mouth
with a bulldozer spoon. Chomps
food like Matsumoto's cow.

Goodness
        "Goodness. Big girls, eh now?"
Miyamoto lady, old-time friend, says my
mother and father are lucky to have two
daughters. Take care of them when old.

Hilo
        They can't think of any
place else they'd rather be.
No place like Hilo town.
Hilo nō ka 'oi.
I ke ou ana i ka nani ao Hilo.
To live and die in Hilo.
"Perfeck place," my father tells me.
"So peaceful, eh."

I
        The I is ego-centered, I learn
at the Buddhist Study Center. We are
imperfect beings. I hate
cleaning my father's shit, seeing mother's
Frankenstein scar—staples that
closed the incision.

Jun ken po
>I kena sho, sucka sucka toe.
An exercise in ki: whoever wins jun ken po
gets to pound a partner's back. Hit
the bad energy out of the body.
Hit, hit, hit, hit. Pain feels good.
I'm into pain; I crave more.
I no longer have to care for my parents.
I saw them through. Everyone dead.

Ki
>You need it to hold up the body.
Tighten the anus and it gives you good balance.
Before, when off balance, I'd have rolled
like a boulder down a hill.
Now, I can catch myself from falling,
from sadness.

Love
>Love—what's that?
The Japanese don't know how to show it.
I embrace my father and he shrinks
like sleeping grass when touched. I ask my mother
if my father ever told her that he loved her.
She doesn't recall.
"My generation," she says, "no one said that to each other."

Mothers
>We are all mothers. M—for the million things.
No one is not a mother, all these women in our family.
We outnumber the men.
We give birth to nothing but girls.
Our gender takes over like a field of flowers.
The men we have left, die
before us. We will soon lose
even our family name.

Naturally
    "Naturally, I going marry the handsome one."
November is my mother's birthday and I feel
her presence in the house. Her perfume
moves in the air like the brush of a sleeve.

Organ
    Organ music and my mother's
best friends sing a hymn for her in memory
of her long-time companionship.
They want to sing it so perfectly. So into it,
they have no time to cry or say a prayer.

Poor
    Poor. Always so poor. They never get over it.
Even when they're both old, they still saving
for a rainy day in Hilo. Later, we find money in my mother's
suitcase. We learn it's insurance against
being put in a nursing home.
"No daughta of mine going put me thea."

Quiz
    I pop one on my students.
"No fair," they complain.
"Nothing's really fair," I say. Really nothing.
Neither life nor death,
the Pure Land, Matsumoto man's cow,
Mick Jagger hopping across the stage,
the shape of my nose,
the size of my chuts.

Rest
    Put your shoes in the geta bako.
Pour the tea. Take sips, breathe deep.
Don't have sex. Let the head droop
like a flower in the sun's heat.

Sex

My mother makes a confession.
After my father got diabetes she says,
"Daddy can't get it up, anymore."
They're in their seventies. She says
this with a great sense of loss.
Did they really have this long a sex life?
She could be pulling my leg.

Tall

This is what I always wanted to be.
Everyone is tall in the family. I get called
short stuff, short-stop, small pint, small feet.
"Can't have small feet and be tall," my father says.
"Fall down bum-bye."

Universe

In intermediate school
you say you're part of the stars.
Your classmates think you're a bit nutty
for talking philosophical. They avoid
you in the hallways, move over in the cafeteria,
don't greet your parents like they used to.

Violet

One of the colors of the aurora borealis.
Young girl time, in California,
mother claims she saw one, looking north
one night in Santa Rosa. "So magnificent," she said
and rode off on a boyfriend's motorcycle
as if she had been touched.

Waistline

Watch it. My parents thickened like
rubber tires—layer of insulating fat
from the cold of age and sickness.
I tighten my red cinch belt. I want
to be wasp-waisted like Karen Omine.
Beats getting fat. Maybe beats getting old.

X it
    The cat howls. The vet says it's a hairball.
"You don't want to X your cat just for constipation, do you?"
she asks my husband. I ponder the implication
of what she had said.

Young
    My parents were—my age perhaps—in Osaka.
This picture shows them happy, their faces
in the holes of a picture cut-out—
my father the rickshaw driver hauling my mother
in the backseat.

Zucchini
    With pieces of pork, sato-zyoyu style, so ono, you know.
My father eats like there's no tomorrow.
"Eat plenty. Take some more on your plate. Here.
You only live once. No shame. Why you yosha for?
Enjoy yourself," says my mother
in a stream of clichés that has governed their lives.

MAKING HISTORY MEAN

After mumbling through the instructions on the back of the bag, Mr. Kaneshiro rose from his little wooden stool and liberally tossed the fertilizer over his entire tomato bed. He groaned as he sat back down. Puzzling once more over the mystical directions, he finally shrugged, then spread more pellets around the largest tomato plant, working them into the soil with his weeder. A sudden sharp pain made him sit up straight. Reaching for his lower back, he rubbed hard. Some days he thought he might break in half at the waist. But he knew in the end all pain was a small price to pay: this year he could probably win every tomato contest in town. He tossed his weeder to the ground, grabbed at his back with both hands, and stretched, up and backward. "Uh!" he grunted, thinking about how good it was to be young. Eyeballing his prized tomato plant, he smiled.

"Grampa!" Kenny called from the back porch. "Ready?"

The old man pivoted slowly and raised his right hand. "Since da day before yesterday," he answered.

His grandson turned, whipped open the screen door, and came running back out before it could swing shut, cold Budweiser in hand. He ran up to his grandfather and held out the sacred twelve ounces. The old man grabbed the beer and swallowed deeply, his head and gray, short hair tilting back and glinting in the sinking sun. "Mmmmm," he muttered after downing half the can. "I evah tol you what a good boy you?"

The boy looked off to the side to think. "Yeah Grampa, yeah. Like every time I bring you beer."

Mr. Kaneshiro spluttered, choking on beer inhaled through his windpipe. After coughing spasmodically for a few moments and finally wiping his eyes, he said, side-eyeing his grandson, "Well you are."

"Oh yeah, thanks, Grampa. I knew you felt li' dat."

The tired gardener shook his head and sipped again, smiling.

"Grampa, so can boddah you now, or what?"

"Huh?" the old man asked, staring down at the sprouting son of his number-two son. "What you mean?" He rolled his wrist, sending the remaining beer into a circular counter-clockwise motion. "Boddah me how?"

The boy toed the perfectly manicured grass. "You know," he said. "You tol me no boddah you until you went pau da yahdwork. So now you pau an I get one question fo' ask."

Grandfather finished off his beer. He burped loudly. "How much?" he asked.

Kenny looked shocked. "Not money, Grampa. I mean, not right now anyways. Right now what I like ask you is fo' tell me one of your great stories."

"Why?" the old man demanded, staring down again, his keen black eyes boring like laser beams into Kenny's forehead. The boy took notice of something on the red-orange horizon off to the left. Old Mr. Kaneshiro shook his head and smiled. "I tell you what, Kenny. Be a good boy an go get me one more beer. Maybe den we talk."

Kenny flew back to the lanai and disappeared behind the screen door. This time he didn't move fast enough to get back before it closed. This made Mr. Kaneshiro suspicious. He cocked his head to one side and listened hard, but before he could focus on the conversation in the kitchen, his wife pushed the door open. His grandson's head angled out from behind her back.

"No!" she said, not loudly but with some force. "That's all the beer you get until after we eat."

Grampa's shoulders sagged. "But da boy like talk story wit me. How I goin help him wit his school work if my troat stay dry?"

"You buggah!" she shot back, louder and more forcefully this time. "You think I'm going to let you drink more beer by telling me you going help him with school work? How dare! What you tink me, Kenji?"

Grandfather gave a look to grandson for help. The boy could take a hint. "Oh yeah, Gramma, that's right. Grampa wants to help me do good in school, so he needs one more beer."

"The word is well, Kenny, well. He wants another beer so he can help you do WELL in—Ah! You boys!" She shook her head and pointed at her husband. "You two, I swear, you. . . ." Her finger shook but further words eluded her. She did an abrupt about-face back through the door. The man and the boy looked at each other and shrugged. Old

Mrs. Kaneshiro's hand came out through the doorway and Kenny grabbed the cold beer. He quickly ran the sacred can to its grateful receiver.

"But I'm telling you that's the last one until after dinner!" she called out through the screen.

Patting Kenny on the shoulder, Mr. Kaneshiro took the Bud from him. "Good boy. Have a seat, Kenny," he offered with great warmth, plopping back down on his gardening stool and gesturing to the grass with his free hand. "So what you like dis story for?"

"Jes like you said, Grampa, I need um for school."

Sipping his creative fuel, he asked, "So what dat English teacher like you kids write about dis time?"

The boy lay down on the grass. "We suppose to interview one ol—I mean one *kupuna*, an write about one of da great stuffs you can remembah from your own small-kid time. You know, one of da best good old days you had dat gave you planny wisdom so you can pass um on to modern day kids like me who gotta learn important value lesson stuff we nevah learn yet cuz we too young to be . . . you know, wise."

The old man stopped contemplating what he figured had to be a minimum four-pound tomato and tasted his Bud. Shaking his head knowingly, he said, "You pretty wise."

"Huh?" the boy asked.

"Nothing. Nevah mind. So," he sipped, "I'm gonna tell you about something dat happened to me so you can write um down an everybody goin say 'Ho, da buggah must have learned one important lesson from dat. He old, but he wise too,'" he sipped, "'cuz of this great experience.' Right?"

Kenny rolled over on his side and leaned on the palm of his hand. "Yeah, pretty much."

"So in other words, I goin do all da work an write dis story for you."

The boy sat up, shaking his head. "Oh no, Grampa. I not jes gonna make like one tape recorder. I goin make like one . . . like one screen, or someting my teacher said. Not jes writing um down, cuz Mrs. Leslie no like dat. I suppose to make what you say different. Trans . . . transsomething da ting for make um change so da lesson point stay real clear."

"Yeah yeah yeah," Mr. Kaneshiro mumbled, then sipped twice. "Okay, lemme think."

Kenny pondered his grandfather's short gray hair, the wrinkled ear, swollen in spots from boxing, the dark moles that sprouted black hairs on his cheek. He looked deeper, watched the gears spinning toward something good. Mentally, he celebrated with great enthusiasm, happily envisioning the "A" story he would write.

Something sparked in the old man's eye. "Kenny, I tought you said you hated English class?"

"Huh? Oh no, Grampa. Not since da las time. I got one 'A,' an Mrs. Leslie tol Dad dat I doin good now."

"Yeah? What you wrote?"

"Oh, about Joey and, you know, him dying."

Old Mr. Kaneshiro turned to contemplate the memorial shrine of stones that marked his favorite bird's grave on the side of the garden. "Joey," he sighed. "He was a good rooster. I wish I knew how come one day he so damn healthy an da next day he so damn dead."

Kenny looked away. "Oh, yeah, me too, Grampa."

The old man snapped around to look at the boy. "What you wrote about Joey? How come you nevah tol me about dat?"

Kenny continued looking away. "I, uh, wrote about how—I mean—dat he died. I went write about Joey, ah, an also about you an Gramma."

"Me and Gramma? What da heck you wrote about us?"

The boy swallowed. "Ah, not too much."

"An da English teacher liked it?"

"Oh, uh huh, Grampa. She said you and Gramma must be, ah, really int'resting."

Mr. Kaneshiro stared at the boy. "Intahresting. What you mean intahresting?"

"I don't know, Grampa. You know dese teachers. Da comments dey write so out of it. Who knows what dey talkin about."

The old man nodded and returned attention to his prized tomato in the making. "Yeah yeah yeah. Well, at least she tought it was good."

Kenny looked at the old man now. "You said it, Grampa. She really liked it. She tol Dad. She said it was really, really, really good."

Mr. Kaneshiro grunted. "Dat good, huh! I like read um sometime."

"Oh, uh, okay, Grampa. I bring um to you, uh, real soon. First chance I get. No worry." The subject changed quickly. "What about what you goin tell me now?"

"Oooookay, Kenny. I get just da story for you." The boy sat bolt upright, his face glowing with anticipation. "But first, you gotta sneak inside and get me one more Bud." The boy's head sank to his knees. "Right now, Kenny."

Kenny stood up slowly and sauntered over to the lānai. He stopped. Instead of boldly marching up the stairs, he suddenly dashed around the side of the house. "Das my grandson," Mr. Kaneshiro whispered, knowing that the next beer was only moments away.

A few minutes later, Kenny came barreling around the side of the house, running with his hand under his shirt. He produced the beer. "I tol Gramma I needed more toilet paper, so she went upstairs fo' get um."

"Good job, Kenny boy," Mr. Kaneshiro said, beaming. He popped the pull-tab. "Now what you planning for say when she come down with da toilet paper?"

"I goin say I used da Kleenex, of course."

The old man chuckled. "But get toilet paper in da bat'room, right? How you goin explain dat?"

"No more, Grampa, I hid um."

"Kenny?" came the call from inside. Mrs. Kaneshiro stuck her head out the screen door. "What are you doing out there?"

"Oh, I jes went use da Kleenex. Tanks, Gramma."

The grandfather listened to his wife's low mumbling and chuckled quietly. When he heard the screen door close, he said, "Okay, now fo' one story." He sipped and contemplated his big tomato. "Hmmmmm, let's see."

"I tought you said you had da story?"

"Huh?" The old man looked up. "Oh, yeah, but you took so long fo' bring me da beer I went lose my train of . . . I forgot." He sipped. "Lemme see."

Kenny waited. Time passed.

Finally the grandfather spoke. "Okay, I get um. I ever tol you about da time your granduncle an me broke into old man Chang's car an hid one dead rat under his back seat?"

Kenny shook his head. "No, Grampa, you nevah. What kine lesson you learned from dat?"

"Oh, yeah, sorry. I forgot about da lesson part. Let's see."

More time passed. More beer disappeared.

"Okay. I evah tol you how your granduncle an me burned down da storage shed behind da Chang's house?"

"No, Grampa, you nevah tell me dat one either. What lesson you learned from dat?"

"Simple an crystal cleah," said the old man. "No put out cigarettes on one old mattress. Da buggah goin burn forevah. No make diff'rence if you spit on da burning part an look extinguish. Da buggah still keep smoldering even if look like da fire stay out." He stopped.

"Oh, okay, Grampa," Kenny said slowly. "But I don't think Mrs. Leslie gonna say dat lesson is *kupuna*-level wise."

"Yeah, Kenny, you right. Lemme tink some more."

The sun had almost set. Kenny still waited. He noticed that his grandfather began swaying slightly on the stool.

"I got it, Kenny boy. I evah tol you how me an your granduncle pulled all of the nails out of old man Chang's outhouse? Sheez. He was da las holdout in da whole valley fo' get one inside toilet. When Mr. Chang wen open da door, da whole thing went collapse."

The boy blinked, then slowly nodded his head. "An da lesson was . . . ?"

Mr. Kaneshiro snorted then sipped. Smacking his lips, he said, "Revenge is sweet."

Kenny slapped his hand on the grass. "Grampa, I canna give Mrs. Leslie one li' dat either. Gotta be more nice kine, you know? Like one good an happy lesson."

The wise one nodded. "Maybe I bettah tink about some stuff besides da Changs, yeah?"

"Yeah, Grampa, good thinking."

Mrs. Kaneshiro flipped on the outside floodlights. Kenny watched his grandfather continue to sway in the dim spotlights.

"An I musta tol you about da camps already, yeah?"

"Sand Island?" Kenny asked.

"Yeah, Sand Island."

"An how you met Gramma dere?"

"Yeah yeah yeah. How I met Gramma dere."

"Yeah, Grampa, you tol me all about dat planny times already."

The old man sighed. Beer blurred the memory sometimes, but no matter how blurry, he could still see the rows of canvas cots in rows of canvas tents, the smoking lamps with their blackened glass, the armed guards. And yes, he'd met Thelma there. In the camps. The only clear memory. All the beer in the world would never erase that.

Suddenly he sat up straight. "Okay okay okay. You know da guys who sell da useless newspapah on da street corner? Well, had one guy, kind of not too smart. I think his name was Bobo. My dad, your great-grandfather, always use to buy da useless newspapah from Bobo. Da kid was nice but kinda slow. Oh yeah, I said dat, yeah? You know what I mean, right? Well, had lotta mean kids who use to make trouble to Bobo. Always boddah him. Always call him lōlō an stupid an dummy. I felt pretty bad for Bobo. So one time I asked my mom fo' make him one great hat all made outta beer cans. Da next time my dad went buy da useless newspapah I gave Bobo da hat. He tought was Christmas an New Yeahs an den. Boy, he nevah took da hat off.

"Den one day, some mean guys pulled up to Bobo in their van an took his hat—"

Old Mr. Kaneshiro blinked, then sipped deeply from his can. He held the beer out at arm's length, squinted at it, and shook his head. Kenny stopped breathing, waiting to hear what the mean boys had done to Bobo and his beer-can hat.

"Ah, sheeeeet!" Mr. Kaneshiro cursed. "Das not from my small-kid time. I tink maybe somebody tol me dat story. Maybe was your dad."

He glanced, beer-dazed, at his grandson. "Nevah mind, nevah mind. Das not my story. Erase. Erase. Now you know why I always tell you no drink when you come my age. Pretty soon you ain't gonna know what from what."

Kenny slapped the ground with both hands. "Man, Grampa, sounded so good da story. Tell um anyway. I like use dat one."

"Eh!" Mr. Kaneshiro spoke sternly. "Das not my story. Das some-body else story. You canna use um. Bad enough you using me fo' write your story. At least you should try for tell my own story."

"No mattah, Grampa. I can change um. Like I can say you gave him one hat made out of 'opihi shells or whatevahs, or one jacket, an he use to sell flowahs or somet'ing, an da mokes rode up on one horse or somet'ing."

This made the old man more upset. "One horse! Eh, had cars, gonfonnit!"

"Oh, okay Grampa. So dey had one car back den. Tell da resta da story."

The old man shook his head. "No no no no no! No good. Das not good, Kenny. Like lying. Or stealing. Like lying and stealing at da same time. Das not my story. Das not what I did myself. I nevah learn any lesson myself. Das not one real experience for make me one wise *kupuna*. Would be shame, Kenny. Big, big shame to steal someone else story."

The boy was upset. Bobo's story had sparked his interest and he wanted it. Mrs. Leslie, he figured, would never know the difference. "Come on, Grampa, please. Das one great story. Please, Grampa."

The old man cleared his throat noisily. "I said no! And no means no. I like tell my own story."

Kenny shook his head. "I no like hear your story, Grampa. I want dat story."

Mr. Kaneshiro stared at the boy, speechless. Furious, he turned his attention back to his future champion tomato. "Don't wanna hear my story, uh?" he mumbled. The tomato grew larger before his eyes. Suddenly he laughed out loud and slapped his leg.

"What, Grampa? What so funny?"

"I tell you one story. Dis one is real. Gonna kill your teacher. Make you forget about Bobo when you hear um cuz so damn scary."

Kenny said nothing; he wanted Bobo.

"When I was one small kid, old man Yamamoto," he pointed to the house across the street, "was one great gardener. He grew every vegetable you could tink of, and every vegetable was da best vegetable you ever seen. Anyway, had one contest coming up over at Pālama Settlement.

"Dere was one noddah great gardener named Souza—yeah, dat was his name. Mr. Souza. He lived over by Kawānanakoa, I tink. He also had da idea he would entah da contest and win wit his tomato.

"Both Souza and Yamamoto nevah let nobody see their tomatoes for two months. Even their wives couldn't get a good look at their tomatoes.

"So da contest day came. Yamamoto picked his best tomato, put um in one box, and hauled da buggah down to Pālama Settlement. In da dark, even, cuz he nevah like nobody see. When came time fo' judge da tomatoes, Yamamoto went bus um outta da box. Everybody's eyeballs went pop. Was five pounds fo' sure. And jes when Yamamoto tought he had da prize, Souza came limping in, flew open his box, and heaved his tomato on top da table. Nevah need weigh um. Da Portagee had um by eyeball. Was two pounds more at least. An Souza got da first prize."

He looked at his grandson. "So what, Kenny? You tink Yamamoto was happy with second place?"

Kenny stared blankly at his grandfather.

"You tink so?" the old man demanded again.

Blank stare.

Mr. Kaneshiro downed the last of his beer and crushed the can in his hand. "You see da Yamamoto's lychee tree?" He pointed toward the thirty-foot high tree surrounding the amber streetlight. The boy's eyes followed to where the index finger pointed. He nodded yes. "Da very nex morning, real early, Yamamoto's wife found him swinging from dat tree. Da buggah was all yellow an purple an black an green. Mrs. Yamamoto screamed so loud everybody woke up. Nobody knows what happened to da tomato. Or da second place ribbon. But dat made me wise, sonny boy, taught me one lesson Mrs. Leslie gonna love. Maybe, maybe not, I one wise *kupuna*, but I learned a whole lot about life from dat." He stopped speaking and continued to crush the can.

Finally Kenny couldn't wait any longer. "So what, Grampa, what you learned from dat?"

The old man gave the boy a long, hard look. Pointing to his largest tomato, he said, "What I learned? I learned dat what I got right here, well, it ain't good enough. Not yet, Kenny boy, not yet. But planny fertilizah goin make what I get grow into one goddamn winnah." He continued to stare coldly at his grandson. "Now go home an write my story."

"Huh?" The boy was confused. "Grampa, so what you went learn exact—"

"I said go da hell home already!" shouted Mr. Kaneshiro. "I tired talk." And with that he stood up quickly from his stool, turned, and trudged toward the house.

"But I don't get it, Grampa. What—"

"Figure it out fo' yourself." Without turning, he gestured with his hand for his grandson to depart immediately through the side gate. The screen door slammed shut behind him.

"Don't want my stories, huh?" He yanked open the refrigerator and pulled out another Bud. Jerking back his chair, he flopped into his place at the dining table.

His wife stirred something slowly on the stove, listening, waiting. "Where's Kenny?" she finally asked.

"Who cares? I sent Bobo home. He get homework. He can eat dinner with his own goddamn father."

"Bobo? Kenji, what happened?"

Mr. Kaneshiro pounded his beer down on the table. Shooting up from his seat he stomped out into the living room. After rifling through his pile of newspapers he uttered a triumphant "Ah hah!" and strode back into the kitchen. He jammed an old copy of the *World Enquirer* in his wife's face. It was the only paper he read. Often he referred to it fondly as "the scandal sheet."

"Das what happened," he said, pushing the paper between his wife and her steaming pot.

"What?" she asked again.

"Read it! What does it say?" he demanded.

She read the headline aloud: "Second-Place Winner in Big Tomato Contest Commits Suicide." She shook her head. "So?" she asked. "So what?"

He crumpled the paper and tossed it toward the trash can. The ball missed and rolled into a corner.

"Das what happened is what," he mumbled. He swept his beer off the table and returned to the living room. Through the picture window he saw his grandson standing under the Yamamoto's lychee tree, staring up into the yellow-lit branches.

For a moment the old man felt a twinge of guilt; he closed his eyes. But the beer still tasted very good. "Das exactly how it happened, Kenny boy," he whispered. He pulled the curtain across the window and flipped on the television.

TURNING HAOLE

The first time I came home for vacation
one of my worst nightmares proved true.
How come you talk like wun haole? my uncle said.
So I spoke nothing but pidgin for three whole months.
No more phone up there? Too good for us now, yeah? my friends said.
So I drank beer with them and jammed to Jawaiian.
You so pale my grampa said.
So I burned at Sandy Beach daily.
How come you los' weight? You no eat rice anymore? my aunty said.
So I ate poi and laulau and gained it all back.
What, you get haole boyfriend? my cousin said.
So I never called or wrote him the whole summer.
Hope you nevah lose your roots my dad said.
But I left this island,
I got away, I broke out.
You lucky you live Hawai'i my gramma said.
So I just nodded,
I know gramma, I know.

ROCKS

Wednesdays I go
to Kāne'ohe Boys' Home
to see my brother.
He got caught with his friends
for stealing a car
and beating up a retarded boy
in a chicken suit
in front of KFC.

This place is worse than home
he says,
and tells me about the ones
who cry at night
in their sleep.
He says the food's bad,
and that's when I give him
the *poke* and Twinkies I've brought.
They let him out for 30 minutes
and we go to the side of the mountain
and sit savoring
the fresh fish and seaweed.
He eats one Twinkie
and trades the other one
for a cigarette, I know it.

We just sit
and look up
at brilliant grey clouds.
He throws pebbles over the edge
and says he doesn't know
when he'll be out.

His time is up,
and he starts to head back.
But I do not move.
My life is here
throwing rocks off this cliff
with you.

WALTER K. LEW

MĀNOA RUN

If I stretch it out, turn and go

Up the hill, the circling road
behind the widow's house

I will see an ocean sunset, flotillas

Of cirrus blazing in their chassis.
I will follow the curve, the lush bend up into the better

Neighborhood: silk dogs, children tumbling like deaf-mutes,

The crying paradisial flora
shrubbed and rinsed and shaken clean.

A cold flame of wind will grab fallen, lung-sized

Kamani leaves and gust them into
A walking companion

Rushing and treading beside me, at shoulder-height:

Its head's milled peat, belly, shins
Unceasingly thrashed and shat into each other,

As if this were no mere exercise

But a face of the hidden urge, whispered
Mind of things to pace and speak with us;

By this I will be made helpless, and jog on

Knowing like a scar, that I cannot remember, cannot
say the spell exactly, or dare to embrace

The falling figure, weep and pray

For the burning prisoner kneeling into his
dissolving shins. *Grandfather!* I may whisper, *Father!*

My father says all his life here. The flame withdraws,

The head keels, flops open like a gourd
Into a hopping gyre of mute leaves

On the black road, if I stop and turn around.

SEPTEMBER, 1997

Death surrounds us. On television
the blonde princess lies splayed
in her casket, gutted like a huge caught fish,
no sound, no air, only
the stench of a spent life.

She lies unburied in London,
from where my wife and daughter and I
have just come—
where its heat, like a noose,
still seizes us. I remember
watching Shakespeare
in a pub without air conditioning,
the audience packed like corpses
in the sarcophagus of a grand cathedral,
not daring to move,
not daring to even sweat.

In this nave of this church
the mother of my friend, this red-faced nun,
gazes out at us
from her young photograph,
her black hair cropped back,
her forehead shining.

Just before our trip
another friend's father also died,
his insides turned hollow and light.
There were only tears and lamentations
reverberating at his service
as we came forward, like children, one by one
to offer incense

to his spirit departing.

The priest called us to the sacraments,
the immanence of body and blood,
but I sit in a stupor
partly from jet lag, partly in prayer.
The mother's mind had become brittle.
I reflect on her daughter's request
when I hugged her; she wondered
if I might write a poem
like those others I wrote before
recalling when my mother died
when I was sixteen
and near the age of the princess' son.

It was so long ago.
I can only think of regrets
for the dead and for their children
of not having lived fuller lives,
of all the stupid mistakes made,
of the hurt caused, and received.
We should travel around the world,
spend more time with our spouses,
apologize more,
write more poems, believe in God.

My thoughts swirl
through the sorrow of smoke dissipating
in front of her black and white image.
It is as if I were a child again
when I had my tonsils removed.
The surgeon told me
to count backwards from 100;
but I did not remember anything past 97.

Someday, another poet told me,
each of us will just fall asleep
but not wake up—
like sleek electricity

in this typewriter
which will one day cease,
the ink which will dry up and fade,
this dull paper
which will curl and flake away.

Read this, my fifteen-year-old daughter.
Read this before it is too late.

THIS LANDSCAPED HOME

"What did she see.
Wet leaves, the rotten tilted-over
over-heavy heads
Of domesticated flowers.
I knew Indian Paintbrush
Thought nature meant mountain,
Snowfield, glaciers and cliffs,
White granite waves underfoot."
—Gary Snyder, "The Old Dutch Woman"

I live in a box enclosed on two sides
by clumps of areca palms in the back
and on the street
a fence of butterfly hibiscus
tall and bushy
with pale pink flowers peeking out.
Inside we have planted
a gnarl of poinciana
three types of shower trees
baak laan and lung ngaan
the portly bottle tree palm
Queen Emma lilies (the color of eggplant)
mei su laan and kwai fa for fragrance
and the dark sharp sheaves of giant mondo
to serve as ground cover
lining our paspalum lawn.

It does not matter
that my palms now have scales
my hibiscus leaves white pustules
for which I have to spray
time and again.
I have accepted the fact

that kiawe have emerged
near my neighbor's garage
and that the wind from the mountains
has thinned out our crista-galli.
Because I tried to poison out the weeds
our lawn now sports brown spots
where the grass too has died
—a consequence of my overeagerness.
The bamboo I wanted to have
has rubbed off roof shingles,
and the angel's trumpet
which we never liked has run riot.
But to me these are minor irritants.

From my second story window
I can see above the rooftops
into the far reach of the valley
where two walls of green converge
catching and reflecting
different shades of light
revealing a thin fissure of water
dropping precipitously
until it disappears behind the treetops
merging we know with other rivulets
to form the coil of stream
that I grew up with
that passes by
two blocks from where we now live
—this landscaped home
our approximate attempt
to savor the natural world.

WILLEM THE WETBACK

—for Jeff Baysa

Willem DeKooning was an illegal alien
An FOB who literally jumped off a ship
in New York
and the rest as they say is
art history

If he had done his jumping off the boat
here in sunny San Diego
the success story as we know it
would be just another immigrant dream

because here in sunny San Diego
wetbacks aren't allowed to paint
unless it was some richman's
beach house
wetbacks aren't allowed to sculpt either
unless it was Mrs. Shoresman's
hedges and overgrown bushes

Instead of being the best
American painter
DeKoo would be the busboy
clearing the dishes

only he would be the one drawing
a still life with his wet rag
while wiping off your table

Instead of hanging out
with Jackson Pollock and Jasper Johns
he would be standing
at the corner gas station
with the other wetbacks
waiting for some rich but cheap
Rancho Santa Fe Zoe Baird type
to come and pick him up for the day
to clean some horse stalls way out in the
middle of nowhere
but DeKoo would be the one
making a mandala out of
hardened horseshit and taking his time

around these parts
they don't like his kind
but they can't live without him
they've grown accustomed to a
certain way of life
after all this is the South
of California

like chasing the cats out of the barn
they can't because then who is going
to chase the unwanted rats

here in sunny San Diego
where even the retired old geezers
have rabid Republican hearts
they can be meaner than
a Tijuana sewer dog

they even want to send their
gardeners back
(but only after he's done all that leafblowing
and grooming of their ten-acre yard)

they hold candlelight vigils
chanting
"send back the wetbacks"

it's funny
these white people
truly think
they own the place

DeKoo was a real life
illegal alien
Willem the Wetback

the same people
that would've sent him back
wouldn't know a DeKoo
if it grabbed them in the nuts (that is after all
what a DeKoo painting will do to you)

Even if they could recognize a genuine DeKoo
they wouldn't be impressed at all

their idea of art
is a Holiday Inn seascape
that matches the colors of
their drapes

colors colors colors
finally we'll see a finale
where DeKoo will be running from
colors

he would forever be running
from the pasty green Migra van
and that jungle fatigue green
that the Migras wear as uniform

he would be running and running
not because he's afraid of
getting caught and being sent back
but because he can't stand
that pasty dead green on the van
he'll be throwing up all the way
to the border

NOEL ABUBO MATEO

A FILIPINO HIPPIE'S LAMENT

—for Jessica Hagedorn

the '60s were a wonderful time
the demonstrations on the streets
against the Tutas
fighting off the Metrocom police
getting detained in Camp Crame
and while in jail
trying to convince PMA cadets
to join Taruk's huks in the mountains
instead of getting their heads cut off in Mindanao
and coming home in a box
we sang peace songs to them
and let them have a toke of damo
they started singing along

the '60s were a wonderful time
until Imelda and Bong-Bong
spoiled it for all of us
they ruined it for the Filipino Hippies
the Pinoy Ipis

the Beatles snubbed Imelda
so she chased them out of the country
Bong-Bong said he liked the
Rolling Stones better anyways

well that was the end of us
we wanted a Woodstock in Manila
we lived for the music
we were the best Beatle imitators in Asia
given the chance

the fifth Beatle
would have been a Pinoy
Ringo, Paul, George, and Carding

Imelda went and ruined it for us
her favorite Beatle was Yoko

we waited for that moment for so long
so what does she do
she and her ignorant
probinciana sensibilities blows it
for a whole generation

you know we could forgive her
for the three thousand pairs of shoes
we could even forgive her for
the five hundred black bras
but depriving the little brown
copycat Pinoy Ipis of
a glimpse of the Fab Four

that we will never forgive

YOU GOT IT ALL

—for John Nelson

a perfect California morning
a seeing-eye dog shits
the blind man pulls out
his plastic bag
somehow he knew
something about a keener sense of smell
he gets down on his knees
he starts searching
for the droppings
picks up one big mound
after another
seeing-eye dogs are not
the small and delicate types

he slips each one into
a bigger plastic bag
he feels around the dog
some more
to make sure
he didn't miss any last minute drops

a visiting New Yorker who happens
to be watching all this
from across the street
a jaded Manhattanite
so used to stepping
on dog shit in the park
because owners
with perfect twenty/twenty
vision

turn a blind eye to
the three pounds that
their beautifully groomed
pedigreed purebred kennel charge just laid
on the bike path

this New Yorker
so used to scraping his shoes
yells at the blind man
across the street
YO! YOU GOT IT ALL MAN!

APRIL JACARANDA

—for Aileen

Over the wide pond
raucous ducks
clammer into torchlight.
A small boy
tosses bits of bread
he tears from
a tightly woven basket
on a table on
a nearly empty lānai.
His parents smile
beyond an open candle.
Feed that one alone
there, his father says.
You are younger now
than ever I remember,
standing beside me
on a spillway where dark
gathers in water
rising to our bare ankles.
This is the Hilo flood
of 1941, you explain.
That spring you died
these hills turned violet,
all the brittle branches
exploded in blossoms
and what I say since
comes mostly in dreams.
Years in dark and silence
led to this birth.
The old lānai has been

boarded up for decades,
ducks moved to quiet
condos on the far shore.
In dreams I weep for
what I cannot understand,
and blooms of bright
jacaranda greet the sky.

EIKO MICHI

BETWEEN THE SHEETS OF ICE

I'm sorry, father—
We couldn't even cremate you;
there was a bad storm.
The road to the crematorium was blocked
and the building blown away.

You counted on a family burial—
ashes in the urns,
some for the family altar,
and some for the grave.
But death did not grant that modest request.

We did have a funeral.
The men put you in a pine box,
roped it onto a horse-drawn sleigh.
But they came back, said they couldn't
get through.

Mother had them take you down
where you loved to fish for salmon.

    —Take those heavy iron bars, she said,
    you will need them to crack the ice;
    sometimes it freezes in layers.

    Put the box between the sheets of ice,
    he'll not melt until Spring.
    And when the river swells,
    it will surely carry him along.
    It's good that way—
    he'll be with the salmon.

I saw you once harpooning
with a pair of big black rubber boots
that came to your hip.
How magnificent you were!
and the salmon, leaping silver in the air,
rush—rushing against the stream,
driven with the promise of birth and death.
The lance flew, flashing back the moonlight—
silver to silver, piercing the fish.

Now your pine box bobs up and down,
down that river.
The salmon swarm around you
bump against you,
jump and fly over you—
some going up, some going down
in your common dream.
Live and die, live and die—
Rush—rush down the river—in the Spring.

WRECKS

Outside our house on Pūpū Street,
I play with my Star Wars figures.
I went cut holes in the Styrofoam Big Mac container,
make space ship, ah.
Ho, I make Luke Skywalker fly all around,
Darth Vader no can catch him.
My father, he yelling at my mother again.
But me, I just keep playing,
pretend I get deaf ear.
Luke, he the best pilot in the galaxy,
fly around the tree,
over the flower bed,
through the rose bushes.
Luke, he fly across the yard,
he think he lost Darth Vader,
but then, lasers start shooting at him.
He make any kine moves for dodge the blasts.
Can hear my mother yelling at my father now,
she asking him for put something back.
Luke, he turn around and fly straight into Darth Vader's ship,
can hear glass breaking,
then my father come out of the house,
punching the screen door open
and fling my mother's bird on the ground.
The buggah went skip on the concrete,
look like one pebble on water.
I look at my father,
can hear my mother crying inside,
he look at me,
I get one smashed Styrofoam spaceship in one hand,
Luke's undamaged one in the other.
His eyes come small,

looking straight at me he say,
"That fuckah never going fly around my house again.
Shit on everything.
Fricken bird."
He look at me little bit more,
no blink,
his tongue digging the inside of his mouth.
My mother start cussing at him from inside the house,
he go back inside,
ready for continue the battle.
Me, I go look at my mother's bird,
all hamajang,
the wings spread,
the head crooked to the left—
still twitching.
My stomach come all funny kine,
like when I like beef with somebody at school.
I start making fists,
the Styrofoam space ships popping between my fingers,
my hands shaking.
Before I could stop,
I went fly my spaceships across the yard.
Went get stuck in the rose bushes.
I look down at my mother's bird,
the thing stop moving,
the feet all curl,
get feather skid marks
and blood on the concrete.
I touch the wings and think,
at least you had one chance for fly.

MARIE M. HARA

TOM OKIMOTO: THE ICONOCLAST

Although the working artist who manages to survive in Hawai'i more often than not wears multiple professional hats, Tom Okimoto still stands apart.

As one who doesn't welcome the label artist, Okimoto has travelled several paths directed to helping others, particularly as a long-time teacher of art at the Hawai'i State Hospital for the mentally ill. Here he won the hearts of his troubled students as he showed them how to use their deep energies in creating with paint and clay. Although the years Okimoto spent teaching at the institution took over his vital career time, he still managed to continue developing an expertise in specific media, kept on track by his desire to create a body of painting and sculpture. This is what Okimoto has continued to do with admirable success. Even after 38 years of painting, he maintains a private persona which allows him considerable freedom from being recognized or stereotyped.

The ironic result of Okimoto's multi-duty roles as teacher, advocate for the arts and student of many cultural directions was a stronger, clearer vision. According to painter Russell Sunabe in reference to Okimoto's 1995 Kapiʻolani Community College Koa Gallery show *Continuum . . . Representation to Abstraction*, "Tom forms a bridge from today's younger Hawaiʻi-born artists to local boys Isami Doi, Keichi Kimura, Tetsuo Bob Ochikubo, to only name a few. And it is of particular historical interest . . . that this legendary group in their heyday revolutionized painting and sculpture in the islands, incorporating their Hawaiʻi roots, ethnic backgrounds and the formation of modern art in a local hybridization of sorts into artworks unique to but first and foremost 'of Hawaiʻi.'"

Okimoto doesn't dwell on his numerous awards and achievements. He says of his highly praised efforts, "All I can do is paint." Okimoto's focus is directed to process itself and only then, the signature products of such a unique mode of expression. The magnetic blank canvas inevitably challenges him anew. On any given day three to six acrylics or oils, the ones he is continually re-working, await his full attention. Of these two or perhaps three will be finished at the end of each year. He says simply, "I just paint." Ultimately his luminous paintings which include vibrant watercolors as well as his striking ceramic pieces can and should speak for themselves from Okimoto's view. They exist in their own right without the usual intercession and rhetoric of the maker or the critics.

Here in his own words is a strongly individual or iconoclastic view of art: "I find it easier to disclaim the label of 'artist' than to assume the identity.

"Ideally, one does artworks simply because of a wish to express oneself, detached and unfettered by values external to oneself.

"The style, media, or subject of an artwork need not be overly important if the results are worth viewing. In one's capacity of creating, the artworker relates to the art viewer—who has a creative capacity in the process of perceiving. The context of art may then be seen as a shared experience; a non-verbal dialogue.

"Perhaps art need not be explained, having a being and a voice of its own. A work of art, speaking for itself, relieves the artworker of rhetorical explanation, as well as the viewer, the pain of such monologue."

With uncommon deference to the immediacy of insightful feelings and with great humility, Okimoto eliminates the gloss of verbiage surrounding his efforts. As he invites the viewer to participate in experiencing his offerings, he gives rich gifts for the human spirit to anyone who will but stop awhile and take a long look.

Ironwoods at Mokulē'ia
Acrylic on canvas, 1983
10" x 14"

Monterey
Acrylic on canvas, 1986
11" x 14"

ROY ONOMURA

ATTACHED TO MY CAR

I sit in my car with two heavy bags of groceries.
I devise a plan to exit my car with groceries in one trip.
Open the door with both bags on lap.
Lock car door and stuff car keys into pocket.
Pivot on car seat and step out.
Standing with both bags of groceries,
Slowly back up and use butt to close car door.
My plan almost works.
The door isn't fully closed.
Frustrated, I slam my butt against the door.
Suddenly, there is an intense, searing pain.
So intense, tears roll down both cheeks.
I try to turn, but I can't.
A chunk of my butt is caught in the door.
I try to bend forward to put the heavy bags down.
I cannot, the pain is too intense.
I am stuck.
Just drop the bags.
No! The glass jars will break.
What an embarrassing scene.
Standing, slightly bent forward carrying grocery bags.
My butt is caught in the door.
In pain, trying to hold back tears.
The door is locked.
My car keys are deep in my pockets.
I hope my neighbors don't see me.
With all my strength, I clutch both bags with my left arm.
I fish for my keys in my right pocket.
No! My keys are in my left pocket.
Oh, the pain!
With every last ounce of strength,
I carry both bags with my right arm.

Quickly, I fish for my keys in my left pocket.
Finally, I get them out and unlock the door.
Ah, freedom!

ROY ONOMURA

CHICKEN FARM

My father owned a fighting chicken farm in Waipahu. He brought me to the farm everyday when I was about five years old. At this age, I wasn't very quick in catching chickens to play with. But one day, I caught one. He wasn't fully grown and he had something slimy all over his body. I didn't care about what he looked like, or even that he felt kind of icky; I caught him and he was mine. My father walked by and said with a firm voice, "Roy boy, put that chicken down. Can't you see that he has medicine all over his body? He's sick." I realized now why I was able to catch him. I put the little black chicken down, but soon after my father had walked away, I ran after the chicken and picked him back up. It was about the third time that I was caught with my little friend that my father's famous samurai attitude erupted. He was very angry with my disobedience. He yelled, "What did I tell you? Don't pick up the chicken because he's sick!" At that moment, my father took my sick little friend away from me and carried him by the feet. He walked to an elevated chicken coop, and began whacking the chicken against the hard wood. I still can remember the chicken screaming and its feathers exploding off its body. My father looked like a baseball player pitching the chicken against the wooden wall over and over again. He wanted to demonstrate that his word was law and was above the life of this chicken. After the chicken died, my father threw it into the bushes. I felt terrible for the chicken. I just stood there and watched him die. If I had listened, maybe the chicken would have lived. Although I didn't show any emotions, I felt very sorry for my friend.

Not long after my father killed the sick chicken, his famous samurai attitude erupted again. This time, he ordered me to feed the chickens, particularly the roosters. He was proud of his roosters and he enjoyed showing them off to his friends. These roosters were the ones he would train to fight other roosters, and they were very expensive. I answered my father by telling him that I didn't want to feed them because they would bite me. He assured me that they wouldn't, but I was too scared. He got upset, and I was more afraid of his anger than the roosters. I then picked up the bucket of chicken feed and walked down the row of chicken coops. An excited rooster stuck his head out through a four-inch-by-four-inch feeding window to get at the food. I was very scared, and this made my father disappointed. He yelled, "Just put the food in his bowl!" I did and the rooster pecked at my little hand, which at six years old was painful. I cried loudly and I yelled back, "See, I told you he would bite me!" My father walked away and came back with a loaded rifle. He stuck the rifle barrel through the feeding window and aimed at the chicken's breast. As the excited rooster backed up against the corner of its cage, he shot the rooster. The rooster's blood splattered all over the walls of the cage. I rubbed my hand and looked at the lifeless rooster at the same time. Its blood was draining out of its body and was making a thick red pool in the cage. I wasn't sure what to do next. That poor chicken was now dead.

My father looked over to me and said, "Now go and feed the rest of the chickens."

THE WHIPPING ROPE

Al Khardz Jail
Kingdom of Saudi Arabia
May-June-July 1985

I

The whipping rope,
forty-eight inches long,
is slender,
and tapers at the end.
But, uh-uh, don't ever
underestimate
its sublime strength
my friends.
When it strikes
the target point,
all the nerves in that area
lose their throbbing
innocence.

How I know?
It's like this:
For almost a year now
in these brutish sands,
the lengthy hours of our toil
have come and gone
including the dreary days
of winter and summer
and we are still farming for
our paychecks,
still eating rotten fish with
gritty grains of rice.

(How lucky are the bees!
They are gladly received
when they drop by
to drink
the sweet fluid in the pistils
and stamens of flowers,
do not have anybody
to boss them
around,
even have their sting
just in case somebody
tries to inflict harm
to them.)

My conscience tells to
myself:
"You must stand up,
not sulk nor grumble!
Forget about working
anymore.

If the watermelons,
If the cucumbers,
If the tomatoes,
If the cantaloupes die,
then so be it.
If you are brought to jail,
then so be it."

II

Every Friday at nine a.m.,
the day designated for praying,
we, prisoners,
herded like smelly goats
from our holding cells
to the main square,
must take our individual

punishment
for the perceived
or real crimes we committed.

Twenty-five lashes on my back
while my hands
are tied
to a black-painted post
are among the rudimentary
ways our tormentor brings
torment to us
as he looks
into our eyes
with such sharpness,
with that unmistakable cruelty
partly hidden
in his wind-burned lips.

I feel somehow that he strongly
feels I am not scared
so he makes sure
that every whip is stronger
than the previous one.

III

Every time the whipping rope
lands on my back,
sometimes
even on my right or left
shoulder blades,
How I want to cry or scream!
But I know the Lord is watching,
It's a disgrace
for Him to see me screaming
and crying.

Every time the whipping rope
lands on my back,
sometimes
even on my right or left
shoulder blades,
it's just natural that I clench
tight my fists as I endure
the taunting
and the jeering
and the mocking
of the whipping rope: I love
your muscles, boy!
I'll make them more tender
and supple.
I love your nerves, boy!
I'll make them more sore
so you really suffer.

So every time the whipping rope
lands on my back,
sometimes
even on my right or left
shoulder blades,
I realize how simple
and unassuming its nature is
and the extent of its power:
These deliberate blows
rattling me to my senses,
at the same time,
wishing me good days
and good nights
of lying on my chest
on that urine-smelling slab
of concrete
as I indulge in this
nerve-jerking, gut-twisting pain.

empty shell

where are
you

sea snail?
i am

distressed
to hear

only your
whisper

in your
empty shell.

ELMER OMAR BASCOS PIZO

BLACK DOG
[pinoy style]

Beloved Frank de Limas, Willy Ks,
every time you meet me on the narrow
streets of waipahu or ewa or kalihi,
in wedding celebrations or birthday parties,
in the mortuaries or pharmacies,
in the supermarkets or churches,
even in the schools or cinema houses,
you never fail to ask me about that
                              black dog.

There's not a need to defend ourselves.
It's impractical, it's useless!
Yet, I, a typical pinoy dog eater,
considered the most shameful remnant
of this human race, still need to set
this black dog thing in a more relevant
perspective.

The smell of dog adobo floating lightly
through your aquiline noses is way,
way different from the real feeling,
from the real thing.
May it be tame or wild dog,
May it be trained or neglected dog,
May it be smart or idiot dog,
May it be rice-fed or chow-fed dog,
May it be pure-bred or native dog,
May it be yellow or brown dog,
When you roast them, their skin always
turns black anyway.

ALSHAA T. RAYNE

COLLATERAL DAMAGE

Some things are meant
to be broken, targeted from great distance
smashed without warning

The air is thick with buddhas
luminous, silent
I think nothing of breathing
right through them
trampling beads, offerings
of freshly picked flowers, rice

Behind me
an army of spirits, ancestors
in their silks and linen, frowning
clicking their teeth on chopsticks
of ivory and precious silver
pointing to empty bowls
their powdered concubines holding on
to robes, combs
threatening to come loose
being pushed from behind by peasants
groaning under foul loads
midwives keening, merchants, lepers
beating on half-rusted cans, murderers
stone throwers, sailors, ex-husbands
soldiers, hordes
and hordes of strangers
fornicating
spitting curses
like loose dogs

And I think I act alone

HUNTER GATHERER

WE EAT TO LIVE & LIVE TO EAT
— I'M AHUNGERED — I GO
AHUNTING & GATHERING — AS
IN A DREAM I ENTER A SUDDEN
BARREN WITH BOREAL LIGHT &
PILES OF FROZEN ANIMAL CARCASSES
— RIGHT OFF I FIND CARCASS OF
RABBIT SKINNED CUT UP DRESSED
STEAMING WITH COLD — THO
RABBIT IN HAND STIFF &
MARMOREAL I SEE BRAISED
RABBIT — I WALK PAST BANK
OF FLOWERS LIKE FUNERAL
DISPLAY FOR DEAD ANIMALS —
I HEAR MUZAK LIKE DIRGE FOR
FROZEN COMPATRIOTS OF
COMMON ANIMAL FATE —

IT IS ONLY A SEEMING TO
BELIEVE WE ARE NOT CANNIBALS
PLENTY FLASHY THE ANTHURIUMS
ORCHIDS THE ODD PROTEA CHRYSANTHEMUM
DAISY LILY OF THE VALLEY BIRD OF
PARADISE — A WORTHY DISPLAY OF
FLORAL — THEN I STEP INTO MOIST
COOL CORNUCOPIA LIT BY BOSKY
UNDERSTORY LIGHT THAT ENHANCES
GREENY VEGGIE WORLD — VEGGIES
DEAD BUT HELD IN FRESHNESS BY
COOLNESS & FREQUENT SPRAYINGS
OF WATER THEY STILL CRAVE
CUT OFF FROM ROOTS AS THEY
ARE — IN HUSHED INTELLIGENCE
OF CUT OFF FROM ROOT BUT
NOT YET DEAD THEY WAIT
TO BE CHOSEN PURCHASED &
CONSUMED BY US SO WHAT WE
ARE AS WE ARE SUSTAINED FOR
ANOTHER DAY & NIGHT —

AH SACRIFICIAL LEAFY GREENS
& YOU THE VEGGIE FRUITS
LIKE PEPPERS EGGPLANTS BROCCOLI
ARTICHOKES GREEN BEANS &
THE LIKE — PLUMP MAUI ONIONS
IN YOUR DRY CRISP SKINS — CLOVES
OF GARLIC PACKED IN BULGING
HEADS — STARCHY TUBERS
WITH EARTHY FORMS — Q —
DO POTATOES DREAM — ASSORTED
FUNGI — BURDOCK ROOT & KABOCHA
SQUASH — SLEEK LEEK WITH
ROOT TUFT — GINGER ROOTS PULLED
FROM GROUND WASHED & LAID
IN PILES AISLESIDE NEXT T.
LEHUA TARO — THEN APPLE ORANGE
BANANA PAPAYA STRAWBERRY
PINEAPPLE PLUM PEAR MANGO
LYCHEE ETC ALL TRYING THEIR

BEST TO LOOK REAL & DELICIOUS—
I THINK RABBIT BURDOCK ROOT
KABOCHA LEEK SHIITAKE
GINGER ONION GARLIC SALT
PEPPER ALE MIRIN SHOYU IN
DUTCH OVEN 325° F TILL
DONE— / STEER TO BANK
OF LIGHTED FROM WITHIN GLASSED
IN FRIDGE ALTARS FILLED WITH
BOTTLES OF THE LEGAL NECTAR
& TAKE OUT FROSTY BOTTLE
OF LIME] LITE ALE — THEN AS
WAKING FROM A DREAM I LOOK
AROUND & SEE MANY OTHER
ANIMALS OF MY SAME SPECIES
OF ALL AGES & VARIOUS GENDERS
LIKE ME UP ON HIND LEGS & EACH
DRESSED DIFFERENTLY DOING JUST
WHAT I AM DOING AS QUIET
ALERT & KNOWING AS MYSELF

WRIT BY HAND

GUESS I'M OLD FASHIONED I'LL
ALWAYS WRITE BY HAND — USING
MY BUILT IN FREE MIND EYE
HAND COORDINATION CIRCUIT
INVISIBLE MIND WITH PHYSICAL
PERIMETERS — I PRESS MY MARKS
WITH PENCIL ON PAPER — IT
IS MY TRAIL — THE ONE I
LEAVE AS I FOLLOW SCENT OF
INNER WILD BEAST THROUGH
BUSHY GRAMMAR OF CIVILIZATION
— I SET DOWN ALPHABETIC MARKS
SO I DON'T GET LOST — SO I
CAN FIND MY WAY OUT — I AM
AN INNER VISION MAN — EARTH
FEEDS ME SYMBOLS OF ITSELF

— BUT SET ME BEFORE A
MT & TELL ME TO DRAW IT
& I WILL DRAW YOU A MT
THOUGH IT MAY NOT LOOK LIKE
A MT TO YOU — PERSONAL
MEANINGS ARE MY GAME —
MEANINGS I GARNER FROM THIS
24 HOUR A DAY GREENWICH MEAN
TIME NON STOP GRUNT IN
BEING WHAT WE CALL ALIVE —
THIS LONG HELD BREATH TO THE
POINT OF BURSTING — WRITING
BY HAND WITH PENCIL ON PAPER IS
THE CHEAPEST FORM OF ART
NEXT TO DRAWING & SINGING
— INNER VOICE EYE HAND MIND
COORDINATION A FREEBIE &
MUSE DON'T CHARGE — OUT
OF POCKET EXPENSE FOR

THIS HOBBY MINIMAL — I WRITE
IN A 288 PAGE 144 SHEET 8½"X 11"
SKETCHBOOK COST ME #11.49 —
THAT'S ABOUT 4 CENTS PER EACH
RECTO ~ VERSO — THE PAPER
IS REGULAR DRAWIN' PAPER — MY
PENCIL IS A PENTEL MECHANICAL
USES 0.5MM LEAD SO NO NEED
EVER SHARPEN — I USE 2B LEAD
WHICH IS SOFT ~ DARK — .
PENCIL HAS REPLACEABLE ERASER
— PENCIL WITH ERASER HEAD IS
RIGHT UP THERE IN MY LIST OF
GREATEST ACHIEVEMENTS OF
CIVILIZATION — THE PENTEL
PENCIL COST $2.59 — A LIGHT
WELL DESIGNED PRODUCT THAT
WORKS — FITS NICELY IN HAND —
MADE IN JAPAN WHERE THEY ONCE
BRED FOR EYE HAND MIND COORDINATION
— MY FAVORITE PIECE OF
SINO JAP CALLIGRAPHIC ART

IS RYOKAN'S — 二 三
1 2 3 ICHI NI SAN — GREAT
CALLIGRAPHY MAKES TEXT LOOK
LIKE WHAT IT MEANS —
SO FOR TOTAL CAPITAL OUTLAY
OF $14.08 I CAN DO MY ART+
THE HIGH OF WRITING FOR ME
IS WATCHING WORDS FORM ON
PAPER AT PENCIL POINT COMPLETE
WITH MEANING & NO AUTHOR

RYAN SENAGA

A LITTLE CRUSH

I first saw her when I took Math 100 in my junior year. She had the kind of bleached brown hair and that deep kind of tan that came from tons of days spent at the beach. She was Asian although something about her straight nose bridge gave me the idea that she had some haole blood. She kept in good shape too: way solid breasts and these really nice smooth legs usually ending in slippers. The part of her I always liked though, was her back. Strong-looking with little ridges of muscle. She always wore these tight tank tops that showed a lot of skin below her neck. I had this feeling she surfed. She looked about 22 and most people who looked like that in Hawai'i surfed.

She always came to class by herself. She never said hi to anybody even though the room had choke people in it. Sometimes she came late and sat down, long sun-bleached brown hair in a ponytail and Oakleys still covering her eyes. Her eyes weren't large. They were slightly narrow, not cute Bambi eyes. There was something a little more serious about them.

I ate lunch with Tyson on the steps of the Campus Center at UH. He was dressed just like me, in his usual Quicksilver T-shirt and board shorts, except he probably washed them way less. We scarfed Mos Burgers and watched people walk by below us.

Some of the red salsa-like goop fell out of Tyson's burger and onto the concrete.

"Ho Dan," Tyson said. "Dat looks like da painting you when do fo your class."

"Shut up."

"Nah, fo reals, Dan." Tyson stared at the Mos Burger filling. "You went school fo almost six years fo learn how fo draw someting dat looks like dat?"

I was used to him teasing me about my major. "Just shut da fuck up already."

"What da fuck you going do wit one art degree anyway? Go teach elementary school kids how fo finger-paint? Ho, imagine if you was one teacher." Tyson raised his hand and began talking in a little kid's voice. "Mr. Matsumoto, Mr. Matsumoto! I when shit my pants."

I threw a french fry at his head. "At least I not going be one accountant."

Tyson picked the French fry off the ground and ate it. "You jealous cause I going make more money den you."

I didn't say anything to that one because she was walking towards us. I last saw her on the day of the final in math class two semesters ago. She looked the same, tank top and Roxy board shorts, real high cut. She walked right up the steps and in between us, heading towards University Ave. I kept my eyes down, looking at my burger. She had a puka-shell ankle bracelet and it looked real white against her tan.

Tyson slapped the back of my neck. "In your dreams, fuckah."

"Fuck you."

"Nah," Tyson said. "She's pretty fucken nice, yeah?"

I nodded and shoved a fry in my mouth.

Tyson pushed my shoulder. "She must be pretty nice if *you* when fucken look. I mean, what? You and Wendy? Like you married already."

Four years.

I finished the last of my burger and balled up the wrapper and beaned it at Tyson's head. "At least I'm faithful. You only act. If you talked like dis in front of Jamie, she'd kick your ass so hard."

Tyson dropped the balled-up wrapper into his Mos Burger package. "Yeah, well, you know dat chick you was scoping? At least I got to see her butt-naked."

"Bullshit." I nearly choked on the soda I was sucking through my straw and some of it spilled out.

"Yups." Tyson smiled big now.

"You lie."

"She's one stripper, Dan."

"No ways."

"Ways boo."

"Where you saw her?"

"Rock-Za's. I went down couple months ago with Eugene dem. Her name is Kianna."

I shook my head. "No ways. Dat's not her real name."

"Oh yeah. She probably made em up but who gives a shit when she's fucken spreading her—"

"Why you nevah call me when you guys went?"

"Oh please. Like you would go. Wendy's got you so fucken whipped. You cannot even go beach wit us anymore." Tyson laughed. "Ho, you should have seen her but. . . ." He stood up and started gyrating. "She was fucken jammin on da stage. Had dat Janet Jackson song 'I Get Lonely' and she was mouthing em and. . . ." He started rubbing his hands on his chest.

I slapped his knee. "Knock it off already."

Tyson sat down, laughing hard. "Yups, she's pretty mean. She was just fucken sliding up and down dat pole."

"You lie."

"I shit you not. Go ask her for one private show."

"What?"

"I'm serious, boo. You know Brian? He paid three hundred bucks for em. Rented one hotel room too. Perverted eh?"

"What she did in da private show?"

"I don't know. Maybe she when just give em one lap dance, maybe she was all fucken finger cuffing or someting. . . . He never say, but I bet you da fuckah was whackin off for weeks after."

I shook my head again. "Dat's nuts."

"You like me hook you up with her?"

"Fuck you."

"I can. C'mon, Dan. I know you like. I just ask Brian. He probably get her number. Fuck, he probably know everything about her."

That night, by the time I got to Wendy's house, it was almost eleven thirty. Her Chihuahua Sammo jumped at my legs and I picked him up and took him into the living room with me.

Her parents were sleeping and Wendy sat on the couch, watching reruns of *The Golden Girls*. She wore a long Winnie The Pooh T-shirt, her sleep clothes.

"Eh," I said, sitting down next to her. I put my face out to kiss her but she kept watching TV.

"I'm gonna go to bed soon," she said.

I put Sammo down and he ran back to his bed area by the front door. Even he sensed trouble.

"Sorry," I said. "I got off late."

"No kidding." She pointed the remote control and began flipping channels. "If you want dinner, I made Hamburger Helper. Go heat it up."

As I scooped Hamburger Helper out of a Tupperware container, Wendy shut off the TV and the lights in the living room. She leaned her arms on the counter and watched me through the opening that separated her from the kitchen.

"Andrew stopped by work today," she said. "I got him to bring me an application."

"Who was Andrew again?"

"He works for the graphic design company I was telling you about?"

"Oh yeah." I Saran-wrapped my plate and stuck it in the microwave. "How come you made him bring you an app? I told you I not leaving my campus job."

"You don't think Andrew's place is closer to your major?"

"Yeah, but I'm already on campus anyway. It's more convenient. Easier that way."

"After you graduate, you're gonna have to leave, you know."

I shrugged and opened the fridge for a soda. "Come on this side and talk."

She stayed on the other side of the counter. "At least look at it?"

"I'll look at it."

She shook her head. "I'm going to bed. Shut off the kitchen light when you're through."

Once the microwave dinged, I brought my plate into her room. Wendy laid in bed either sleeping or pretending to.

I knew she'd get mad if I went home early. She liked me to be there when she fell asleep. I wasn't really tired so I turned on her computer to check my e-mail: Aimee wanted to borrow my *Bulworth* soundtrack, my sister was freezing her ass off in Spokane, Todd told me to return his *Gran Turismo* cheat codes, and Michelle said Christy was probably gonna break up with Michael to go out with Darren but only if Darren drops Sheree.

Tyson e-mailed me too. All it said was, "I'm gonna get you all hooked up."

Oh please, whatevahs.

I got up and sat on the edge of the bed next to Wendy. She always slept on her stomach. I moved her hair out of her face. She was out cold, mouth a little open, long wrinkle on her eyelids. The next morning, she'd wake up with the meanest double eyes.

I slowly moved my finger down her cheek and she twitched her head a little. Her face filled out a little rounder since we first started going out. Then again, whatever abs I had were totally gone already.

Wendy finally felt me touching her face and she inhaled loudly. "If you're gonna come to bed, take off your shorts first. They're dirty." Then she rolled over and faced the wall.

I went back on the computer and checked out web sites for *Starcraft*. After about an hour, my eyes burned and I was ready to go home, but I checked my mailbox one last time. More stuff from Sey, Eric, and Stacey, and one from an address I didn't recognize. The user name was Surfgrl. The subject was Looking 4 Me? I clicked on it and read the message. A file was attached and I downloaded it: a picture of Kianna, standing on some rocks barefoot with the ocean behind her. She wore only a fluorescent green g-string and she had her arms wrapped around herself, covering her breasts.

"Tyson you fuckah! You smoking crack or what?"

We sat on the steps of Campus Center again, eating Mos Burgers. Tyson had half a bite in his mouth and he began cracking up, trying to breathe through his nose.

"What?" he said, still laughing. "I tole you I was going hook you up."

"I taught you was jus fucking aroun." I whacked his shoulder. "I was at Wendy's when I downloaded em."

"Wendy saw em?"

"No. You lucky. She was sleeping."

"Well den, it's all good, right?"

I told him about the picture of her on the beach, wrapping her arms around herself. "I had to go delete the file and everyting."

"She probably takes dat kine pictures for modeling or something eh?" Tyson began laughing at me again. "Oh shit, you must've popped one boner behind Wendy's back."

"Shut up."

"So what? She when write anything?"

I fiddled with the straw on my soda cup. "Not much. Just how she heard from couple guys that I was interested in her. Fuck, how many people you when tell?"

"Oh, I was just talking with a couple people. I figure, ho, when Dan's checking someone out, everybody going wanna know eh?"

I shoved some more fries in my mouth. "I can't believe she's on the Internet."

"Fuck yeah boo. Kianna's world-wide." He paused and took a sip from his soda. "You when write back to her or what?"

"Hell no. You tink I nuts?"

Actually, I did write back.

Once I got home from Wendy's that night, I checked my account from my own computer. I re-read her message and stared at her picture again.

I heard you were asking about me.
Do you like my pic?

I tried to place her voice, what it sounded like. The way her eyes stared at the camera and that smile with just a bit of teeth. Real confident. She knew she was bad.

Have we met at the club before?
I'm working till closing Mon.-Fri.
Come down. We can talk more.

This chick was just so out of my league. Granted, she probably expected money, but. . . . The way she looked. She looked so local, like she probably went to one public school and she hung out at Ocean's on Thursdays and she cruised Tower Records every once in a while. . . . She was bad, but I just couldn't believe she was a stripper.

When I got home, before I came inside the house, I rummaged through all the CDs tossed in the back seat of the 4Runner. I knew Wendy had left a whole bunch back there and after a little while, I found it. The Janet Jackson CD with the song Tyson said he saw her dancing to.

I stuck it in the computer and listened to that "I Get Lonely" song and tried to imagine her dancing like that, on a stage, with the metal pole. . . .

I shook it off and wrote a real fast reply to her mail. I explained I seen her around school a lot and that my friends blew things out of proportion. I just had a minor crush on her. That was it. I didn't mean to waste her time and I apologized. Then I sent the mail, turned off the computer, and after a while, I stopped hearing that Janet Jackson song in my head and I fell asleep.

The next night work let out early so I got to Wendy's at a decent hour. I figured we were gonna go movies or something but she didn't feel like going out again. We just ended up watching volleyball until the game finished.

"I want ice cream," Wendy said.

We went into the kitchen and she was dumping strawberry cheesecake into a bowl.

"You want?" she asked.

"I'll just eat off yours." I moved behind her and put my arms around her waist. She held the spoon behind her neck and I ate the remaining bits off it.

She stood at the counter eating. "Me and Lorna were the only ones at the office today and the Fed Ex guy came in. Yum."

I began rubbing her waist and I rested my chin by her neck. "Shut up."

"Well he is," she said, smiling. She fed me another spoonful. "I'd leave you for him in a second."

"Uh huh." I began nuzzling the side of her neck.

"Cold lips." She bent her neck away from my mouth.

I slipped my hands under her Winnie The Pooh shirt and slowly rubbed my hands on her waist. "You wouldn't leave me. I can flip the perfect omelet."

"Your only talent."

"Uh huh." I let my hands travel and began messing with her neck again.

"So you're gonna be an omelet chef?" She started using her playful voice. "Everyone else's boyfriends are gonna be raking in the big bucks while you're standing around flipping your eggs all day."

"Yeah, but are they really gonna be happy?"

"At least they're gonna be able to move out of the house."

"Excuse me?"

"You never thought of that?"

I pulled my hands out from under her shirt but kept my chin on her shoulder. "What do you mean?"

"C'mon Dan. I'm just messing with you."

I placed my hands on her hips and rubbed them back and forth over her butt. "Should you really be eating ice cream?"

"Shut up."

"Seriously babes. You better start jogging with Jamie again."

She rapped me on the forehead with her spoon.

"Hey," I said. "I'm just messing with you."

"Uh huh." She began dumping the rest of the ice cream into the sink. "Lorna's boyfriend's gonna be teaching at Wilson Elementary this fall."

"Big deal."

"Yeah, it is a big deal. Have you even thought about what you want to do after you graduate?"

"Das a while more."

"No it isn't." She was running the water, washing ice cream down the sink. "Maybe you should start looking into some things. I was thinking about it and you know what? I think you'd make a really good teacher. I can picture that."

"What?" I said, pretending to laugh. "You my maddah now?"

She turned to face me. "No, I'm just saying. That's all."

"So what?" I kept the smile on my face. "Unless I'm making bucks, you not happy?"

She slapped my shoulder. "Knock it off. I've just been wondering lately."

"About what?"

"Whether you know what you want. That's all."

I opened the fridge and began looking for a soda. "I know I don't want to talk about this already. You want a 7-Up?"

"No." She paused for a bit. I couldn't tell how her face looked cause my head was still in the fridge. "It's late. I better take a shower." Her feet slapped on the tile as she left the kitchen.

I went to her room and crashed on the bed. After a little while, I felt her get in next to me, smelling clean, like that Ann Taylor shower gel she uses. I kept my eyes closed and eventually I felt her fall asleep next to me. 1:00 a.m. I think when my head was in the refrigerator, I knew what I was gonna do. I got out of bed quietly and left her house.

I didn't want to go into the bar so I just kinda waited, walking back and forth on the sidewalk. Even though it was really late, a lot of people hung out by the entrance: military grunts with their buzz cuts, a few guys around my age in T-shirts and shorts, huge Hawaiian bouncers with arm band tattoos and biceps filling their shirt sleeves.... Lots of cars still moved on Kapi'olani and I watched their headlights flash by, hands in the pockets of my denim shorts.

After about fifteen minutes, I noticed the dancers coming out. Long poofy hair, huge tits, really short shorts, and they all carried gym-looking bags that probably held all their extra clothes, towels, and stuff. Even in the dark with only a bit of purple neon and the orange street-lights, I could make out Kianna's silhouette.

I called her name and she looked towards me. I jogged up to her. She wore her usual high-cut board shorts, slippers, and a tight black tank top. Her long hair was pulled back away from her face into a pony-tail. She just kinda stared at me with those slender eyes.

"Hey," I said. "I'm the guy you wen e-mail the other night."

She nodded and stuck out her hand. "I thought you changed your mind."

I shook her hand. "I'm, uh, well, you know...."

She nodded again. Her voice wasn't quite how I placed it in my mind. It had a slightly higher, more feminine pitch than I imagined. You could tell she talked pidgin but she was trying to sound haole.

Her friends waited behind her, mostly young blond haole chicks, probably dancers. Most of them looked like they had fake breasts, too round and huge to be real. Kianna told them to go on without her and they left, turning back to look at us as they walked away.

"So you're the one who's been asking about me," she said. "You wanna talk for a little while?"

"Yeah. You got time?"

"Where'd you park?" she asked. "Gimme a ride to my car."

We walked to the 4Runner and I let her in. She gave me directions to a beat up white Toyota Celica parked on the street by Daiei. She did-n't say anything besides the directions. My windows were up and I could smell a little bit of perfume, sweet, something I sniffed in a mag-azine before. I could also smell some alcohol coming out of her.

"Just pull up behind me," she said.

I stopped behind the car and killed the engine.

"So," she said. "Your name's Dan right?"

"Yeah."

"Brian's friend."

"Well, he's a friend of a friend."

She nodded and spoke with her eyes closed. "You've seen me around school a lot?"

"Yeah. I had you in math classes."

"Oh okay." Kianna opened her eyes and stared at me. "I've never seen you before." She smiled. "So what can I do for you?"

I took a deep breath. "I know this sounds totally weird, but seriously, I just wanted to meet you."

"What?"

"I don't know." I ran my hand through my hair. "I never did anything like this before. I just was really curious."

"What do you mean?"

"Well, I always saw you around in school and den I found out you were a stripper and you know. . . . I just never figured." My fingers drummed the steering wheel a bit but then I managed to stop. "And den you e-mailed me. I mean, you know. . . . I didn't know you even had one computer."

She laughed a bit. "I'm real popular cause I'm local. The whole surfer-chick thing. You have a girlfriend?"

I nodded.

"I can tell," she said. "So wait. You basically just wanted to meet me?"

I laughed a little to myself. "It was just a crush, you know? I never was supposed to actually get to meet you, you know? Does that make sense?"

"Yeah, that makes sense." She shook her head. "So you just wanted to meet me?"

"Yeah."

"What do you want den?"

"Huh?"

"I don't mean to be a bitch, but I'm kinda busy, you know. I'm supposed to meet my friends at the Wave after."

"Oh, yeah, I understand. Look, I'm sorry. I'm just wasting your time."

"If you want to ask me anything, ask me now cause I'm here and I'm not gonna do this again cause I'm really kinda busy."

I sat up straighter. "Whoa. Look, I never mean to piss you off."

"I'm not pissed. I just like know what you want."

She kept staring at me, closing her eyes, then staring at me some more. A little pink flushed her cheeks beneath the dark brown tan. She was drunk.

"Umm, look," I said. "I'm real sorry. It's late. I should be going."

She closed her eyes and rested her head on the seat. "Oh God, the bartenders make the drinks so strong." For a second I thought she fell asleep but then, she opened her eyes again. "Dan, right?"

"Yeah."

"What high school you went?"

"Kaiser. Why? Where'd you go?"

"Kaiser," she repeated to herself. "I went 'Aiea."

"Hey, can I ask you something?"

She looked at me. "Go."

"Is Kianna your real name?"

"No." She smiled. "I not telling you."

"Oh okay. I understand."

"Nah," she said, touching my leg for a second. "It's Dana. Dana Hashimoto."

"You related to Robin? She went Pearl City, I tink."

"No," she said shaking her head. She began to laugh. "On the mainland, no one asks you questions like that. Small island, you think everybody's related yeah?"

I laughed too. "So what you taking at UH?"

"I'm doing some business classes. I wanna open my own club later on."

"Cool."

"Open the window." She took out a pack of Marlboro Lights and she lit one. "You want?"

"Nah, das okay." I turned on the ignition, rolled the all windows down. Without the tint from my windows, more streetlight came into the car. I hoped the cigarette didn't make everything too stink.

She blew smoke. "So why'd you wanna meet me?"

"Well, like I said, you were in a lot of my classes—"

She interrupted me. "But why me?"

"Like I said, it was just a crush. I mean, I don't got no money so I wasn't planning on getting one private show or whatevahs." I took a breath out of my side of the window, trying to get some non-smoke air. "I'm not some perverted stalker or something. I mean, I got a girlfriend. I shouldn't even be talking to you. It's just, I don't know. You just looked really normal. I mean, it just really got me all shocked when I found out you were a stripper."

"Do you love your girlfriend?"

"What?"

"I mean, I know what it's like." She ashed her cigarette outside my window. "You want the whole thing and the white picket fence and all dat shit but you know, you do what you gotta do. I don't have to answer to nobody and I pay all my bills and I paying for my school and. . . ." She took another drag from her cigarette. "Do you love your girlfriend?"

"Yeah, I guess."

She smiled. "Then why are you here?"

"I don't know."

She took another drag and flicked her cigarette into some bushes. "You just wanted to meet me." She shook her head. "That's so cute."

"I mean, I just thought you were really attractive. I was just curious."

My hand rested on the gear shift of my truck. She slipped her fingers under mine.

"That's so funny," she said. She wasn't quite holding my hand, more like she was touching it, palm to palm, pressing my fingertips with her fingertips.

"You know, I haven't had a boyfriend for a real long time. I don't wanna get intimate right now."

"I guess I can understand that." Warmth came out of her hand and onto mine. "What happens in those private shows I keep hearing about?"

She laughed. "Why?"

"I'm curious about that. I keep hearing about them."

She began making a fingering motion. "Basically I just get off. Bring in some music, dance, strip. Then," she gave me a look and made the fingering motion again, "you know." She was smiling but then she came serious. "But no contact with the other person."

"Oh nah. That's not dangerous? I mean, the guys and all?"

"No. Usually I have an idea where I want them and how I want it to be." She paused and smiled. "Why, you interested?"

I shook my head. "No. I can't."

She nodded and stared at me. "Can I ask you something?"

"Yeah."

She shook her head. "Nah, I cannot. That's too horny."

"What?" I asked.

She shook her head. "Nevermind. Too horny." She closed her eyes again.

She still had her hand under mine, not quite holding it, just pressing against it, and her tank top was tight on her breasts. She had her gym-looking bag on her lap and her long brown legs started down from there. Her legs were really smooth, almost shiny, ending in the white puka-shell anklets. I wanted to know what her question was.

"I should go," I said.

She opened her eyes and let go of my hand. "All right." She put her bag's strap over her shoulder again.

"So," she said. "Is that all?"

"Umm, yeah," I said. "I guess so. I'm sorry I just wasted your time."

"Do you love your girlfriend?"

"Yeah, I do."

She opened the door and stepped out. She had to balance herself a bit since my truck was kinda high.

"You can drive okay?" I asked.

"Yeah," she said, slamming the door. She looked at me through the passenger window. "Decide what you want. If you change your mind, you know where to find me."

She didn't say bye. She just opened her car, threw in her stuff and drove off towards Waikīkī.

I ran a hand through my hair and sat in my truck for a little while. Her smell was still there. The perfume, the bit of alcohol and cigarette smoke. . . . I had the Janet Jackson CD with me. I considered putting it in and listening to the song she liked to dance to.

Instead, I just drove home all the way to Hawai'i Kai in silence, not even with the radio. I left the windows open and I let the wind whip into my truck, hopefully blowing all traces of Kianna's smell out.

THE MAORI DOLL CALLED RUTH

I was six years old when my self-image underwent serious tweaking. It never occurred to me that people who looked like me could live in such different worlds. I was isolated. What did I know? I was six years old, and the only people of significance in my life were my large extended family: redheads, blondes and brunettes, mainly women—five aunts, my mother, and two uncles. And of course the patriarchs, my full-blooded *Tainui* father, and my grandfather, *Poua*, one quarter *Ngai Tahu*.

My father was accustomed to the formal attire required at dinner at my grandparents' home, which led me to the inevitable conclusion that everyone was like us. Shirt and tie for the men and boys, jacket optional, except if there were guests. Dresses for the women and girls. White starched and ironed linen tablecloths and sterling silver cutlery, crystal glasses and Royal Dalton china, thin see-through saucers with solid gold edging and delicate tea cups with pink roses on the inside as well as the outside. Three Christmas trees. Large formal all-day long Christmas dinners, not including pudding, that I took for granted every year.

Stuffed mushrooms, shrimp cocktail, clear soup, cold soup, hot soup, roast duck or goose or both, turkey, roast beef, fresh ham, leg of lamb, roast potatoes and boiled minted new potatoes, fresh peas—sugar sweet and minted, asparagus, pumpkin and yams, silverbeet and brussel sprouts, rich brown smooth gravy, hot rolls with whipped butter balls, vinegary but sweet mint sauce.

Steamed pudding spicy and sweet, smothered with hot thick yellow custard; large white pavlovas, crusty and formal on the outside, with melt-in-your-mouth soft white meringue in the middle, covered in whipped cream and fresh strawberries or kiwi fruit. Trifle, coconut macaroons dipped in chocolate, brandy snaps, custard squares, cream puffs. And of course that ubiquitous marzipan covered confection—rum soaked, gaudy Christmas cake.

Christmas Eve we walked to the Anglican church for midnight mass where we lit candles, sang hymns, marveled at the miracle of the virgin birth, promised ourselves to do good deeds and help others, came home and drank eggnog with or without alcohol, and were allowed to open one gift before bed. I loved Christmas in the cool summer evenings of December. The days may have been warm and mild, but the evenings were as crisp and cool as autumn. Breath we could see. Thick knitted jackets with mittens or gloves at night. Crunchy grass. Christmas lilies.

And it never once occurred to me, in those days of innocence and childhood, that my father's drunkenness was anything more than what happened on Christmas Day. After all, he knew the hymns, chose the right fork, drank the wine, and wore the shirt and tie. He smiled and charmed all the ladies in that estrogen-dominated home. So there were *Poua*, Bob (my father), my younger brother Jack, and the two uncles, Dan and Brian, five aunties, Grandma, Mum, and me. And a partridge in a pear tree.

Poua was a big man, tall and strong and omnipresent. He was the center of the family around which the others orbited. When he moved from Dunedin to Christchurch for work, we all followed. I was four, my brother half that. It was Christmas Eve when we hopped on the train and headed off to a new life in a new city, hundreds of miles north.

That Christmas Eve I was both sad and excited. I was convinced that because of that long train ride, Father Christmas would not be able to find us and our stockings—those pillow cases that we hung on the ends of our beds would not have the usual lollies and oranges and apples and gifts.

But Father Christmas was a myth that hadn't yet let me down, and was not about to. He gave me my heart's desire—a new doll, with clothes, and a blue plastic carry cot and blanket. Her name was Ruth. There wasn't anything better than that brown rubber doll, a *Maori* doll dressed in a blue knitted dress with a flared skirt and white stripes going all around it, a blue and white matching knitted hat, white knitted pants and petticoat, a whole ensemble. A *Maori* doll named Ruth in knitted fashion.

Ruth was my constant companion for two years, until the time we went to visit some cousins I had never met, on my father's side.

"Now kids, your cousins live in Sheffield. Be polite, and don't stare. Be polite."

Whatever "polite" meant.

"Your uncle's name is Boy. His wife is Aunty Mabel."

Now what kind of man is called Boy? I wondered.

"And they have four children."

The town itself was no more than a pub, a few houses, a dairy and a railway station, in the middle of lush fields and farmland. Uncle Boy's house was near the track, off a dirt roadway. Dusty and dry unpainted missing picket fence, gray clapboard house, patches of brown grass in the front yard, a dog house with a chain, no dog. A football on the cracked concrete path, a dry flower garden by the front door. We pulled up next to the fence. Dad got out of the car and shouted at the large figure that filled the front doorway of the house, who waved back at him.

We got one more warning from Mum.

"Be polite. That's Uncle Boy."

Uncle Boy looked like my father, just not as handsome. A little older, with a big puku, blood-red eyes, and black circles underneath them. He was wearing a black singlet and his Wranglers hung below his large gut. Dark skin. Unshaven. Not a trace of Old Spice or even toothpaste. In fact he smelled like beer—and it was only 10 in the morning.

"Come inside, *haere mai, haere mai*. Ya want *kai*? Mabel, get up!!"

We looked in the front door. Cautiously, we went inside and stood around the walls, afraid to step anywhere. Aunty Mabel was on the couch, snoring softly, mouth slightly open with her false teeth on her chest, rising and falling in time.

From the front door we could see the whole house—living room and kitchen ahead, and to the left a bedroom with a mattress on the floor. There was a sheet strung up on the window in the living room, and an old black roll-up blind on the bedroom window, ripped at the bottom.

We could hear the crackle of frying food. Uncle Boy was back in the kitchen cooking. Liver. Onions.

"Uncle Bobo, Uncle Bobo!" the kids yelled.

Four bare-assed, snot-nosed children, and cats, lots of cats, and lots of unbrushed cat and child hair. Cat and child piss and crap on the cracked lino floor. Cat shit, kid shit, I couldn't tell the difference. Brown lumps on the lino. Golden puddles near the mattress. Liver. Onions. Piss. Crap.

Who the hell was Uncle Bobo?

As four children piled up on Uncle Bobo, it became obvious. My father was Uncle Bobo. Bob. Bob was Bobo.

"Watch where you step, kids!" mother hissed at us as she stepped in some wet shit right by the front door. With as much dignity as you can muster with shit on your white pumps, she walked back out of the house and used the tap by the dog-house-with-no-dog to wash her shoe off. This was the house of my cousins.

It smelt like the barn at Lorna's house, the barn where we watched our father, who art now in heaven, and Mary's Little Lamb.

A butcher by trade, he had gladly offered to reduce Lorna and Arnold's flock. Lorna and Arnold were friends of our parents who owned a small farm about 15 miles from our house. Their house was a two-story fairy-tale Victorian with a wrap-around porch at the end of a long driveway. Behind the garage was an old barn. To the right of the barn was an apple orchard, and to the left of the house were the animals, the cows, sheep, and horses. We usually took off when we arrived, to play War amongst the trees, or Sir Edmund Hillary up the hay bale. But not that Saturday.

He picked the sheep up by its hind legs, tied a rope around the haunches and hung it on a hook he'd attached to a rope thrown over a branch of a large oak tree. He grabbed the squirming animal by the nose and ran a knife across its neck, spouting blood all over his blue and white striped butcher's apron, and his white butcher gumboots. He didn't take his eyes off us, grinning at the spectacle he produced, the spurting blood and the cringing faces. When the blood flow slowed, he took the smaller knife from his apron and peeled off the skin, slowly slicing the hide from the flesh and carelessly tossed the skin over the wooden fence. Then he took the big knife again and slit its guts all the way from its bum to its hanging neck.

Sheep guts are green, and stink.

Shit and farts and the sulphur soaked smell of geothermal *Rotorua* and the abattoir, all in close range.

Yards of tubular green things and round green things. Gallons of pinky green wet stink guts.

Buckets full of offal.

I developed a new respect for my father and his knives that day. He was grinning with the pride he felt in a job well-done. He lectured while he worked about keeping the knives sharp and to not use his knives for anything else but this. Fear and revulsion and a sick fascination on everyone's faces that day.

"That's what sheep are. *Kai*. Why ya look like that? Where d'ya think chops comes from, ay? Or mutton? Or those bloody slippers you wear at night?"

Uncle Boy's house was heavier on the shit, lighter on *Rotorua*, but the feeling, the queasy disgusted stomach wrenching stench was the same. Only the sick revulsion and fascination was missing. Jack and I stood still right by the door, looking at the sleeping form of a toothless, barely clothed woman.

Ruth. Thank God for the strong smell of rubber *Maori* dolls named Ruth. I buried my nose in Ruth's hair and inhaled deeply. All Jack could do was hold his nose between his fingers.

The Aunty woke up.

"Come, give Aunty a kish, honey. By golly, you bloody buggers are big now, ay? *Haere mai, haere mai!*"

I felt my mother nudge me gently on the shoulders. I took one look at my mother and took off, my lungs bursting for fresh air, out the front door, Jack right behind me.

How long are we staying here? I'm not kissing her. I'm not playing with those kids. They've got no clothes on. Let's go home. I'm hungry. It stinks inside. I hate liver!

"Kids," she said, "Remember what I said—be polite." She went back inside to greet her sister-in-law and to apologize for our bad manners.

Polite means stepping in shit and not being horrified; it means not holding your nose with two fingers when you can't stand the smell, but holding your breath instead. Polite means kissing a toothless wild-haired boozy-breathed stranger whom we had to call Aunty. It means eating liver and onions for breakfast. It means eating at a table in a room that smelt like the pub. Fuck polite.

Mabel hung her head out the sheeted window and yelled at us, "Kids, you want *kai*?" Mum was standing behind her glaring—Be Polite said the glare.

"No thank you, Aunty. We're not hungry. We ate before. We'll stay outside and play."

Polite was not easy. Not even when Mum came out of the house and grabbed me by the arm and tried, halfheartedly, to drag me inside. It's not that she couldn't drag me, or pick me up and carry me inside. It's just that half of her was being polite, and the other half, the bigger, stronger half, was jealous of our rudeness, admired our bad manners.

After they all ate liver and onions, and the aunt and uncle smoked a couple of cigarettes, Dad and Uncle Boy went off somewhere. We'll be right back, he said.

We waited outside, by the dog-house-with-no-dog. The railway station was off limits, the road was too dusty. There was no park or playground or anything. So we kicked around the football in the front yard.

"They just want to play outside. Why don't you join them, kids?" Mum looked in the cousins' direction.

Luckily they were shy, just watched us from behind the strung up sheet in the living room.

Saint Mum stayed inside and helped the Aunt clean her house. What really happened was Mum cleaned; Mabel smoked and moved dirt around. Mum mopped floors, washed dishes that were piled in the sink, scrubbed the sticky cupboards and counters, the oven and the fridge, washed the sheet that was lying under the one dirty mattress. The kids scooped up cat/kid shit and emptied buckets of water. I was going to offer, but decided that I would just get in the way. And Mum did not insist. So she scrubbed and wiped and soon the smell was gone and the floors were no longer sticky. She washed the kids' clothes too. By hand. Three shirts, two underpants and a couple of pairs of shorts— for four kids.

"Oh, if those buggers go to school, they wear something of Boy's or mine, ay? But them buggers hardly go to school. Bit like us fellas, not too bright. Heh, heh, heh." After she cleaned the house, it was the kids' turn. This was no small task—they had no Lux, no Breck, no combs or brushes. So she used the Sunlight on the kids. She dug an old comb out of her purse and tried to get the tangles out of their hair. She backed away quickly when, later on that afternoon, they offered the comb back to her.

"No, no, that's fine. We have others. You keep it. Please."

Which reminded her of the bag of our old clothes she had put in the trunk of the car. They must have thought it was Christmas—four kids stood in the living room, grinning and clutching the new old stuff, hand-me-downs. I thought that now that they had underwear and shoes they might, just might want to go to school, if for no other reason than to get away from the cats, and Mabel.

Bob and Boy had not returned. Mum assumed that they had moved on to the pub. It was getting dark. The day was long, and not only were we hungry, but I badly needed to pee.

"No you cannot go to the railway station. It's getting dark and we're going home soon. You never know who's at the railway station, hiding, waiting for kids like you to show up."

Kids like us?

What was it about us that bummy old child-snatchers wanted? And who the hell would hang out at the train station in Sheffield waiting for us? We were in the middle of nowhere, and not one car or truck had gone by all day. Occasionally we'd hear the sound of a fire truck or ambulance on the highway past the trees, to remind us that there was a motor way just beyond the pine trees, but in Sheffield there was nothing, at least not this Sunday.

But I could not delay any longer. I went inside the now clean house to find the toilet.

"Oh, ya see the shed over there? Out back? That's it."

A long-dropper. Great. I would rather have pissed myself than use one.

I knew the shed would be dark, with holes in the wood where daylight crept in. And there would be no seat. Not that that was a problem really—Patty had trained us that one never sat on a public toilet seat anyway. But sometimes, you just gotta. A wooden plank with a hole in it that you squatted over and did whatever you had to do. Hard brown toilet paper and the strong smell of Dettol. Just made me sick thinking about it. In retrospect though, there was probably no disinfectant in that loo.

I held myself and jiggled until the feeling went away.

My endurance was boundless.

After they were cleaned up, brushed and bathed and dressed in our old clothes, I let the girl hold Ruth. My doll, my Ruth. Clean, tired, hungry, bored, disgusted, needing-to-piss, showing her manners *Maori* girl. My rubber smelling *Maori* doll dressed in a new pink dress and lacy knickers.

"Don't suck on her, don't drop her. And don't let your brothers near her."

About that time their dog came bounding in the yard, saw that the girl Mabel (junior, I suppose) had a new toy, and ripped it out of her hand. In my struggle to wrest Ruth from the jaws of the little black flea-bitten mutt, she lost half her right arm, her left eye and all of her toes on both feet. Ruth died an ugly and premature death that summer day in the country with the cousins from the boonies. *Maoris*. Poor. Shy. Dirty. Drunk.

My father's blood.

Outsiders we were, in this dusty country cat-piss-kid-shit-no-underwear-Ruth-shredding world—just as he was in Patty's linen-crystal-sterling-silver-three-Christmas-trees-suit-and-tie world. I just never realized how far apart the two worlds that we inherited were. How very disparate the blood. The rainbow crystal, the rose tinted prism that was my world had all of a sudden separated the cafe-colored life that was mine into the black and white that was reality.

SHE MEANT TO SEE CHINA

She meant to see China as if China were an old rerun
she could always catch at the Princess Theater,
a matinee she may have wandered into as a child
in the only picture I have of my mother from that time.

Nine years old,
squinting into the sun,
she stands straight, her back to a wall.

She meant to see China with her two daughters,
ride a river boat past ink-washed mountains,
the long braids of her daughters' hair
whipping like banners in the wind.

She stands against a wall,
hair cut
neat and practical,
chopped blunt as a boy's
as if the amateur barber knew
haircuts for this child were few.

She meant to see China with her two daughters,
visit the flickering shrine of an ancestral village,
knock on the door of a distant relative,
see the resemblance.

Mug shot pose, so serious, thin
shift of a dress, thin bare arms,
she stands, her back to a wall.
Motherless, Fatherless,
she squints into the sun.

She meant to see China,
walk the great structures,
the dragon tail of the longest one
visible from the moon.

Who cut my mother's hair?
Who sat her on the crate and draped
a cloth across her shoulders?
Who told her to sit still
even though a warm wind blew
hair into her mouth, hair
stiff as the burnt offerings of joss sticks,
hair that blew into my mother's mouth?

She meant to see China with her two daughters,
ride a river boat,
walk the Great Wall,
take a picture of some old resemblance,
pay her respects.

Someone swept the black leavings
off the back porch.
A warm wind blew the burnt sticks
across the lane of feed stores, butcher shops,
soda fountains, tiny dwellings, temple bells,
sounds of orphans, derelicts, philanthropists
and angels
ringing in that tiny bell.

She meant to see China,
buy velvet slippers, the ones that make no sound,
bring back to School Street a suitcase full of red ones,
red and beaded, swirling with dragons.

Someone cut my mother's hair,
dusted behind the ears,
shooed the child into the street,
pressed into her hand
a fortune

so she could catch the movie,
buy something to eat.

An extravagant sum,
a warm steamed bun.

My mother clanked down the long stairs of the wooden
walk-up
visible from the moon.

Someone mumbled a prayer.

Someone threw in
the sweet sour reminder,
Good daughter,
Take care.

CATHY SONG

THE LAND OF BLISS

Rain that falls and has been falling
is the same rain that fell
a million years ago. To think not
a single droplet has been lost
in the articulate
system of our blue planet
wrapped in its gauze of atmosphere.
Like breathing, the planetary breath
draws oceans, rivers, lakes,
and even these ponds,
cradling gold fish.

After a night of rain, the benevolent eye
of morning glistens a fine mesh
between ferns.

Last night I climbed the ladder
to the loft, tired in a way the bones
liquify after a day of doing
the work one has set out to do.
I had worked mindful and steady through the hours
on a poem not quite done.

The thought that there would be
more work of the same to do
when I woke up,
that there would be
that poem waiting,
made me happy.

I sank into bed, cradled by the sound
of rain filling the night: wet leaves
and old gold ponds.

I drifted before entering the body of sleep,
the breathing slowing down to a quiet
web of vibration, quiet
to the point of stillness,
as if I held my breath to swim
toward dreams waiting on the other shore.

The Pure Land is empty.
There's nobody there.

FORCE MAJEURE

I quickly tired of watching my big toe nudge air. And after finishing my third bag of fried pork rinds in one sitting while flirting with ancient water buffaloes kicking up the dust in front of my grandmother's porch, I decided to concoct some diversion on my own rather than rely on Mama. She was still engrossed in deconstructing my grandmother's career as a loan shark.

I was visiting Santo Tomas because Gran was ailing; my mother was trying to get an advance on her inheritance by determining which villager owed what. We all expected Gran to greet St. Peter shortly and enter the Big-Post-Office-in-the-Sky. Gran had loved to hang out in the post office with a huge, rattan purse that contained the pesos she would lend at rates sufficiently usurious to make my otherwise jaded Mama salivate. Since the northern part of the Philippines had been wracked by hurricanes and volcanic eruptions over the past five years, Gran had gleaned quite a few clients from farmers whose crops were decimated by *force majeure.*

But the waiting was tedium. So I told my cousin, Donna, to plan an excursion to Baguio City. That's how I met Nickie, my husband and with whom I came to join the illustrious list of Imelda Marcos' afflictions.

Baguio City is the Philippines' "Summer Capital" for its pleasant weather year-round, even when the rest of the archipelago sweats under a heavy blanket of heat and humidity. Popular with tourists, it is famous for shops specializing in wooden souvenirs carved by the artisans of *Igorot, Ibaloy, Bontoc,* and other tribes living in the mountains surrounding the city. I thought I might try chasing down a carved chess set whose figures evoked native tribesmen battling Spanish colonialist invaders. Besides, I needed an excuse to leave Santo Tomas for a brief period; its sun was turning me as black as a tobacco farmer.

No, Nickie was not one of Baguio's unemployed actors, bookies, or gamblers who hung about Burnham Park concocting schemes that would allow them to afford their favorite habit: beer. I first noticed

Nickie after one Romeo Pascual, a bald and rotund lad whose life's ambition was to visit Graceland, overheard my Americanized English and insisted on making me the target of fake but immediate adoration. That day, despite the combination of my overflowing belly and virtually non-existent breasts, I offered the unique merits of correct citizenship with whom marriage could provide entry to the land of Elvis Presley's birth.

Nickie came over to the huge acacia tree that shaded where I sat fondling the chess pieces and nibbling fresh coconut slices as I concocted for Donna a feminist theory for the Queen's powers versus the sluggish chess steps of the King. We were also being treated by the improbably named Romeo to his egregious Elvis imitations. Leave, Nickie ordered Romeo, otherwise Romeo would find himself doing the jailhouse rock for harassment, noise pollution, and spitting on the ground (the latter charge being particularly frowned upon by Baguio's earnest cops, according to a sign by the park's entrance). At least, that's what I assumed Nickie told Romeo since he spoke in Tagalog, the Philippines' national language that I do not understand, having been born after my parents emigrated from Santo Tomas to San Francisco.

"Thank you, Nicolas," Donna said gratefully. I had been amusing myself by offering smiles and flirtatious glances from beneath my stubby lashes to encourage the lout with the voice of a tuba, or *"loko-loko"* as Donna muttered under her breath; thus, my cousin was much relieved by Nickie's intervention. Nickie's real name is Nicolas Cosmo Cabiling. I call him Nickie because the diminutive is my way of responding to his irresistible charm.

In any event, as he confronted the *loko-loko* trying to flirt with my heart and passport, I noticed Nickie for the first time and felt a certain stirring in my loins. I hadn't felt that simmer since five years earlier when I developed a mad crush on Dr. James Pix, my former dentist. Like "Pixie," Nickie had glossy, black hair poorly cut to hang about a narrow, angular face with cheekbones as chiseled and perfectly aligned as those of Ivan Lendl's. Like Pixie (and Ivan Lendl, had he been unable to afford well-groomed hair), Nickie evoked a Russian monk I once saw while playing tourist in St. Petersburg. The Russians were celebrating Easter and I was in church because it was on my tour group's itinerary. Since the monk was both Orthodox and behind a cross, I left him alone. Pixie, I didn't leave alone. But after making me suffer through ten dental cleanings in one month, he finally suggested the name of a female dentist who was also covered by Blue Cross; I took Pixie's hint and gave him up. As I watched Nickie increase the intensity of his glare against Elvis Imitator Number 798, I began to shift on my seat from that long-dormant simmer.

"Who is this utterly delectable guy?" I whispered to Donna as Nickie carefully watched my would-be suitor slink away.

Donna looked at me strangely and said, "He's our driver. You sat behind him for six hours from Santo Tomas to Baguio."

Hmmmmm, I thought. He's from Santo Tomas, too. All of a sudden, waiting for Gran to die didn't seem as tedious as before.

*   *   *

The following day, Nickie sat on Gran's dining table decorously sipping the hot chocolate I insisted he try because I proclaimed it was the best Switzerland had to offer. Before leaving San Francisco, I had packed some provisions I didn't expect would be available in Santo Tomas: Mallomars and the Swiss Miss brand of powdered chocolate mix (the latter is actually made in Cleveland but I assumed Nickie would be ignorant of that fact). Nickie was visiting at my request because, ostensibly, I was looking for a driver for another excursion—this time to visit Marcos' embalmed body in one of his childhood homes located three hours away in the town of Laoag.

"It's richer than local brands," Nickie said after a cautious sip at Swiss Miss. Then he smiled briefly at me. In the future, he would admit he didn't care for chocolate but decided it was more prudent to be polite. Nevertheless, he smiled and, though brief, that smile sufficed to make me feel once more that certain stirring in that netherward region of my newly-sensitized body.

"So, what do you do when you're not chauffeuring tourists around?" I asked, crossing my legs and pushing forward a plate of Mallomars. He must have been thoroughly disgusted by the cookies and marshmallowy goo generously encased in thick, dark chocolate.

"I plant vegetables," he said.

Nodding enthusiastically, I brilliantly asked, "What kind?"

"Tomatoes."

"Rea-a-a-ly? How very interesting," I replied and drowned myself in the depthless pools of his brown, brown eyes. His eyes woke me to the wonders of the color brown.

When I surfaced to breathe, Nickie was looking at me as if it was still my turn to speak.

"I beg your pardon?" I breathed, suppressing the urge to fling myself at him and crush my breasts, such as they were, against the muscles evident under his thin, white t-shirt.

"When would you like to visit Ferdinand Marcos?" he repeated.

"Tomorrow?" I said, trying to disguise the hope in my voice.

"That's fine," he said, rising from the table. Because he readied to depart, my heart plummeted like an overripe mango from its branch.

I also thought Nickie was an absolutely brilliant conversationalist.

*   *   *

I long suspected Imelda Marcos was off her rocker. Peering at Ferdinand Marcos' body embalmed in wax and lying in a room with a set temperature of 58 degrees, almost half the outside temperature of Laoag that day, I ruminated once more that Imelda should be the one knocking on St. Peter's gate to put the Filipinos out of their misery which, contrary to her frequently touted belief, had never been alleviated by watching her dress up in thousand dollar *terno* gowns and dia-mond-pelleted rosaries before going disco dancing with George Hamilton.

"Oh my god, oh my god," Donna kept exclaiming as we walked around Ferdinand's body. Imelda must have visited Lenin's Tomb dur-ing the years she forced herself into the role of the Philippines' senior diplomat and came to fancy the manner in which the Russians immor-talized the guy who unnecessarily killed the Romanovs. I tried to hide my irritation as Donna kept comparing the dead dictator to the most supreme of deities; many residents of the Ilocos region, which includ-ed Santo Tomas, still worshipped Marcos, who was born and raised in their midst. Totally aggravated, I left the mausoleum to look for Nickie, who was waiting with the van outside.

"Bastard," I hissed as I slid into the front seat, still thinking of the man who exemplified Aristotle's claim that absolute power corrupts absolutely.

Seated behind the wheel, Nickie coughed. I looked at him in dismay.

"Sorry. Did I say that out loud? I didn't mean you," I quickly said.

"Did someone offend you?" he asked, staring past me towards Marcos' childhood home. He frowned as if he expected to see the glistening scalp of Elvis Imitator Number 798.

"Oh, no, no. I was actually thinking of the man whose body now lies all decked out in pompous ceremony back there. . . ." I broke off and quickly shook my head, determined not to let thoughts of Marcos ruin a moment with the subject of my dreams. I woke that morning entangled in soaked bedsheets and sucking a raw knuckle.

I looked at Nickie's eyelashes: dark, thick, long—the curl on their tips evoking waves exactly at their peak before breaking to cool a shore of heated sand. Sitting on my palms whose fingers ached to ride those waves, I suggested, "Let's not talk about him. Let's talk about you."

"Why?" he replied, raising an eyebrow (perfectly-shaped and as lustrous as a crow's wing, quite unlike the mess of fuzz capping my eyes).

"Oh, I don't know," was the best I could manage. That, and a stupid, silly giggle.

After a brief silence as I nibbled at the manicure that Donna had given me while we passed time on Gran's porch, Nickie said softly as he stared ahead through the windshield, "I didn't care for him either."

Startled, I spit out a Royal Cranberry flake and asked, "Who?"

"Ferdinand Marcos, of course," Nickie said as he looked at me. He smiled and added, "The bastard."

I would insist for years afterwards that it was at this moment that Nickie fell in love with me.

*　　*　　*

Conveniently, Donna needed to run some errands in downtown Laoag. So we dropped her off as I pretended that I needed to stop by the local airport to check on the schedule of flights to the United States.

"Are you sure you'll be all right?" Donna asked earnestly as I shooed her out of the van.

"I'll be fine," I insisted, waving her off.

"Besides," I added, glancing at the impassive man by my side, "Nickie will take care of me."

After agreeing to meet later at the same spot in three hours, we zoomed off from Donna's sweating face.

It was Nickie's idea to sabotage the electric generator that cooled Marcos' mausoleum.

"Imelda hasn't paid the electricity bill for at least six months. Bastard can fry," he rationalized to my willing ears as we planned our escapade. He pronounced "bastard" with relish, drawing it out as "baaas-taaard" as if he had never heard of the word before and found its taste irresistible. In response, I opened my lips and found myself short of breath. I still respond the same way today. Sometimes, when he's addressing that certain stirring in my loins and the moon is full beyond our bedroom window, I ask him to say the word: *baaas-taaard*. But I remain too embarrassed to tell him why, no matter how many times he asks me to explain my strange predilection.

I had noticed that the security was quite lax around Marcos' childhood home. Enrico, the guard, was usually asleep—easy enough to determine as his snores were the type to rattle the *capiz* windchimes floating over his station. As for Innocencia, the salesgirl who sat behind a small table peddling old postcards and browning photos of the once-cute-but-now-bloated Ferdinand "Bong Bong" Marcos, Jr., she usually spent the day bowing her head over her crocheting. We tip-toed past the near-sighted Innocencia as shells tinkled to Enrico's vibrations of his soft palate—a symphony that masked any sound from our steps as well as the choked laugh I loosened when Nickie inadvertently kicked a mangy lizard that appeared from nowhere.

The generator was housed in a shack in the backyard. The door wasn't locked and we quickly stepped into the dimness. Nickie confidently opened a box and traced his fingers over the thing-a-majigs that laid there. I knew nothing about electrical circuitries and such, but insisted on accompanying Nickie. Though silently bemoaning my eyelashes' deficiency, I couldn't help batting them as I simpered, "Please don't torture me with the suspense of waiting while you endanger your life."

Then I raised a hand (trembling slightly) over the flat breast over my heart as if it was threatening to explode at the thought. Nickie offered a bemused look before quickly looking away. Months later, he revealed that he responded to what I thought was a becoming maidenly fluster by wondering whether the heat or my over-sugared diet had addled me.

After checking a few of the electrical thing-a-majigs, Nickie said softly, "This should be it."

He placed a hand over an orange lever. It was positioned by an "On" sign; pulling it down would position the lever by an "Off" sign.

I placed my hand over Nickie's palm and, with silent apologies to Nike, exhorted in a hoarse whisper, "Just do it."

His hand quivered briefly under mine, surprised by my touch. He looked into my eyes and, this time, I couldn't hide how I felt about him. I've long felt that when we both pulled down the lever, it was the first time we made love.

*　　*　　*

Much to the Imelda's dismay, visitors long had stopped trekking from any of the country's 7,000 islands to genuflect before Ferdinand's waxed body. The man who once claimed it possible for an honest Filipino to earn $10 billion had become merely a tourist attraction in a dusty region with limited competition. The next time Enrico opened the mausoleum, it was five weeks after our visit.

"*Was ist los*, what is wrong?" the German tourists gasped as they entered the room. With its failed air conditioning, the mausoleum's thoroughly sealed walls made the interior hotter than the 110 degrees then boiling Laoag. The mauseoleum also offered a stench that a newspaper reporter later likened to "a fruity mix of bananas, coconut oil and star apples underlaid by whiffs of spoiled eggs and rotten frog meat."

"*Que horror!*" Enrico, who was once gifted Spanish lessons by Imelda, exclaimed and bolted towards the direction of Marcos' body. Clamping their fingers on their noses, the Germans heaved curiously in his wake.

The wax had melted off Marcos' visage, leaving behind a skull with hollowed eyes peering out of the stiff collars of his yellow tunic. Out of each sleeve, the bony fingers looked incongruous against the still puffed out torso. Imelda's cohorts must have stuffed Ferdinand's suit with something more robust than wax to enhance his body's appearance.

After Marcos' stinking—no pun intended—body was discovered, Nickie began stopping by every evening to share that day's coverage by the *Ilocos Bulletin*. I attribute the reduction of my belly to those evenings of prolonged, wheezing laughter as we savored every word of every article. In particular, we scoffed at the photo of Imelda's outraged mien topping an immense bunch of microphones; its caption featured her lashing out, "The Philippines has never known such tragedy!"

"Yeah, right," I pithily mocked her words.

"Baaas-taaard," Nickie agreed, quickening my breath and parting my lips. That's when we shared our first kiss.

*   *   *

I freely confess that I seized on Gran's impending death as the excuse to march Nickie to the altar of Santo Tomas' church a few weeks after our first kiss. For the first time in many months, Gran's eyes sparkled as, seated in a wheelchair bought for the occasion, she watched me walk down the aisle festooned in lace, silk, pearls, and pink baby roses. The whole village turned out to cheer one of their sons finding wedded bliss with one who had returned to her cultural origins. My bridal gown naturally was dazzling white and, forgetting my difficult romantic past, I was ecstatic I could feel sincere about the color. My happiness was so contagious Mama announced that she was forgiving everyone who still owed money to Gran (I think Mama also finally accepted defeat in deciphering Gran's scribbled records as to which farmer owed what).

Nickie claims no regret over our hasty nuptials, even though Gran has recovered sufficiently to spend her days again wandering the halls of her beloved post office. To Gran's irritation but my amusement, there is limited demand for the contents of her purse. God seems to be in good humor, with nature's moods quite benign of late.

Meanwhile, I have acquired a goat whom I tend while eating raw tomatoes, freshly plucked from the vines climbing our new residence in Santo Tomas. They taste as sweet as Nickie's lips, sweet enough to overcome my dismay at my complexion, newly-darkened by the sun that remains consistent in its brightness.

DA MAYOR OF LAHAINA

My faddah from Lahaina sai. Ass wot I tell my friends wen dey all ass me hakum we going Maui. "Maui?! Why you going Maui fo'?" dey all ass making faces. Nobody stay jealous. Dey say, "Mo' bettah go mainlaaaand." I tell 'em, "Cuss, at least we going someplace, bully. Going someplace is beddah than going no place." Sometimes I wish we wuz rich like Steiler Shintani guys who go like Disneyland like every oddah year and Disney World like every oddah oddah year in between. Wot's wrong wit Maui? Good Maui. Maui get Planet Hollywood now. Ass wea my Uncle Stoney guys ran into da Barbarian Bruddahs lass year wen dey went right aftah da special openings. Maybe, if da timing correck, if eh-ry ting wuz all synchros, maybe me and my faddahs might bump into Bruce Willis, or dat "Sly Guy" Sylvester Stallone, or maybe even Ah-nold—da box office behemoth himself. And das like ten thousand times way mo' bettah dan da washed up has-been Barbarian Bruddahs. Wotchoo tinks, cuss?

I wen go lock pinkies wit all my non-believing, thunder-stealing, so-called friends of mines and I toll 'em, garans ballbaranz bully, full-on fo' sure to da infinite power kine, me and my faddahs going run into SOMEbody famous. And jus so no mo' arguments, no mo' debates, no mo' one shadow of one skepticism, fo' make 'em one full-on, full-fledge facial disgracials I going take some picture perfeck photo-graphics fo' make 'em ALL witout one doubt, proof posi-ma-tive.

At first wuz go, den no go, den go again. My maddah wen make my faddahs take one physical last month wen we wuz planning dis trip and I guess da doc toll him he bettah lay off da cigs cuz my Puff da Magic Dragon faddahs used to smoke like two packs a day and now he no smoke nahting. He get couple pills he gotta take too, but dey no like tell me wot ees fo'. My maddah wuz all worried if he could han-dles going on dis trip, but he sed no mattah wot he wuz going.

My maddah da one always flip-flopping. Jus like wen she drive. To moss people one yellow light mean slow down, cuss, slow down. To my maddah one yellow light mean stop, go-stop, ah mo beddah GO

I tink so. In da end my maddah wen decide fo' stay home save money. Gotta tink da future she sed, plus she had fo' watch my kid bruddah. So wuz jus me and my faddah on dis plane ride.

Usually me and my faddahs no talk nahting. Not dat we hate each oddahs. Jus we no mo' nahting fo' say. My maddah da one get da motor mout, talking on and on to da endless power kine. My faddah sez her mout only good fo' complain, complain about how everyting so expensive nowadays—I dunno why, but only recently my maddah sez cannot afford da kine Kellogg's Cereal Variety Packs. Get mo' bang fo' your buck she sez if we buy one big box of generic, look like, but not Cheerios and so I gotta eat 'em everyday fo' da whole month until by da end of da first week da fake Cheerios no seem so cheery anymo', but too bad so sad fo' me cuz das all I getting, cuz das all get, and das all I going get until I finish dat big buffo bargin size box.

My faddah sez da plane ride going take only like twenny-thirty minutes. And dis flight attendant stewardess-man is jus one rude dude, cuss. Ees like he tink I looking him WOT, so he looking me WHY, only I not looking him wot, I looking him, I THIRSTY WEA MY DRINK, cuss. My troat stay all dehydronated. At least I practice da kine good kine mannahsrisms at my house. Cannot be rude, cuss. Wen all my friends come ova, da first ting I do is offah dem drink and someting to eat. "Kyan, Ryle, you guys like Cheerios? Now hurry up eat 'em befo' my maddah see."

Pre-soon I could see Maui and my faddah wen reach over and point out da window, "Sonny boy, look 'em look 'em, dea Māhinahina. You see Maui grandma's house?" I get all confuse, bu's. "So if you wen grow up Māhinahina den hakum wen people ass you wea you from you always say Lahaina?"

"Cuz moss people dunno Māhinahina. If you say Honokōwai den maybe dey know, but Māhinahina, da strip is only about a mile long. You blink your eye, you pass 'um. Māhinahina, Honokōwai, Kā'anapali—das all part a Lahaina," my faddah sez pulling out one map from insai da airplane magazine. "See stay between da two rivers—da boundary go from da mountain, to da ocean," he sez pointing wit his finger.

"Aw, das jus like da ahupua'a system, yeah?" I wen go add on, making all intellectual cuz das we wen learn last year, seven grade Hawaiiana wit Mr. Oba. Ho, I know 'em ah cuss. Badness.

We wen touch down and my face came all frown cuz my faddahs. I dunno how we wuz going make all style profile in dis sorry-sad looking blue-grey Geo, no mo' powah, junk-a-lunka rental car. I wuz hoping fo' one ultra-bad, ultra-rad, spitfire red Pontiac Sunbird convertible fo' make da kine full-on fo' sure tourist kine action, but my faddah sez coss too much, gotta save from now. Aftah we wen pass through Lahaina town, mostly had jus sugarcane. Ten thousand miles and miles of sugarcane-sugarcane and ocean. I tot wuz going have some sights fo' see and I had my camera all reddy spaghetti, but nevah have nahting fo' shoot. Sadness.

My faddah grew up in da lime green house right by da beach. I only went dea couple times wen I wuz small. I only remembah going down da beach and picking pipipi while my faddah guys wen mo' down fo' catch eel.

"You remembah da time you caught one ghost moray," my faddahs wen ass me outta da blue kine like he wuz tinking my tinkings.

"No. Who I wuz wit?"

"Cousin Rip."

"I get one Cousin Rip?"

"No wait. Das MY cousin, so das your . . . second cousin? Third cousin? I dunno, get 'em written down. Wen we go home try go ask grandma if she still get da family tree."

Den my faddah nevah say nahting again cuz I guess he wuz trying fo' figure out all da relations. Wuz quiet in da car and could only hear da sound of him chewing his nicotine gum fo' help him quit smoking. I remembah my faddah sed dis road used to be da main road befo', but ees only like two lanes, one way-one way, but befo' wuz considered part of da highway until dey wen make da join mo' insai. Finally aftah driving fo' like fo'evah and a day my faddah pulls off to da side of da road.

Could hardly tell dat da house wuz dea. Da mango tree outsai wuz all growing wild, one wall of weeds wen take ova da driveway— wuz like Maddah Nature wen eat my Maui grandma's house. She wen sell her house chree years ago fo' like million trillion dollahs or someting to some guys who wuz going build someting on top da beachfront property. Das planny money, bully. I could buy like ten thousand Richie Rich comic books wit dat. She wuz one of da lass peoples to sell. Practically along da whole stretch a road only had condo condo condos. But I tink so doze investor guys wuz experiencing da kine financial depletions cuz me and my faddahs could see dey nevah do nahting yet. Chree years and da house wuz still dea. Still standing. But all boddo boddos now, da windows stay all boarded up jus like da place wuz haunted.

I wen take one picture of da house fo' go show grandmas. We wen walk back across da street and my faddah wen turn da car around. I dunno why, but my faddahs wuz starting fo' get mo' and mo' walkie talkie now. Muss be da Maui air I tot. My maddah sed da fresh air wuz going be good fo' his health. He wuz all reminiscing about da mountain apple and guava dey used to go get from up da mountain, da pigs and chickens dey used to raise. Full-on E-I-E-I-O action alreddy.

Nevah get nahting fo' see on da way back. Only da same sameness. "No mo' too much cars yeah dis road," I made color commentaries.

"Ten o'clock no' mo. Ho, morning time, I hea get some planny traffic I tell you boy. Everybody work at da hotels, eh. Jus like Honolulu alreddy."

So we spent da whole day driving, driving, driving all around, driving all ova town—jus looking fo' see wea tings used to be. Me, I wuz born O'ahu so I wuzn't feeling dis kine full-on nostalgias dat my faddahs wuz feeling. "Dis used to be da hardware store. Ovah hea had da Queen Theater, and ova dea wuz Pioneer Mill Theater." Boooring. I wuz starting to wish dat my maddah and my kid bruddah all came on dis trip too cuz den maybe we could make like da kine Scooby Doo action and split up into groups—da grown-ups can go all sight see and da kids can go play Street Fighter someplace.

"Your faddah not going always be around you know. You listening to me, Sonny boy?" my faddah wen boddah me as I wuz tinking of whether I should use Ken or Chun-Li fo' beat Bison.

"Wen we going Planet Hollywood?" I wen ass my faddahs again as I noticed dat we wuz getting mo' farther and farther away from da ocean, away from da town, away from Planet Hollywood.

"I go take you go someplace first." All right, cliff hanger-anticipation action, I tot as we wen go up da hill. But da expectation of eventual showtime excitement wen only last fo' all a two seconds cuz we wuz alreddy practically right dea by da place he wanted fo' show me. His old school—Lahainaluna c/o '59. Dis is wea he spent da bess years of his life he sed. Wea he met my maddah in automotive class. High school sweethearts.

"Twenny-one years of happy marriage. You no can beat dat," my faddah sed all looking up to da sky. I wuz jus nodding, leaning against da car. Den all one time he wen jump on da hood and stretch his arms out. "Smell da AIR," my faddah sed making all one wit da wind. "AIR. Das life. Good ol' country life. Dis da air dat make you feeeel—FEEL ALIVE. You no feel 'um?"

"Yeah yeah yeah," I toll 'em, taking one deep breath, making all like I wuz feeling invigorated too. And den he wen go off on how school wuz so diff'rent befo' time. To go school hea he sed, dey had to milk cows and stuff and dat used to pay fo' their room and board. Wit a moo-moo hea and one moo-moo dea. Hea a moo, dea a moo, every-wea a moo moo man, like big-whoop-d-doo, bu. Da gate wuz closed so wuz like so lame. And I nevah even see one cow cuss, not even ONE, bully.

On da drive back to town my faddah wen ass me wot I wanted fo' do in Lahaina. I toll 'em "I-ro-ro," like how Scooby Doo sez I dunno to Shaggy, cuz I figgah my faddah wuz tired hearing me nag wea I like go, wea I like go, cuz he knew wea I like go. He knew I wanted fo' go Planet Hollywood, and maybe if get time, Hard Rock fo' mingle wit Axl Rose, Slash guys. Befo' we got on da plane I had fo' explain to my fad-dah dat Hard Rock is one fancy rock-n-roll theme restaurant, not one newly discover natural geographic rock kine formation dat he nevah evah heard about befo'. He so not-hip sometimes.

"Oh I know, you wanted fo' go, wot wuz, Planet Holly-Rock, eh?" he sed making pretend dat he forgot, but saying 'em incorreckly wrong, probably not on purpose kine, but jus cuz he too old fo' remem-bah new stuffs cuz he getting old so his synapses stay all hammajang, so to him Planet Holly-Rock sound mo' correck cuz get dat Fred Flintstone caveman kine ring-a-ding to 'em.

We wen park along Front Street in Lahaina town. Nobody in back got mad wen he had fo' reverse and parallel park. Everyting so slow motion dis town. Da cars is slow. Da people slow. Even da tourists all stay taking their time. I can see da young guys being slow, cuz dey get like all da time in da world. Old guys, dey bettah hurry up, ees like any minute dey could die. My faddah put money in da meter jus half a block down from Planet Hollywood. Shmall kine tourist. I needed one Planet Hollywood shirt. I jus had fo' bring back one Planet Hollywood T-shirt cuz sez Maui on top. My faddahs wen suggest getting one of those chree fo' ten dollahs, el cheapo generic white shirts dat sed Maui on top wit bright neon pink and blue lettering. Sometimes I dunno if my faddah is joking or if he really has no sense of style. I toll him we jus had fo' get da shirts from Planet Hollywood cuz wuz like da ultimate in cool. Ultra badness, ultra-radness. Ho, going be so killah wen I wear 'em next week on da first day of school. Blow da doors off Kyan and Ryle's Bigfoot da monstah truck shirts dat dey got from da car show lass year. And ees like way mo' awesome opossum dan Shimomi's over-size Cats T-shirt. Anybody can get dat kine. Well, anybody who like pay seventy bucks fo' go see one stupid show and get suckered into paying one noddah twenty five bucks fo' one shirt and one noddah thirty bucks fo' da CD so dey can relive da excitement ovah and ovah again.

I couldn't relate to my faddahs jus how much I had to have 'em, and I nevah like get into da discussion on da difference between needs and wants so I jus toll my faddahs, "Mom sed can." Das all I had fo' say fo' get my faddahs to forget da chree fo' ten dollahs babies. Planet Hollywood all da way, cuss. Ultra-badical, ultra-radical. Two shirts fo' me, one for my maddah, and one fo' li'lo kid bro even though he too young fo' appreciate da coolness of it all. Wuz crowded but so my faddah nevah go insai da restaurant, he jus bot us shirts from da front window li'dat. While he wuz all making da cash transactions, I took my camera and made one quick trip walk around insai fo' take some candid camera shots. I wen take pictures of da frozen Sylvester Stallone from Demolition Man hanging from da ceiling, da fake life-size plastic Predator, and da giant sword on da wall, da one Arnold wen use in one of his Conan movies. Had planny trippy stuff, but nevah get no Hollywood celebrities eating dea. Wuz kinda dahk insai, but I can tell celebrities wen I see celebrities and I nevah see no celebrities. Dis place wuz mo' like Planet Haoletourist than anyting else.

I went back outside to da front fo' go see wea my faddah went. I tot maybe he wuz cruising, shmoozing, maybe talking stories wit some minor, major motion picture moviestar, but he wuz jus waiting outside wit da bags all by himself. He got me one separate bag. He sed I gotta carry my own. I nevah care dat we nevah eat dea cuz hamburger is hamburger. Nobody going ass how wuz da food. And if dey do, jus go "ah, I dunno, not bad I guess," and make sure you say "I guess" cuz das not lying if you state dat you jus guessing.

Still had chance fo' see some stars walking around town. Cuz I know dey like go look around aftah dey pau grines. My faddah wuz glad I nevah care if we ate dea or not cuz he saw da menu in da window and sed too much price escalation action. So he took me down to da closest McDonald's. He wen order da food while I watched da table. I held da bags in between my feet and I jus stared out da window. At least some of da Planet Hollywood wives should be all shopping around, somewhere in da town. Maria Shriver, Demi Moore, wea you guys stay?

Den out of da edge of my eyeball I wen happen to spahk some b-buzzin swarmin' stormin' kine action. Tourists wuz all surrounding dis one Bob Marley-looking guy who wuz kinda caught in da mid-jle. Looking in between all da haole heads I could kinda sorta see dat wuzn't Rastafari Bob Marley. Wuzn't even Ziggy Marley. Wuz jus one Local-looking homeless guy. He wuz kinda tall and had all shaggy shag, all stay tangle and mangle, long black and silvah hair. All his bangs and bushy bush beard wen go shade his face and make him look really really dahk. But he looked pretty clean from far, like he somehow took a bath everyday kine. Only his feet wuz kinda dirty cuz he nevah get slippahs. And he had on one navy blue Local's Only T-shirt and red flower print surf shorts. Pretty stylin' his clothes, wuzn't all buss up like how you would expeck 'em fo' be.

Aftah awhiles da bummy looking guy wuz leff by his lonesome hanging around in front McDonald's. Kinda looked like he wuz playing with toys or someting I couldn't see.

"Dey should clean up dis neighborhood," I sed tilting my head toward da trippy bum guy outside as my faddahs set down da tray.

"You know who's dat, eh?" he assed me knowing I nevah know, attemp-ing to make conversations wit me. "Das da Mayor of Lahaina."

"Linda Lingle?! Linda Lingle is really one man??!"

"No. I mean, I dunno. I mean, das not Linda Lingle."

"He one former politician?"

"No."

"Den how he got to be da Mayor of Lahaina?"

"Cause. He jus ack dat way, so people call 'um dat," my faddah sed all pointing, making undahstand rubbahband wit his finger. "And he no scare away da tourists. In fack, him da numbah one tourist attraction ova hea. See, look 'um Sonny boy. Dey taking picture wit him. Fo' some reason everybody like take picture wit him. Must be he some good looking guy, no?"

While me and my faddahs wuz all grine-ing our burgers I couldn't help but stare at da Mayor's face. Wen da sun struck 'em at da right angle, you could see da waves of wrinkles break on his face. His face had character, but I dunno wot wuz da secret to his box office drawing power and star appeal. During da time we wuz eating, I counted like chree diff'rent groups of tourists who took pictures wit da Mayor. I can see why da second and third group wen go take pictures cuz ees like monkey see, monkey do, but I dunno wot wen possess dat dummy initial first group fo' go make all picture postcard? Maybe *Maui This Week* wen go liss him in their brochures as one must-see tourist sideshow attraction?? But what would dey bill him as??? Da Mayor of Lahaina—Hawai'i's only homeless man??

No, get planny homeless mans. Unsolve mys-try, cuss. My faddah wuz all talking about his yout again, oblivious to da inquiring-minds-wanna-know, Scooby Dum look on my face dat screamed "Dum dum dum dum," tell me about da Mayor.

"Eh, da guy work or wot?" I assed, cutting my faddahs line.

"Uhhh, I heard he used to get planny degrees—business, agriculture, law, but one day he jus wen geev 'um up and decide fo' live da way he live."

"But how he eat?"

"Das a good one. I dunno wot he do now. Maybe he go down da beach like grandma/grandpa kine catch fish. Befo' time Lahaina wuz small town. I remembah he could jus walk into any restaurant and he nevah haff to pay. Everybody knew him. Everybody knew da Mayor. And den I guess wen he got tired of bacon and eggs people say dat he used to go hunt da kine pig li'dat."

"You mean he get hunting dog and da kine gun?"

"I dunno fo' sure cuz I nevah seen, but I heard he used to make da kine 'ōkolehao and soak 'em insai da bread. Den he wen up da mountain sai and feed 'em to da buta. Da pig come so drunk dat can jus walk up to 'em an cut da troat."

"Das gross. And wot, he no get sick or wot da guy?"

"K, once again, I no can say fo' sure, but da rumors wuz dat he real good wit da kine nature kine stuff. He da one wen teach Uncle Buzz and Auntie Tipsy how fo' fix 'em wen dey get hangover. He know all da traditional Hawaiian medicinal kine herb. So wen he get sick he boil da kine leaf li'dat make tea, den pau, sick go away."

"Trippy," I tot as we wen pau eat so we wen stand up fo' scram. Rocking to get da momemtum and wit both hands on his lap my faddah pushed himself up, making dat ol' people stretch kine sound effecks. My faddah muss be coming old. We wuz walking down da boulevard and I could see jus up ahead dat da Mayor wuz sitting on da sidewalk in da shade taking some kala-koa objects outta one bag. I wuz walking on wen I heard one "ayeeeee whatchoo doing hea." My faddah all stopping back in da distance fo' to talk to somebody he knew from befo'—probably somebody from da ol' cow country. I know dat soon as we go home my faddah probably going back look in his yearbook see who in all reincarnation dat wuz. He ehrytime forgetting people. He really getting old—I tink so sometimes he forget my name too, das why he always calling me Sonny boy.

I stood around by my faddah fo' couple minutes jus shuffling my feet. My camera still hanging, dangling from my neck, ready fo' da kine quick draw celebrity shoot-out. I twisted round and around, looking at my feet, wishing fo' one famous amos celebrity close encounter, but real willing to settle fo' one casual corner kine meeting wit Glenn Medeiros or even dat Local girl who wuz in Karate Kid II, da one who wen go ring da bell. Slowly, swizzle stick swirling, twirling away from my faddah I heard, "Eh, boy. Boy."

Da Mayor couldn't have been talking to anyboy else. I wuz da only boy around. I walked up closer to see wot he wanted. Maybe he wanted bus money I tot, but den I remembered no mo' bus on Maui, cuss.

"Boy," he sed again. "You one tourist or one Local?"

"Um, I guess one Local tourist."

"Das a good one," he sed smiling one perfeck toothpaste commercial smile. "We no get too much a dat around hea. Wot you bot?" he axed pointing to my package.

"Planet Hollywood T-shirts."

"Oh," he sed looking kinda disappointed. Maybe he wuz hoping I had food. I wish I nevah indigest all my hamburger. He turned his attention away from me as he looked down at someting and continued doing wot he wuz doing—drawing little squares on top da sidewalk wit da edge of one sharp stone. I nevah know whether fo' make like one Van Damme and split or stay and talk to him sa'more. I turned and saw my faddah wuz still talking to his friend, so I figured I'd make all Magnum P.I. action and solve dis mys-try.

"So wot you get in your bag," I sed pointing wit my chin.

Den his face wen go come all lite brite as he wen turn around fo' grab his pupule purple sack from in back. All proud wit proudness he took out his collection of da kine McDonald's Happy Meal toys and he wen go slowly arrange 'em on da sidewalk. "You like play chess?" he asses me as I noticed da squares he wuz drawing wuz one checkerboard pattern. He wen carefully arrange his colorful Disney toys, making sure da placement wuz all correck. Snow White wuz now one queen. Some of da dwarves wuz pawns. Captain Hook wuz da black king and I guess in dis game he wuz married to Ursula da octopus even though dey wuz in different movies and different species. I sat down opposite da Mayor, looking back at my faddah making sure he could still see me.

"You can go first," he sed. Da Mayor ended up making da first move cuz I wuz too scared. I nevah know if he wuz serious. As we played he assed me wea I wuz from and stuff. I toll 'em Honolulu. Wuz hod playing wit him cuz I kept mixing up Tigger and Winnie da Pooh—da bishop and da horsey-man.

"Which is da knight?"

"Jus remembah, Pooh is da paniolo."

I only talked wen I had one question pertaining to da game. Felt weird wen wuz quiet, but I guess chess you not 'post to talk too much. I wuzn't sure if he wanted me fo' talk to him. I wanted to, but couldn't tink of wot to say. Took me like forevah and a day fo' tink of someting to make da conversations. "Eh, s-s-so wot you do," I assed him, not knowing wot he wuz going say.

"I live, live life."

"Oh. But, wot you do, fo' one living?"

"I no mo' one job, if das wot you axing."

"But how you make money?"

"Sometimes I sell these Happy Meal toys. People buy you know chree dollah one. Das mo' than da meal. Onreal, no?"

"But you no work? I heard you used to get all kine choke degrees."

"I free. I not one slave to my job like da ress of da peoples. I not into accumulation of status. In fack, my money, I gave moss of 'em away. Planny people tink I homeless, but I not homeless, I get one home. And I used to get one family. Till my wife wen die young. Yuuup, I used to get one beeg family." Aftah he sed dat he jus closed his eyes, like he wuz going cry, but he nevah. Wot he wuz doing I tot, maybe he wuz going sleep I wen stay specu-ma-late, but den he starting chanting, chanting someting.

Maybe he wuz calling his chess 'aumakua or someting cuz I jus ate his Fox and da Hound. Fo' couple minutes he went off and I nevah know wot he wuz going do next. I tot of ditching him, but he opened his eyes again and continued talking sa'more.

"Everyting changing around hea, boy. I been hea while da world fought two, chree, no four wars. Every morning you can count on me being somewhere along dis strip. I no tink dis town would be da same witout me. I can tell you everyting dat happen hea in da lass seventy-six years. Da whole history of dis town stay in me."

"So wot going happen wen you die?"

"I'll still live on in oddah people's memories. You die da true death wen you are forgotten," he sed all nodding his head, agreeing wit himself.

Das wen my faddahs cot up to us and looked at us like wot we doing. Fo' one second I tot of assing my faddahs if we could take pictures wit da Mayor, cuz he wuz famous and all. I looked at da Mayor den I looked at my faddahs. I froze not knowing wot to do. During dat split second of indecision my decision wuz made wen my faddah wen go tilt his head "WE GO," so I left da Mayor hanging even though wuz still my turn. I wuz going geev da Mayor da k-dens catch you latah shaka, but he nevah look up.

As we wuz walking away, I nevah know I wuz making all room-a-zoom-zoom Speed Buggy and I wuz all passing my faddah's pace so I wen slow 'em down so my faddah could keep up. I noticed, he wuz all sucking, sucking, sucking wind, like he wuz on his lass breath alreddy so I wen step da brakes. I wen realize dat I leff behind my prize Planet Hollywood package. Looking over my shoulder I wen change my mind ten thousand times, I tot, geff 'em, no geff 'em, go geff 'em, tinking of how pissed my faddah wuz going be. Finally, I wen jus leave my shirt fo' da Mayor fo' choose how fo' use as he saw fit. Before we wen turn da corner, I wen go snap one picture of da Mayor all staring at da board so I had someting fo' da purposes of preservations. I walked on, den I looked back again fo' see if da Mayor wuz going look up, but he jus continued playing, moving my pieces fo' me, as if I nevah left.

NOT-SO-REMOTE CONTROL

Look at how this man in my house
insists on holding that little black box.
No one else dares vie for its possession.
His fingers stronger than ever—
even in sleep, his limp body
and heavy breathing are just a guise,
as I fail to pry his fingers
free from his tiny instrument.

I've checked with other women,
and all of us think this
obsession peculiar to men;
just to keep peace in the nest,
we relinquish the remote control
to our husbands and lovers.
And if they're not at home, we notice
it's our sons, not daughters,
who wrangle and wrestle
for next-in-line rule.

It reminds me of childhood
before TV had taken over our lives—
my entire family followed an unspoken
ritual for viewing the *Sunday Times*.
No one could touch the paper before Father,
who'd read it in the same precise sequence.
Once he'd drop a section to the floor,
we kids scrambled, hoping
to fish up the funnies.

But times have gotten scary—
this multifunction electronic weapon

so much more sinister, family upon family
subject to the whims of its possessor
and his psycho need to jump
from baseball to animal documentaries,
jumble in some *Jeopardy*,
speedclick to basketball,
old black-and-white love flicks,
football replays, even
random channel checks
just to make sure he won't miss
anything important.

Whenever I try to tease him,
playfully demanding a woman's turn
to push those buttons,
he always gives me the same look,
silently warning
there are just some things in the world
a man shouldn't have to explain.

THE RETURN

There was an old woman whose hair was long and black and
beautiful. She drew it around her like a shawl and so divided
herself from the world that not even Age could find her.
—N. Scott Momaday, "The Colors of Night"

I stay in the city. Not for the usual reasons. It has something to do with an old woman with hair to her waist. She wears an unsashed kimono, carries a ceramic bowl containing water from a stream. She only visits when I am alone. On the mountains just north of the city, I see her dancing under the light of moon. From the nearby coastal shore, fog moves in and around her like a lover. And then she is dancing by herself again. Sometimes she rides on the hood of my car. Her hair streaming across the window, she keeps laughing. One August I find myself in a tropical jungle. All day the sun and rain and eyes of children follow me. That night I leave the jungle on a crowded bus; everyone sleeps but me. The only light comes through the headlights, a bare yellowish path through the black night, and a lucent white from the moon. The old woman is sitting beside me, teaching about the people of each place in connection with all things. Then the old woman asks me again, "How strong is your love?"

POSTMODERN X: HONOLULU TRACES

"Since Copernicus man has been rolling from the center toward X."[i]
—Friedrich Nietzsche, *The Will to Power.*

Once there were 'neighborhoods,' like Kaimukī.

Explain yourself in plain English. *Art House. Artwear.*

Deployed as news or fashion, postmodernism was beginning to feel like a problem of discursive overload, too much information coding the individual head.

"I, author-function."

"I" "was" "suffering" "from" "a" "case" "of" "semiotic" "overload."

Location became a question of continuity, like how do I get from one day to the next that was not a function of lyric mood. The problem of living within non-narrative was gleefully read as decentered pluralism, first-person-singular "rooms with a view."

Some were attacking 'theory' for premature totalizing: "Jameson's Restaurant" (North Shore), "Lentricchia's Bar & Grill" (Durham). Some were fed up with the will to theory: "we have a hunger for examples."

"I, author-function" was suffering from a case of semiotic overload, so I headed home to the Island Colony to drink some Japanese beer with Hawaiian labels (surf scenes of Waikīkī Beach minus the hotels).

The assembling and disassembling of a poem was related to a helicopter hitting the beaches of Nicaragua, though this was my own projection.

Eventually the question of postmodernism came around to the wonders of dining at McDonald's, though I tried to point out the pseudo-vernacular styles spelled the death of regionalism in simulacrous copy, the emptying out of local creolization: koa wood counters for Waikīkī, Peggy Hopper prints for Mōʻiliʻili, pastel sailboats for Hawaiʻi Kai, Elvis posters for Bamboo Ridge.

The Kodak Hula Show which has existed in Honolulu since 1937 could now begin to function nicely as a postmodern art-form, phasing out so-called real hula, or at least desacralizing it in the context of mass images, a trillion copies, flash bulbs popping from Pearl City to Rochester. So the postmodern became a function of image displaced from prior context, force severed from history, sign floating in the free market of commodity exchange. A kind of sublime infinitude.

It was simply, the man said, a matter of imperial burlesque, *not* a matter of choice, tone, or mood. You were both exhilarated and weirded-out, over-amped and emptied, filled with a million exchangeable signs with the inability to do any thing about it except keep on exchanging them, even in a Mānoa zendo.

"Products from all over the world lie available to you on the shelves [of the Waikīkī Duty Free Shop]. What do you reach for? Do you think about climbing on board your jetliner with a newly purchased six-pack of Coke? No. But what about a Gucci bag? Yes, of course. In a sense, duty-free shops are the precursor to what life will be like in a genuinely borderless environment."[ii]

The 'ontological hunger' you felt for the sacred displaced itself into a search for private truth. She became your signifier/signified, "Hiroshima Mon Amour." 'She' alluded to an infinite range of lexical possibilities, metaphors, cottage-industry truths, site of tropological production.

My fellow Americans, you had a nostalgia for master narratives, a longing for mountain grandeur and paternal households across the prairies of Iowa, so the political unconscious invented Pat Robertson ("I, Pat Robertson, do solemnly swear. . .").

Her anger was not cold war paranoia, simply an accurate consciousness of events. As for 'reification,' why do these people have to use such foreign-sounding words to talk about such simple things?

The bottom line is.

"India and Pakistan have fought two of their three wars [since 1947] over the Himalayan state and continue to skirmish daily along the 'line of control' that [since 1971] divides Kashmir [between the two]. . .The airstrikes, the first in Kashmir in 20 years, have escalated tensions between the two nuclear powers in South Asia and alarmed world leaders."[iii]

Eric Chock. Robert Chalk.[iv]

I filled my cramped study walls in the Island Colony with postcards and pictures of Emerson, Kenzaburo Ōe, and Montgomery Clift, and a gleaming photo of a red 57 Chevy convertible I had wanted as a kid back in the downsizing Brass Valley of Western Connecticut. I longed for time to stand still, back up, leap, rewind, fast forward.

Father Marx. Father Freud. Mother Nature. Mother Goose.

My disgust at sublime commodification was based upon a lapsed-Catholic abhorrence towards a de-sacralized world.

"They alarmed me."

Whatever happened to the Kuhio Grill?

Wallace Stevens' "Anecdote of the Jar" began to look like an air-raid drill on slovenly, Third World natives. Haiku read like suicide dives into the Pacific, ethnic pacification.

The aura must die and be reborn as signs. The aura of a billboard for designer jeans. As for the symbol, what would be left to symbolize?

Each day postmodern English deployed itself in expanding territories. Time was wrapped in clear plastic at Liberty House in Ala Moana, readying the planet for Easter Clearance Sales. Space was a detailed regret for the billing lading.

We locals fondly called the thirteen nuclear submarines the 'old blues' and 'old salts' of Pearl Harbor. How many Hiroshimas squared? The state had plans to evacuate the citizens of Honolulu to the kāhuna-laden "friendly island" of Moloka'i. There would probably be a traffic jam on the H-1 freeway going out to the airport. Remember the last *tsunami*-scare?

---

i   Friedrich Nietzsche, "European Nihilism," *The Will to Power*, trans. Walter Kaufmann and R. J. Hollingdale (New York: Vintage, 1968), p. 8.

ii   Kenichi Ohmae, *The Borderless World: Power and Strategy in the Interlinked Economy* (London: Fontana, 1991), p. 34.

iii   "Pakistan claims 2 fighters downed," Associated Press wire story, *The Honolulu Advertiser*, May 27, 1999: A1.

iv   Eric Chock is co-editor of Bamboo Ridge Press, to be sure, and author of the cautionary collection of poems on the death and rebirth of the Honolulu local, *Last Days Here* (Honolulu: Bamboo Ridge Press, 1990); "Robert Chalk" is Rob Sean Wilson, author of this mongrel essay/poem on the disappearance of the Honolulu local as a fate of postmodern de-sacralization. On this global/local fate of place-imagining in Hawai'i, also see Rob Wilson, *Ananda Air: American Pacific Lines of Flight* and *Automat: Un/American Poetics*, forthcoming; and "Seven Tourist Sonnets" on the www internet journal from Australia and England, edited by innovative poet/editor, John Tranter, *Jacket* 7 (1999) (http//www.jacket.zip.com.au).

ROB WILSON

WAYS OF HEAVEN

In the first way of heaven I follow the trusty
sayings like "We don't want to give up
the family store to those forests, now do we, son?"

In the second way, I invent tiny headlines like
"Man Swallowed By His Own Emptiness, Waiting
for Autumn to Descend upon O'ahu."

In the third way, when I talk you talk,
In the fourth way I talk, I listen.

Outside my window some magpies splash in a morning puddle.
In the fifth way of heaven, I stop talking.

THE HUNT

5:30 a.m.
Dollar bills?
Check.
Flashlight?
Check.
Plastic grocery bags?
Check.

I weave my way
past the Oroweat Thrift Store
the new old Hata Building
I am Bible and
Reuben's Mexican Restaurant.

People start up their cars.
Their headlights spotlight me.
They leave as I arrive
dollar bills
flashlight and
grocery bags in hand.

My strategy:
    Case the place first.
    Check out who and what's where.
    Banana man
    Kea'au corn man
    The Pavaos
    Check out what's going fast.
    Papaya man with the cigar box cash can
    Get that first.

Ha much dis one, Tata?

Dis one por por one dollar, Ma'am.
Dis one pibe por one dollar.

My Maglite beam bounces
as I squat
hover over the black mound of papayas
piled high on the blue tarp.
The beam catches the small patches of yellow
of the ripening ones.
The black mound shines dark green.

I hunt for the ripest.
I survey, sort, lift,
turn, and gently squeeze each one
for the smoothest skin
firm and round.
Each one that passes my test
is nestled in my KTA bag.

I thrust two dollar bills
into Tata's brown leathery hand.
He, in turn, reaches down
to another black pile
and picks up a green torpedo-shaped papaya.
"Dis one manuahi," he says,
bending down to put it in my plastic bag.

CONTRIBUTORS

Margo Berdeshevsky received the *Honolulu Magazine*/Border's Books Fiction Contest Grand Prize for her story "Bats"; published recently in *Many Mountains Moving, Paris/Atlantic, Hawai'i Review, Soviet Woman, Calyx, Women's Voices in Hawai'i, Visions International, Pacific Art and Travel, New World Magazine,* and *Midwifery Today.* First place fiction and poetry recipient from National League of American Pen Women's Lorin Tarr Gill Competition, scholarship to Prague's Charles University, invited as guest of (former Soviet) Writers' Union to live and work in their House of Creation in Yalta, a Poet-in-the-Schools on Maui for ten years. A photographer as well, her most recent works are collages, a marriage of forms, as she rips apart her own mind and looks for a new integrity. She is presently playing Colossus, one leg in Maui, the other on the banks of the Seine in Paris.

Nancie Caraway is a scholar and writer who lives in Mānoa Valley. Her heroes are: Nelson Mandela, Petra Kelly, and Janis Joplin. Her favorite quotation is from African writer Chinua Achebe's *Anthills of the Savannah*: "Writers don't give prescriptions. They give headaches." A big mahalo nui loa to Bamboo Ridge for doing what it does.

J. Freen spends his days working on his resume for *Baywatch.*

Jacinta S. Galea'i was born and raised in Amerika Samoa. She graduated from Samoana High School in 1985 and attended the University of Washington in Seattle where she earned a B.A. in English in 1989. She taught English at Samoana from 1989–90 and is currently on leave from teaching English at the Amerika Samoa Community College to pursue her M.A. in English from the University of Hawai'i-Mānoa. She is hoping to write both creative and theoretical works in English and Samoan.

Norma Wunderlich Gorst writes poetry and short fiction and is a freelance editor. Her work has appeared in *Chelsea, Bamboo Ridge, Chaminade Literary Review, Cottonwood, Hawai'i Review, Kaimana, Rain Bird, ALOHA* magazine, and *The Honolulu Advertiser.* Her short story, "A Shell for Mrs. Everhart," won first prize in *The Honolulu Advertiser* fiction contest in 1996. She received the John Unterecker Prize for Poetry from Chaminade University in 1991. She has lived in Hawai'i since 1969.

Marie M. Hara, writer, editor, and teacher, wears a t-shirt that says "cultural observer."

Ermile Hargrove, master's degree in Linguistics, is currently working as an independent educational consultant. Her projects have included writing grant proposals in literacy and strategic plans for educational evaluation and program assessment. She is also one of the developers of a website on language varieties (Pidgins, Creoles, and Other Stigmatized Varieties). Her interest in understanding why some local children have difficulty learning to read has led her to pursue a course of study to learn more about reading acquisition and language development.

Jody Helfand received an M.A. in English from Simmons College and an M.F.A. in Creative Writing from Chapman University. His poems have appeared in *Public Voices* and *Rain Bird*, and his first book, *The Nature of Insects*, was published by Nothing Gold Press. He teaches writing and literature in Hawai'i, where he lives with his girlfriend and their pet spider, Gertrude.

Jeffrey Higa: The great burden of my life is that I was born a kotonk. Even though I made it back to the islands within six months of my birth, the damage had already been done. For my family, the fact that I had been born in Duluth, Minnesota, and not in Hawai'i like the rest of them explains a great many things about me: my propensity to lose my tan quickly, my wanderlust which led me through several creative writing programs on the mainland before I accidently graduated at the University of Missouri-St. Louis, and my need, as my grandma put it, to write and "tell any kine people all dakine stuff about our family." True to my kotonk nature, I am currently living in Yokohama, Japan, and can be reached at higa@etrademail.com.

Muriel Mililani Ah Sing Hughes was born in idyllic Lahaina, Maui before the coming of the big hotels. Raised in a plantation community where pidgin reigned supreme, Hughes is now a high school English teacher in Hilo and continues her love affair with reading and writing. She is married and lives in Glenwood.

Laura Iwasaki was born in Hawai'i, spent many formative years in Los Angeles, and now lives in Bellevue, Washington, where lately a line from an Indigo Girls song has been stuck in her head. "Empty pages for the no longer young"... how scary....

Darlene M. Javar has been published in *Growing Up Local* by Bamboo Ridge. Her poetry is forthcoming in *Chaminade Literary Review*, and *Hawaii Pacific Review*. She lives in Hawai'i and teaches at Ka'u High and Pahala Elementary School.

Juliet S. Kono lives and works in Honolulu.

Lanning Lee: Since 1991 I have written 17 stories about the Kaneshiro family. After the first few stories, they moved out of my house and are living on their own these days. Every once in awhile I run into them, usually when I least expect it, and another story presents itself. The more I write about them, the less I think I know them, and the more mysterious they seem to become. I can, however, tell you some "facts" about them. For instance, I know that the grandfather and grandmother, Kenji and Thelma, live at 8421 Booth Road, way, way back in Pauoa Valley. Kenji is the younger of two brothers; his older brother is absent. Kenji and Gladys have a son, Kenji (II), who also has an absent older brother. This older brother had a scholarship to play football at UH Mānoa, but ended up joining the U.S. Army when he was drafted, rather than seek a 2S deferment. His father, a rabid 'Bows fan, has never recovered from this. Kenji (II) is married to a Mainland Caucasian whose name is usually Lisa. They met at the University of Wisconsin at Madison. His father has never recovered from this either. They live above Pauoa Valley on Pacific Hts. Rd. Kenji (II) and Lisa have two children, a son named Kenneth/Kenny, and a daughter whose name changes often. One is older than the other, but that depends on the particular story. Other than that, I can't tell you much more about them. Oh, except that they all lie to each other constantly, and that fabric of untruth seems, thankfully, to hold the clan together.

Tracee Lee: I was born and raised in Kaimukī, and attended Maryknoll grade school, then Punahou school. I graduated from the University of the Pacific in 1995, and then went on to play on the professional tennis circuit for two years. I will be attending the M.F.A. program in Creative Writing at San Diego State University this fall.

Walter K. Lew's books include *Premonitions*, an anthology of new Asian North American poetry, excerpts from: ΔKTH DIKTE, for *DICTEE*, and a forthcoming collection of his poems, *Brine*. He is preparing the selected works with commentary of the Korean avant-gardist Yi Sang, the novelist

Younghill Kang, and the poet Frances Chung, and also co-editing with Heinz Insu Fenkl a historical anthology of Korean American literature. (Editors note: Walter Lew's poem has been reprinted in this issue to correct errors when it first appeared in *Bamboo Ridge* #73. Our sincerest apologies.)

Wing Tek Lum's award-winning collection of poetry, *Expounding the Doubtful Points*, was published by Bamboo Ridge Press in 1987.

Noel Abubo Mateo is a painter and poet who was born in Baguio in the mountains of the Philippines. His poetry has been previously published in *Bamboo Ridge* and included in a number of anthologies. He lives in Southern California and remains a Baguio Boy at heart.

Michael McPherson was the *enfant terrible* of Hawai'i literature in the '70s and early '80s. His book of poems, *Singing with the Owls*, was published in 1982. Nowdays he mellow. He was born in Hilo, and now lives in Kamuela and practices law. His poem in this issue was written for his mother, who passed away in 1998.

Eiko Michi: I was born and raised on Sakhalin Island, formerly the north-ernmost island of Japan. It was occupied by Russia at the end of the war. All Japanese were uprooted and were repatriated with only a knapsack to mainland Japan. Because of my father's position in the government we were detained, and it was only after his death in 1948 that we were allowed to return to Japan. Had he not died at that time the fate of our family could have been drastically different.

The poem "Between the Sheets of Ice" comes from this period of my life where the post-war confusion and trauma had swept all the families who lived under the dangerous military regime of Stalin.

After a time in Sapporo, Japan, working for the U.S. Occupational Forces, I was fortunate to receive a scholarship to study in the U.S. Eventually I received an M.A. in English Literature and Psychology from the University of Oklahoma, Norman. I taught many years in public high schools and junior colleges.

In the last 20 years I have given workshops in the Intensive Journal Workshop and Creative Writing "Wild-Mind" classes.

My teachers include: Anaïs Nin, Deena Metzger, Natalie Goldberg, and Dr. Ira Progoff, the creator of the *Intensive Journal Workshop*.

Tyler Miranda currently resides in Wahiawā. He recently graduated from the University of Hawai'i at Mānoa with his secondary teaching degree. (If anyone knows of any DOE job openings, he'd really like to know about them.) He was lucky enough to work with Lois-Ann Yamanaka for a semester while she was a "Distinguished Visiting Writer" at the University. Although he had experimented with many different forms and styles of poetry, he had never written a Pidgin poem before. Lois-Ann Yamanaka helped him find a voice, one which was yearning to speak for many, many years. And to think he almost didn't take her class! He writes all the time. Poetry, fiction, sad and pathetic love songs, whatever. Tyler is currently working on his first novel, a story about growing up in 'Ewa Beach during the early 1980s.

Roy Onomura is currently a student at Kapi'olani Community College. He enrolled in Leigh Dooley's creative writing class last spring semester to learn about writing stories and poems. At first, he was worried that writing poems and stories for this class would be difficult—much more difficult than his math, chemistry, and medical terminology class combined. What he discovered was that creative writing is fun and that it is a great way to share with people his life experiences.

"Thank you Leigh Dooley, Mavis Hara, Mike Molloy, and Gary Pak for encouraging me to write."

Elmer Omar Bascos Pizo: The hurried sounds of flirting house lizards are most often a source of pleasant distraction when I am trying to organize words into a so-called poem.

Alshaa T. Rayne is a visual artist and a poet. She has been published in *Rain Bird, Hawaii Pacific Review,* and *Hawai'i Review.* She lives in Mililani, Hawai'i, and gives private workshops in Trash Art and "Loose Hair" Poetry.

Albert Saijo recently published *OUTSPEAKS A RHAPSODY,* a collection of prose-poetry, his first solo literary publication since co-authoring *Trip Trap* with Beat writers Jack Kerouac and Lew Welch. He is Nisei, born in Los Angeles, interned during W.W.II at Big Horn Basin, Wyoming, and is a veteran of the 442nd. He attended USC, but dropped out before completing his master's thesis on the partition of Vietnam. His only other publication was a book called *The Backpacker.* He now lives in Volcano, Hawai'i.

Kent Sakoda: Fram da taim ai waz bawn awn Kawai, waz awmos gærenti ai goin bi wan Pijin spika. Ai bin græd Waimea Hai Skul æn den wen go awl da we tu Ayowa fo go skul sam mo. Ai hæd kam bæk go Yu Eich bat. Ai ste lrning linggwistiks nau, æn ai tich wan kaws awl abaut Pijin. Ai ste lrning hau fo tawk Ingglish tu.

Ryan Senaga likes Nintendo games, taro flavored jelly caps, balconies, 24-hour gyms, cows, Steely Dan, Halloween (the holiday), Raymond Chandler, brand new underwear, Jeep Wranglers, the smell of a freshly bathed dachshund, getting caught in the rain, jacuzzis, balconies, Jar Jar Binks, short people, Glenlivet, postcards, and the time to recline on a white chaise lounge on cool, clear full moon nights while pondering why Liam Neeson's body didn't disappear when he was killed in Episode I.

Mei Simon: I am from Aotearoa originally, but have lived in Hawai'i for more years than in my homeland. I am married with two teenaged girls, live in an old plantation home in the country, and I have a day job in Honolulu. I am working on several projects set in Polynesia, one with a plantation theme, and the other a multi/cross-cultural bent.

Cathy Song: Now appearing on buses in Atlanta as well as subway cars throughout New York City, her poetry is part of the Poetry in Motion program.

Eileen Tabios recently released *The Anchored Angel* (Kaya/Muae, 1999), a volume of selected works by Philippine poet José Garcia Villa with essays by prominent Filipino poets. She is currently co-editing *Screaming Monkeys*, a 2000 anthology of prose, poetry and art revolving around cultural portrayals of Asian America. Her other books include a poetry collection, *Beyond Life Sentences*; and an essay/interview collection, *Black Lighting: Poetry In Progress*.

Lee A. Tonouchi is da co-editor of *Hybolics*. He no drink, he no smoke, he no SHmoke, so sometimes he wondah if he can really call himself one writer.

Amy Uyematsu is a L.A. sansei from the '60s—Buddhahead is still a basic part of her vocabulary, along with dances at Rodger Young Auditorium, movies starring Toshiro Mifune and Tatsuya Nakadai, special family dinners at San Kow Low in J-Town, and calls for "yellow power" when Asian American studies programs were just an ideal.

Rob Wilson has published poems and reviews in *Bamboo Ridge* since 1979, and in various journals from *Tinfish, Taxi, Mānoa,* and *Central Park* to *New Republic, Ploughshares, Partisan Review,* and *Poetry*. He is a western Connecticut native who was educated at the University of California at Berkeley, where he was founding editor of the *Berkeley Poetry Review*. His works of poetry and cultural criticism include *Waking In Seoul* (1988); *American Sublime* (1991); *Asia/Pacific as Space of Cultural Production* (1995);

Global/Local: Cultural Production and the Transnational Imaginary (1996); and *Reimagining the American Pacific: From "South Pacific" to Bamboo Ridge and Beyond* (forthcoming with Duke University Press in Spring, 2000) He is at work on two collections of poetry: *Ananda Air: American Pacific Lines of Flight*; and *Automat: Un/American Poetics*, and still plays basketball, pool, and meditates (and prays), each day, in the great void of being and creative bliss. As Jack Kerouac put it in *Dharma Bums*, "Equally holy, equally to be loved, equally a coming Buddha!"

Merle M.N. Yoshida: During the school year, Merle spends more time helping her students at Hilo High School with their writing than working on her own pieces. Her goal is to generate a variety of pieces more frequently, but in the meantime, she continues to jot down ideas and images for future pieces, often at the urging of her husband. Sometimes she just thumbs through her notebook searching for a good laugh.

THE WOUNDED SEASON

KOREAN STORIES OF POST-WAR MEMORY

Focusing on the influence of memory, history, and counter-memory in post-war Korea, MĀNOA presents *The Wounded Season*. Guest-edited by Susie Jie Young Kim, a leader of the younger generation of Korean translators, the feature includes fiction by Im Cheol Woo, Kong Sŏnok, Yi Ch'ŏngjun, and Choi In Hoon.

The Wounded Season also includes Min Soo Kang's insightful essay on the demolition of the Korean National Museum Building as a symbol of Japanese imperialism; a symposium on translating Asian poetry into English; North American and other international fiction, poetry, and essays; photographs of post-WWII Korea; reviews and more. Published winter 1999, $16.

Individual one-year subscriptions (2 issues):
$22 U.S.-Canada / $25 foreign

Institutional one-year subscriptions (2 issues):
$28 U.S.-Canada / $33 foreign

MĀNOA *A Pacific Journal of International Writing*

University of Hawai'i Press
2840 Kolowalu Street Honolulu HI 96822
1-888-847-7377 (toll-free tel) 1-800-650-7811 (toll-free fax)
www.hawaii.edu/mjournal   mjournal-l@hawaii.edu

Issue Numbah
One

Hybolics

geff 'em?

Now axcepting
submissions fo'
Issue #2

Hybolics, Inc., P.O. Box 3016, 'Aiea, HI 96701
TEL: (808)366-1272 E-MAIL: hybolics@lava.net

Hawai'i Review

THE HAWAI'I ISSUE

Subscription rates: one year (1 regular issue; 1 double issue), $20.00; two years (4 issues), $30.00; sample copies, $10.00. Subscriptions will be mailed at bookrate; if you would like your books mailed first-class, please add $5.00 to the subscription price. Address all subscription requests to: *Hawai'i Review*, c/o Board of Publications, University of Hawai'i, PO Box 11674, Honolulu, HI 96828.

Submissions are welcome year-round. Send submissions to *Hawai'i Review*, 1733 Donaghho Rd, Honolulu, HI 96822.

HAWAI'I REVIEW 53 CONTRIBUTORS: Alani Apio, Carol Catanzariti, Gary Chang, D. Māhealani Dudoit, Solomon Enos, Rosa Flores, Joy Gold, Kristen Kelley Lau, Juliet S. Kono, Karyn Lao, Kelly Lee, Ian MacMillan, Joy Marsella, Chris McKinney, Wendy Miyake, Rodney Morales, L. Nishioka, John O'Meara, Joan Perkins, Alshaa T. Rayne, Rowland B. Reeve, David Richardson, Cecelia Gibo Sasaki, c. sinavaiana-gabbard, Joseph Stanton, Carrie Y. Takahata, Lee A. Tonouchi, Lois-Ann Yamanaka, Ida Yoshinaga

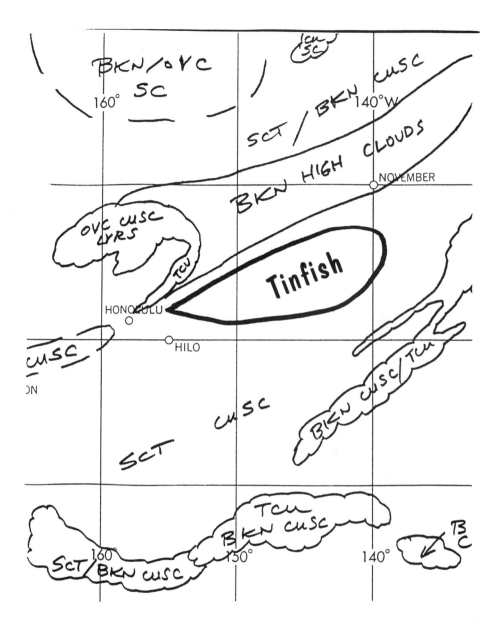

Tinfish: a journal of experimental poetry with an emphasis
on work from the Pacific region

Issues 2-7: $5
Also available: *Voiceovers*, John Kinsella & Susan M. Schultz - $4
                4-evaz, Anna, Kathy D.K.K. Banggo - $4

Order from: Susan M. Schultz, editor
                47-391 Hui Iwa Street, #3
                Kāneʻohe, Hawaiʻi 96744 U.S.A.

Tsunami Years
Juliet S. Kono

Rich in detail, this collection spans three generations and examines themes of childhood, heartbreaks and affinities, family obligations, love and devotion, death and dying. Cathy Song writes, "Juliet S. Kono's language shimmers with multiple, luminescent layers of meaning, each poem a pearl of truth wrested out of the heart of living."

$10.00 (book) ▪ 173 pages
ISBN 0-910043-35-3

$8.00 (cassette)
ISBN 0-910043-36-1

$16.00 (book and cassette tape set)
ISBN 0-910043-39-6

OUTSPEAKS A RHAPSODY
Albert Saijo

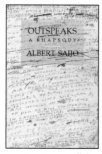

A devout poet-philosopher and practitioner, Saijo is committed to illuminating his vision for others through language. Realizing all the while the inherent limitations of this construct we call language, Saijo expounds upon the ineffable as much as is humbly and humanly possible. Lawrence Ferlingetti says, "Albert Saijo has the great vision most poets and painters never had." Saijo is the author of *Trip Trap* with Jack Kerouac and Lew Welch and *The Backpaker*. Of *OUTSPEAKS A RHAPSODY*, Saijo's first collection of poetry, Gary Snyder says: "All CAPS and dashes, Albert Saijo's poem is a great life's strong song."

1998 Small Press Poetry Book of the Year and 1998 Pushcart Prize winner.

$12.00 (book)
ISBN 0-910043-50-7

$8.00 (cassette)
ISBN 0-910043-51-5

$18.00 (book and cassette tape set)
0-910043-52-3

bamboo ridge press

Expounding the Doubtful Points
Wing Tek Lum

This collection of poetry by the 1970 Discovery Award winner speaks of the author's Chinese American heritage: his ancestors in China, his family in Hawai'i, and forging a Chinese American identity. He also speaks of racial discrimination and the obscenity of ethnic stereotypes with astute and unforgiving clarity. "Lum's style is an unembellished line of measured prose, setting out a message in direct declarations…his straight forward descriptions take their impact from that very detachment."—The New Paper

Winner of the 1988 Before Columbus Foundation American Book Award and the 1988 Association for Asian American Studies National Book Award.

$8.00 (book) ▪ 108 pages
ISBN 0-910043-14-0

Subscribe to Bamboo Ridge

All subscriptions are shipped postage paid and are money-back guaranteed.

4-issue (2 year) subscription, $35 (save $15)

2-issue (1 year) subscription, $20 (save $5).

Institutions: $25, 2-issues.

Coming in Spring 2000, Issue #76 *Intersecting Circles: The Voices of Hapa Women in Poetry and Prose,* an anthology of *hapa wo*men writers edited by Marie Hara and Nora Okja Keller.

Bamboo Ridge Press ▪ P.O. Box 61781 ▪ Honolulu, HI 96839-1781
For more information call (808) 626-1481 ▪ www.bambooridge.com

Celebrate Hawai`i
with a red crustacean lei t-shirt

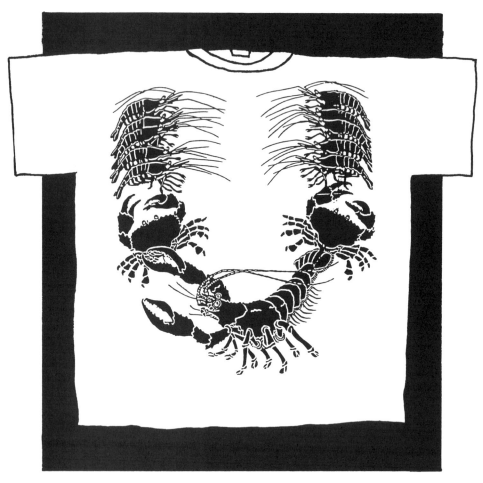

CANE HAUL ROAD, LTD.

since 1977

available at: Native Books & Beautiful Things,
222 Merchant St. and Ward Warehouse